Anita,

Many blessings.

# Snake Walkers

## J. Everett Prewitt

Northland Publishing Company
Cleveland, Ohio

A Northland Publishing Company book
2775 South Moreland Boulevard
Cleveland, Ohio 44120

Library of Congress Control Number: 2004114512
ISBN 0-9761927-0-5

Book design by Janice M. Phelps

This book is dedicated to

the Prewitt family

living and deceased

and especially to

my mother

Margaret Ann Prewitt

And my father

Selmer E. Prewitt

1908—2004

# Acknowledgments

This book would not have been possible without the input of a number of people. I would like to thank my writing workshop compadres, John Kavouras, Kaki Brzytwa, Sarah Crowley and especially Barbara Hacha who gave guidance and encouragement to this rookie writer; my cousin Milford Prewitt, a reporter, whose opinions helped shape the story; Blythe Camenson, Fiction Writer's Connection; and Janis Kearney who provided me with resources for my research.

I would also like to thank Chandra Sparks Taylor, editorial consultant; Sam Fulwood of the *Cleveland Plain Dealer;* Anita Bunkley, author; James Spriggs; my cousin, Montrie Rucker Adams; and a host of friends.

*I have given you authority over all the power of the enemy,*
*and you can walk among snakes and scorpions and crush them.*
*Nothing will injure you.*
Luke 10:19
New Living Translation Bible

# PROLOGUE

*Late Summer, 1948*
*A farm outside Pine Bluff, Arkansas*

The two twelve-year-old cousins raced around the edges of the cornfield as the sun slowly moved across the horizon, changing from a fiery yellow to a burnt orange, signaling its pending departure. The smaller boy, a visitor at his cousin's farm, and the faster of the two, stopped for the third time to wait for his playmate, and to look once more across the rows of corn towards the woods.

As if reading his mind, the larger boy whispered, "The woods are hainted. You don't want to go there. Nobody goes there. That's where the ghost of dead people live."

Anthony Andrews shrugged. He wasn't afraid. "I still want to go. Will you tell?" he asked.

Joe Mathis hesitated, shaking his head at his cousin's bull-headedness. "No. I won't tell."

Without a second thought, Anthony started toward his destination, glancing back to see his cousin standing, arms folded, still shaking his head.

It took longer than Anthony expected to reach the edge of the forest through the endless rows of corn. The trees that appeared so much smaller in the distance loomed over him now like giant guardians to the entrance of some other world. Unfamiliar with his surroundings, he hesitated at the edge of the forest, listening, as Joe's warning of a haunted woods echoed faintly in his head.

It didn't take long for the adventurer in him to win out though. So despite any misgivings, he entered, moving cautiously into the quiet darkness.

Where the cornfield he had just passed through was lively with the sounds of swishing stalks swaying in the wind, accompanied by the high-pitched cawing of crows, the even higher-pitched chirps of the woodland birds, and the faint, lowing of a distant cow, the woods were unlike anyplace he had ever been.

Anthony felt a dampness in the air that seemed to diminish any sounds of life, creating a quietness that settled like a blanket over the towering, majestic trees. Even the singing of the birds seemed muted. He stood still, his hands on his hips. It was as if he had entered another place in time.

Eventually he stepped carefully over the roots that snaked from the huge clustered trunks of the lofty oak trees and moved inward, entering an open area of red and yellow dahlias and white jonquils. He felt more at ease after seeing their bright colors and inhaling their light, breezy fragrance.

Hesitantly, he walked farther past a thicket of brightly colored bushes, where he found a group of smaller pear trees encircled by a blanket of flowers and shrubs. The place was like a beautiful painting. It was better by far than anywhere else he had ever visited.

Anthony decided this would be his secret place, where he would come to be alone and surround himself with the magic the area possessed.

He continued to walk deeper into the woods, through the trees, flowers, and bushes, marveling at the variety of shapes, colors, sounds, and smells. Occasionally he looked behind him so he wouldn't get lost, but he had no intention of going back until he was satisfied he had seen everything. There was a small hill shaped like the letter L that overlooked the meadow. Anthony climbed it to get an even better look at his paradise.

It became dusk quickly, but at that point, for the minutes he stood savoring his surroundings, time was unimportant. *I'll go back in a little while*, he thought as he lay on the ground, hands behind his head, looking up at the stars.

He lingered as long as he thought he could before reluctantly rising, stretching his thin arms and legs to begin his descent. Before he could take his first step, he was stopped by the faint sound of men laughing that drifted through the stillness of the night. It startled, then upset him, that there were other people in the woods, intruding.

The noise came from down the slope on the other side of the hill, accompanied by more laughter and a sound he had never heard before. He lay down on his stomach and eased to the edge, fearful that even the smallest of sounds would alert the men. Brush and other growth along the ridge of the hill allowed him to see, but still remain concealed.

The moon had emerged, and played hide-and-seek, while the darkness made its home among the trees. He could barely make out a group of men with one small torch surrounding a smaller person at the far edge of the woods near the pear trees he had just left. They were walking toward him. Some had what looked like big sticks or baseball bats, and one man had what looked like a rope. All Anthony could make out was that while the other men varied in size and shape, the man with the rope stood out. He was fat and squat-looking, and he reminded Anthony of a picture of an ogre he had seen in one of the books at the school library.

The men stopped near the base of the hill next to a smaller oak tree. Anthony watched as two of them held the person in the middle. The squat-looking man slung a rope over a branch. There was faint whining and sniffling coming from within the gathering. As the men shuffled around waiting for the man with the rope to finish, shards of light from the moon bathed the group in a dull, yellow hue. It made the white rope and the beige-colored baseball bats more visible.

Anthony counted nine men in the group all dressed in overalls and boots as if they had just left their farms. They were white except for the person in the middle. Anthony could see him more clearly as additional light filtered through the trees. The face wasn't familiar, but it was clear he was a colored boy, like him, and young, like him.

The strange noises were coming from the boy.

"Shut up, nigger, and quit your moaning," a tall, pale-looking man growled.

Anthony froze.

"I ain't do nothin'."

A bat interrupted the boy's plea. It hit him in the forehead. A short scream erupted from the young boy as his head snapped back from the vicious blow before he slumped, ready to fall to the ground. A knot as big as a baseball appeared almost instantly on his forehead.

Anthony shuddered and wiped a tear running down his cheek. The sound was the same one his friend Cal Harper's bat had made when he had hit a homerun the week before.

The boy didn't fall, only because two other men held him up.

"Goddammit, Junior. You almost hit me," the taller of the men said.

"But I didn't."

The men laughed.

The squat man pulled on both ends of the rope, inspecting the branch. "It'll do," he rasped in a deep, gravelly voice.

Anthony watched in disbelief as one of the men put the noose around the boy's neck. Three of them grabbed the other end and began pulling the rope. The tree limb creaked from the additional weight.

As the body rose slowly from the ground, an eerie whine punctured the night air, causing the men pulling the rope to stop briefly before tying the end of the rope to a stump. Only a faint gurgling noise could be heard among the jeering laughter as the body that at first jerked spasmodically, barely swung back and forth while the men stood admiring their handiwork.

They then picked up their bats and started swatting at the hanging boy.

Chills rushed through Anthony's body, and more tears poured down his face as the sound of the bats penetrated the darkness.

"You swing like a girl, Tyson," a heavy-voiced man said.

"Oh yeah? Your momma don't think so."

In morbid fascination, Anthony wiped his eyes to look one more time.

"Watch this," the tallest of men said as he swung with full force at the boy's head.

Anthony began to tremble uncontrollably as the boy's head snapped back again. There was another cracking sound. This time the young boy's head fell to the side at an odd angle. What could have been blood dripped slowly from his dangling tongue, which had slipped out of his opened mouth and swung back and forth with the force of each blow.

He watched the men swat at the hanging target for what seemed like hours. The lifeless body began to sway again, creating the same creaking sounds as before, interrupted only by the men's grunts of exertion.

The moon slowly disappeared again, leaving only the smallest slivers of light behind as a witness, while Anthony, still trembling uncontrollably, turned away for the last time.

At first he couldn't stand. His legs were so weak, Anthony feared he would have to stay there all night. He crawled on his hands and knees through the brush and down the other side of the hill until he felt his strength return. Unable to see clearly through teary eyes, he willed himself to run as fast as he could through the woods toward the farm.

He hurtled his thin body through the brush and trees, oblivious to the cuts and scratches from the branches that grabbed him at every step. Noise was of no concern to him now. Anthony's thin legs pumped so fast that he fell headfirst down a brush-covered ditch. A flock of startled blackbirds cawed; their wings flapped angrily as they took flight.

The fall slowed him temporarily, but his feet never stopped moving until he reached the clearing where he could see the lights from his uncle Mathis's house above the rows of corn that were now as still as the rest of the night.

His lungs were on fire as he fell exhausted on the ground. With his chest heaving from both fear and fatigue, Anthony looked back at the edge of the woods, terrified that the same men he watched hang and beat the boy would burst out of the woods and do the same to him.

The grunts and wet thuds made by the bats as they hit the bloodied, lifeless body followed him all the way back to the farm. He burst through the front door and through the house to the bedroom, acknowledging no one. "Where have you...Anthony?" His mother's voice sounded alien and distant.

Bumping his knees on the bed he shared with Joe, he climbed in, shivering, with his clothes still on, pulling every blanket he could reach over himself.

Eventually, there was a quiet shuffle of bare feet as someone else entered the room. The bed sagged from the weight of another person as Anthony slid even farther under the covers.

"I told you," Joe whispered.

PART I

·|·

*January 1961*
*Pine Bluff, Arkansas*

At 5:30 A. M., the two runners had the track to themselves. It was an isolated area surrounding a grass-covered football field at the back of an old brick school. Anthony liked the track since few people used it. Because it was so secluded, there was minimal chance of human contact. That day, though, Anthony wanted company.

The air was brisk with no breeze and a temperature of around fifty-five degrees. The mist lifting from the ground made the men look ghostly. The crunch of their shoes hitting the red cinders was the only sound penetrating the morning stillness. Anthony, the slightly taller of the two, ran with an effortless gait. The shorter, huskier runner with the build of a running back labored as he ran to keep up.

"Anthony James Andrews, if you keep up this pace, you're going to be running by yourself," the shorter one said as he struggled to keep abreast.

"You're the one who ran track in school," Anthony chided his friend Chucky as they turned into the backstretch for the seventeenth lap. Anthony and Charles "Chucky" Aaron White met when they first started elementary school. Their friendship grew on its own, unattended by words, like a cactus would grow unattended by water. Neither acknowledged their closeness in so many words, but both considered the other to be a best friend. Their friendship was the reason that when Anthony called, knowing that even though Chucky hated to run long distances, Chucky would come.

"Yeah, but it was 440 yards, not the marathon," Chucky said puffing, "and I wasn't obsessed with it like you."

Their laugh, throaty but subdued, sounded like it came from the same person. In fact, there was little to distinguish the two except their height. Both twenty-six year olds would be considered attractive with dusky brown complexions, short hair, high cheekbones, and angular noses that stopped just short of the wider noses attributed to their African ancestors. Anthony, however, at six feet was two inches taller than Chucky.

Anthony had to admit that Chucky was right. He was obsessed, and there was a reason. It hadn't been a good night. As a matter of fact, it hadn't been a good week. The nightmares had returned.

A week ago, his father's funeral home where he worked, had received the body of an old colored man who had been beaten to death outside the town of Wynne, Arkansas. After a glimpse at the bruised and mutilated corpse, Anthony experienced his first flashback in years.

It had been thirteen years since the incident in the woods. He had hoped the pain of it would disappear in time, but it hadn't completely. It was still there, lurking in the shadows, waiting, like some gigantic, poisonous viper. At the beginning, during the most dreadful periods, Anthony felt that he was just within the serpent's reach, and if it ever caught him, it would swallow him whole.

It was evident that time would not be his narcotic, so he ran.

Running was redemptive. It cleaned and restored the natural order of things within him. The nightmares, the flashbacks, the nagging fear that something was behind him faded away, at least for a time. The pain of exhaustion temporarily replaced the pain of sadness and powerlessness, but even that dissipated until only the steady, rhythmic sound of his feet was left to propel his mind to a more peaceful place.

"Lost in thought?" Chucky asked, bringing Anthony back to the present as they slowed to a jog to cool down.

"I'm sorry, man. There's a lot of stuff on my mind these days," Anthony said.

"Whenever you want to unload, all you have to do is start talking," Chucky said, tapping Anthony's back in a show of support. "That's what friends are for."

"Thanks, man. I appreciate that."

"Talking about friends. Are we going to see you at Mo's this Saturday?" Chucky asked. "When you don't show, we have no choice but to talk about you. You need to be there to salvage your reputation," he said, laughing and still trying to catch his breath.

Anthony laughed with him. "I plan on it."

"Good. I'm going to get some coffee after I shower. You want to join me?" Chucky asked.

"No. I'm going to do some weights before I head to work."

Chucky turned with raised eyebrows. "Weights? When did you start doing weights?"

"Just recently. Nothing heavy. Just a lot of repetitions."

"For how long?"

"Another hour or so."

Chucky shook his head. "Are you sure you aren't overdoing it?"

"I - I just feel better when I've had a complete workout."

Chucky raised his hands, palms up. "This wasn't a complete workout?"

Anthony took a deep breath. "Not to me."

Chucky looked at Anthony closely. "What's going on man?"

"Everything's okay, Chucky."

Chucky continued to stare at Anthony. "How's everything at the funeral home?" Chucky asked as they slowed to a walk.

Anthony shook his head slightly. "It's fine, but it's not what I want to do for the rest of my life."

"The money's good, isn't it?" Chucky asked.

"It is; but my father and I don't agree on a lot of things," Anthony said as he thought about the old man who was beaten to death and the rift it caused between he and his father. After Anthony saw the body, he had gone home that day shaking his head in disgust at the anguish it caused him and the weakness he felt because of it. As soon as he had entered his apartment, he retrieved the folded yellowed piece of paper he had carried with him since he was a kid. Before the woods, Anthony feared nothing. Now fear, though most times dormant, accompanied him everywhere he went. It scared him most that he wasn't in control.

Aunt Ida, his father's sister who passed four years earlier, used to always say "The devil knockin'" when she began to feel "strange." Anthony didn't realize the significance of her statement until years later when she was sent to a home for the mentally unstable.

Years had passed since the devil had knocked on Anthony's door, but it had come, pounding away, that day he saw the old man's body. He had stayed in his apartment for two weeks. His mother called every day. His father called once, to find out when he would return to work.

The second weekend after he had taken off from work, his mother insisted Anthony come to the house for dinner. It was only the second time during that two-week period that he had left the apartment.

The dinner table had always been where almost all discussions took place. That night was different. His dad's usually caustic commentary was subdued. Even his mother was quieter than usual. Halfway through the meal, Randall Andrews looked up at Anthony. "Son, I don't think you're going to cut it in this business."

"Randall!"

Anthony was startled more by his mother's response than his father's statement. "What do you mean, Dad?"

"You see a dead man, and you take off for two weeks? How can I depend on you if I have to worry about you running off again?"

Anthony shook his head slightly. His father didn't understand. He couldn't understand. "Maybe you're right. Maybe I'm not cut out for this business."

"Anthony! Your father is just upset right now. Don't make it any worse."

A half smile crossed Anthony's face for a brief second. "Dad's right, Mom, but for the wrong reasons."

His father's face darkened as he looked at Anthony closely. "So what's the reason? What's the reason I have to almost turn down business because my son, who would eventually inherit this profitable enterprise, can't stand the sight of a dead body?"

Anthony stood. "You wouldn't understand, Dad, and I'm not going to try to explain it to you."

"What I do understand is that I raised a son to follow in my footsteps, but he can't take it," his father said as he slammed his palm on the table.

A need to fight back coursed through Anthony's veins and settled somewhere near the front of his brain. He couldn't tell if the sudden headache was from anger or fear, but he couldn't show anger. Anger meant you had lost control. He couldn't show fear either, because he was the cub, and the wolf was tougher, and if you cower, the wolf wins.

The wolf and the cub. That was their relationship in a nutshell. How could a father like that understand? All he was concerned with was being right at all costs, running his funeral business and making money.

Anthony glanced at Chucky. He wasn't comfortable sharing his problem with his friends. They all looked up to him. They would be disappointed knowing that a dead body had caused him so much distress. It was a burden he would have to bear by himself, and a problem he would have to solve by himself.

They stopped their walk as Chucky turned to look at Anthony and nodded knowingly. "I can understand you having problems with your dad." He laughed. "I would imagine that anybody who worked for Mr. Andrews would. 'We're the upper echelon of Negro society,' " Chucky mimicked.

Anthony smiled. "Yeah, they even started calling themselves the 'Echelons' until someone told them that the name sounded like some singing group from Detroit." His smile faded.

"You know. I try to please him, but he's convinced that Andrews Funeral Home is my future. I went to school to become a journalist, and that's what I intend to do," Anthony said resolutely. "For some reason, my father doesn't believe I can do it."

Chucky said nothing, prompting Anthony to ask, "You don't either?"

Chucky sighed. "I think you can be anything you want to be, eventually, but the reality is that they're not hiring many colored folks as reporters in any of these big newspapers. You know how it is down here."

The two runners sat on a bench as Anthony shook his head, a wry smile on his face. "Yeah, I know, but somehow, someway, I'm going to break through."

Chucky shrugged. "Well, if anybody can do it, you can."

Anthony nodded. It was just a matter of time. All he had to do was hold it together.

· II ·

I t was a Friday morning, and Anthony had just finished running
seven fast miles alone. He showered and sat in the living room
of his apartment, drinking a glass of orange juice, reading the
paper, and enjoying a moment of peace before dressing to go to
work at the funeral home.

Although the apartment was no bigger than the living room
of his parents' house on Barroque Street, the one-bedroom suite
was sufficient for his needs. It was sparsely furnished, but he did-
n't care. It was home, a place where he could get away.

Anthony reflected on the past months. The possibility of getting a job as a reporter was becoming more and more remote.
Although he remained hopeful, his resolve was waning. The
failed interviews were beginning to weigh on him, and his future
as a reporter was becoming a distant light that was fading into a
dim flicker.

The pile of résumés on his desk was depleted. With no prospects in mind, Anthony had to think long and hard about his future. He was certain he didn't want to remain at the funeral home, but what else was there? Maybe teaching?

So many questions, so few answers.

Anthony took a deep breath and was headed toward the door when the phone rang. It startled him because the phone hardly ever rang.

"Hello?"

"Mr. Anthony Andrews?"

"Yes."

"I hear you're looking for a reporter's job, Mr. Andrews."

Anthony's pulse quickened for a second, then he gathered himself, trying to determine which of his friends was playing games. "That's correct. Who is this?" Anthony asked cautiously.

"I'm William Whiting, city editor of the *Arkansas Sun*. One of my colleagues at another paper gave me your name. Are you interested in interviewing with our paper?"

Anthony couldn't detect the voice, but he had to give whomever it was credit. They were good. "Yeah, right." Anthony laughed as he hung up the phone. Someone was going to pay for this. He smiled as he again opened the door to leave.

The phone rang once more.

"Were we disconnected?" The voice on the other end of the line sounded a little irritated.

Still skeptical, Anthony asked, "How did you get my name?"

"Pardon me?" the man answered.

"What paper referred you to me?" Anthony asked suspiciously.

"The *Mississippi Sentinel*," the man replied hesitantly. "Are you interested in becoming a reporter or not? I don't have time to play games."

Anthony, still suspicious, but now unsure, answered, "Yes, sir. I am."

"Good. Get a pencil and take down this telephone number. Ask for Hannah Dickinson. She'll set up the appointment."

"Thank you, sir," Anthony said as he stood holding the phone long after the other party had hung up.

*That was strange*, he thought. After being rejected by every paper he sought an interview with for the last three years, he received this call out of the blue? It had to be some kind of joke. Anthony gently placed the phone down, not sure whether he should be happy or remain suspicious.

Later that day, after hours of contemplation, Anthony called his best friend. "What do you think?" Anthony asked. "There is a William Whiting at the *Arkansas Sun*. I checked."

Chucky paused. "It does sound strange, but hey, what do you have to lose?"

Anthony related the telephone conversation to his parents over lunch at their house. Anthony's father sounded predictably irritated. "After three years, I would think that you would have given up on this nonsense of being a reporter and settle down into the funeral home business."

"Dad, I went to school to be a reporter, and now I think I'm finally going to get the chance." Anthony looked to his mother for support, but she said nothing as the two men talked heatedly.

Anthony usually listened carefully when his father lectured him on how to conduct himself. Even though he had more questions than his father had answers, he accepted his father's assessment of racial issues and how a family like his was "above the fray," but he would not accept his father defining his future.

Anthony often wondered why his dad and mom ever married. Randall Andrews was rigid and a constant complainer who was always railing against something. If it wasn't the poor niggers trying to get burial services for little or nothing, it was the out-siders coming in and causing trouble with the white man. Mildred Andrews, on the other hand, was a quiet, gentle woman who never raised her voice and listened more than she talked. Whatever peace there was in the house was because of her.

Anthony had more of his mother's characteristics than his father's.

As Anthony drove home from his parents' house, he reflect-ed on the day's headline in the *Arkansas Sun* which blared, "King in North Carolina." The article lamented that Dr. Martin Luther King, Jr., was involved in a sit-in at Woolworth's lunch counter, stirring up people unnecessarily. He read it with inter-est because of his recent conversations with his father and his father's friends. For some time, racial tension had been on the rise, and southern states like Arkansas were feeling the pressure. America was feeling the pressure.

A journalist once wrote in a New York paper that, "Race relationships in the South have always been covered by a thin veneer of southern decorum. Peel the skin off though, and what you find is an unspoken contract between blacks and whites that governs every aspect of their lives."

Anthony agreed, but in the past few years, he noticed that the assigned roles and established relationships were slowly beginning to unravel as more and more Negroes joined the cho-rus of voices seeking change.

Attitudes were shifting—or maybe hardening was a better description. Resentments that had simmered just below the sur-face now erupted like bubbles in the belly of a lava-pregnant mountain, one then another, bursting, subsiding, then multiply-ing in numbers, until it finally overflowed.

The festering rage over the death of young black men like Emmett Till, the discord over Rosa Parks and her refusal to move to the back of the bus, the integration of the schools, and the general turmoil created by Dr. King and his people ignited a slow but steadily growing fire in the South as well as the North. Even among colored folks though, it wasn't a heat that everyone welcomed.

"That damned King!" Randall grumbled one day at the dinner table. "Rabble rousers like him are destroying the very fabric of the South that allows so many of us to obtain a good living. The lowlife and rebellious few that are causing all the trouble should get off the streets, stop complaining, work harder, and achieve. Then there would be no reason to march and cause trouble."

Anthony tried to understand his father's anxiety. Randall Andrews had expressed the same concern when the nine kids integrated Central High. "Uppity Negroes. A colored school isn't good enough for them?" But Anthony had to admire those kids and others like them who felt so strongly about Negro rights that they would risk their lives for it.

The results of this unrest though were the same as if one were to hit a hornet's nest with a stick. Acts of violence against Negroes increased, and tension was so thick you could almost touch it.

There were times during that period when Anthony almost felt compelled to join the quest for rights and freedom, but he was torn. He was torn between his sense of justice for all, the agony of his past, and his own pursuits. In the end, he opted to take the path of personal gain. There were many reasons. Some he couldn't formulate. But at that moment in his life, he decided that if he were to accomplish his lifelong dream of becoming a reporter, he would have to focus. Nothing was more important.

## · III ·

W hile researching the paper, Anthony found that the *Arkansas Sun* was one of the two largest newspapers in the state. It had grown from a small, weekly, one-town paper in the late 1800s to a respected statewide daily in the 1900s. It had a staff of more than one hundred and a reputation for finding the news wherever it was.

Two days after talking to the personnel secretary, Anthony was on his way to meet the city editor. He didn't know what to expect, but even after all the frustration he had suffered, he was still optimistic.

The office was on Scott Street in Little Rock. As soon as Anthony saw the building, he stopped, experiencing the same apprehension he felt when he first entered the woods. He laughed at himself for being so childish and pushed his anxiety to the back of his mind.

What distinguished the building most from the others surrounding it was the grayish stone blocks that covered the front except for the windows. It was imposing for someone rejected as many times as he had been. What awaited him inside?

Anthony hesitated only briefly before entering a small vestibule with a window that allowed the receptionist to greet visitors.

"Mr. Andrews is it?"

It surprised Anthony that she knew his name, until he realized that probably no other colored person would have come through the front door, especially wearing a suit. He bowed slightly, hat in hand. "Yes, ma'am, I am."

The receptionist directed him to sit in the lounge area, which allowed a view of the main floor. This area had hardwood flooring, and the click-clack of heels on the wood would give even a blind person the impression that this was a no-nonsense establishment.

The only sounds beside those heels were of typewriters, telephones, and the hum of conversation. To most, the clatter and chatter would sound like so much noise, but to Anthony it sounded like a symphony orchestra. He watched as people walked briskly back and forth with paper and pen. As his presence became known, it seemed that traffic increased, with each person glancing, if only briefly, in his direction.

Anthony felt William Whiting's presence before he ever saw him. Even the sound of his walk was different from the others. It was distinctively heavier. Anthony could hear the sudden shift in the traffic pattern to accommodate his presence. "Mr. Whiting." "Hi, sir." "Hello, Mr. Whiting." None received a return greeting, at least not verbally.

Anthony stood expectantly.

William Whiting was a commanding figure. He was a large man at six-five and 250 pounds, and obviously a confident one from his bearing. Whiting was a twenty-eight-year veteran of the paper. Anthony learned that Whiting started out as a mail clerk and became city editor quicker than anyone who preceded him. Based on Whiting's status, if he could convince this man, Anthony was probably in.

"So, you're the young man I've been hearing so much about," he said in a deep booming voice as he stuck out a large paw that enveloped Anthony's hand. Although Whiting spoke effortlessly, his words bounced off the walls of the building as if he had shouted.

"I don't know what you've heard, Mr. Whiting, but I'm hoping at least some of it was good." Anthony replied as he returned the handshake.

Whiting's deep laugh reverberated throughout the now quiet building. He waved, and Anthony followed him across the open pits into his office. It felt like every person in that office was staring at his back. That was something he could get used to—if he was hired.

After Whiting entered his office, closed the door, and sat, Anthony took his seat. The city editor pulled out Anthony's résumé and looked at it briefly before laying it on his desk. "Why do you want to become a reporter, Anthony?"

Anthony paused a second before speaking. "It's been a life-long dream of mine, Mr. Whiting. Ever since I was a kid, I've always wanted to write about things I thought others should know."

Whiting slid his reading glasses onto his nose, bent over the desk, and began to read Anthony's résumé carefully.

While Anthony waited, his thoughts drifted back to his childhood. For weeks after the incident in the woods, Anthony had asked his parents every day if they had read anything about a young colored boy who might have been found dead. He couldn't bring himself to say the word *hung*. Did they hear anything about a young boy missing?

The answer was always the same: "No, Anthony. Why do you keep asking?" His mother had looked at him with just a hint of concern in her voice. "Why would you ask about something like that? What did you hear?"

Anthony never answered. He couldn't. It was hard enough trying to sleep at night with the image of the bruised, damaged body swaying back and forth like some apparition, invading his sleep, causing him to sob quietly as he mourned the boy for the hundredth time.

It was then he made a promise to Emmanuel—Anthony had named the boy in his mind, because it wasn't right that he not have a name—that when he grew up, he would make sure no one was treated like Emmanuel was treated in the woods without everybody knowing about it. In Anthony's mind, it was only proper that everybody hear when evil rose from hell like that to strike down a person for no apparent reason.

It was then that Anthony decided to be a news reporter. He would investigate and report the evil that men committed against one another; and maybe if he did, they would stop, and the world would be a peaceful place. Maybe if he were able to fulfill that promise, maybe the images would go away, and maybe he and Emmanuel could finally go to sleep.

Whiting nodded, laid the résumé on the desk and looked up at Anthony. "And what in your experience gives you the idea that you would be a good reporter?"

Anthony paused. "I was a good student, and I received good reviews from my internship. There is a letter there from the managing editor of the *New York Times*, where I interned." A small bead of perspiration formed on Anthony's upper lip. He wiped it quickly.

Whiting read a portion of Anthony's résumé out loud. "First black assistant editor of the *Daily Tar Heel* at the University of North Carolina Chapel Hill's School of Journalism; graduated in the top ten percent of the class and received an internship at the *New York Times*."

Anthony nodded as he recalled his school days. No one ever knew how hard it was for him to achieve academically. For a few years after the woods, school held no interest. He couldn't concentrate, and his grades suffered as a result. Even though his mother, a former school teacher, worked with him to improve, it was Anthony who eventually realized that if he didn't succeed in school, he wouldn't be able to accomplish his ultimate goal of becoming a reporter. Only that gave him the motivation to slowly overcome his lack of attentiveness and push everything else aside, at least temporarily, to concentrate on his studies.

Whiting continued, "Was offered a position, but left because of homesickness. Ha. I like that. New York has to be one of the most wicked places in America."

"If it isn't," Anthony answered, "I would hate to be in the city that was first."

There was never a true job offer in New York. Out of desperation, Anthony had stretched the truth a little. Hopefully it wouldn't come back and bite him in the butt.

Whiting laughed again. "We have our problems, but I'll take Arkansas any day of the week."

Anthony nodded affirmatively. He leaned back in his chair, feeling a bit more comfortable.

"What have you been doing since you left New York?"

Anthony scratched his knee self-consciously. "I worked for my father for a part of that time. The rest of it, I interviewed."

"Anywhere I would know?"

"I'm sure you do. I barely made it through the front door though." Anthony decided it wasn't a good time to inform Whiting that the *Sun* also had his résumé.

"I understand. It's probably hard for a colored man to break into this business, even in the North. You would probably be the first if we hired you, you think?"

"I've heard of one or two others, sir."

"You think you could fit into this environment? It's hard enough doing your job as a rookie reporter without having to deal with all these white people." The slightest hint of a frown formed on Whiting's face as he raised his eyebrows expectantly.

"Sir, if I am given the chance, I'll be the best reporter on your staff. I know that I might not be accepted, but I wasn't accepted at first when I was in college, nor was I accepted when I joined their newspaper staff. I graduated with honors though and became assistant editor. I know I can do the job."

The frown didn't leave Whiting's face. He stood, and Anthony stood with him. "Let me think this over. I'll be talking to some other folks here at the newspaper over the next few days. The decision isn't mine alone, you understand."

"Yes, sir."

"I'll give you a call."

"Yes, sir."

There was no hint of how the interview went, but Anthony was hopeful. If this didn't work out...

He dismissed the thought.

## · IV ·

To most people, the Mo Restaurant in Pine Bluff was only a hole-in-the-wall, greasy spoon restaurant, but to Anthony, it was a major part of his social life. It was a restaurant where you might see anyone from a street sweeper to a politician. Socializing and eating were the only reasons people came to the eatery—and in that order.

Even though the sign on the outside read "Mo," Anthony and everybody else knew it was named for the owner, Moe. The story about the sign was legend.

Ever since Moe was a short-order cook, he had dreamed of owning his own restaurant with his name on a big sign over the entrance. Moe saved his money religiously and after ten years was able to rent a building on Fourth off Main. He hired someone to paint his name, but for some reason painted "Mo" on the sign instead of "Moe's."

Moe had given the cashier instructions to pay for the sign if she approved, but she was so busy with customers, she never went out to check it. Moe was furious. Nobody understood why the missing letters would cause so much fuss, but Moe ranted and raved for weeks, causing the cashier to take a week off due to stress. Word got to the sign painter, and no one ever saw him in the neighborhood again.

Because of the way the painter had arranged the letters, it would mean the whole sign would have to be repainted, and Moe was working on limited funds. After all the years of scrimping and saving, Moe still didn't feel like he got his wish to have a restaurant with his name on the sign.

After sleeping on it for a couple of weeks, however, Moe had a revelation. Instead of having the sign repainted, it would be easier for the restaurant to live up to its new name, so he began to serve larger portions. On Sunday, the restaurant offered an all-you-can-eat dinner. Hence the name Mo took on a new meaning and the restaurant gained a faithful clientele.

Since graduating from the university in 1957, Anthony and four of his friends would meet on Saturday mornings to catch up on the week's events. Chucky White, Albert Alford Gantreau, Donald Reginald Rector, and Anthony's cousin, Joe Washington Mathis, were all there when Anthony arrived.

"Here he comes! The paper man."

Anthony winced slightly. Chucky could have at least waited until he made the announcement himself.

Anthony could hear the laughter from the street. His cousin Joe's voice stood out among the four. He was always so jovial. Anthony often wondered how cheerful he would be if he had gone to the woods with him that night at the farm. But as quickly as the thought flashed through his mind, Anthony suppressed it, shook his head, straightened up, and walked through the door smiling.

Joe stood and was the first to greet him with a hug. He had grown from bear large when he watched Anthony take off for the woods years ago, to mountain large. *We could have stopped that hanging*, Anthony thought. They had only been kids then, though. He tried to clear his mind again.

"The *Arkansas Sun* kid. They move you from the back room closet yet?" Albert asked in a friendly but mocking tone, bringing Anthony back to his friends.

Anthony released a stilted laugh as he slapped Albert on the back. "They haven't even hired me yet, but editor in two years."

His friends laughed with him.

Anthony ordered the Mo Special of biscuits, sausage, fried potatoes and onions, grits, fried eggs and coffee.

Mo was crowded that morning. Even Reverend Rayford Rayburn Riley was there, laughing and telling the type of jokes that made Anthony wonder if he was ever ordained. To hear the reverend tell it, he was the reason there was integration at Central High. And even though no one including Albert, who was involved, remembered seeing Reverend Riley anywhere around that September four years ago when the nine students attempted to enter the all-white high school, Reverend Riley would tell anyone who would listen that he was at the front of that movement. Anthony always wondered about him and whether he was as religious during the week as he looked on Sundays in his robe.

Moe came out to greet Anthony and his friends. Like most elders, he considered it his responsibility to dispense wisdom to the young men who gathered at his place on any occasion he could. He looked at Anthony, cupping his chin and looking like some judge ready to give a verdict. "So you're going to work for that newspaper, huh?"

"I hope so, Moe."

"Well, you know I wish you the best, but remember, ain't nothing in this world free or easy, so when a door opens for you, you damn sure better look before you walk in. Better yet, walk around the whole building and look in the windows before you enter. You need to know what you're getting into. That's what a smart man would do."

Anthony sighed to himself. "Thanks, Moe."

"Smart! He ain't but so smart," Chucky snickered as he looked over Anthony's shoulder. "Somebody needs to teach him how to handle his women," he said under his breath, just loud enough for the men at the table to hear him.

"Uh-oh." Albert muttered.

Moe's smile lit up the restaurant as he watched with everyone else as the shapely woman entered the restaurant.

Anthony looked up, but said nothing.

His friends chuckled quietly.

"Hey, Anthony."

"Hey, Naomi."

"Hello, gentlemen. Hello, Moe."

"Hello, Naomi," they responded in unison.

"Haven't heard from you in a while," Naomi said, trying to disguise her obvious disappointment with Anthony.

"I'm sorry, but this job search has kept me hopping," Anthony said, looking at Naomi with raised hands.

Everybody waited for Naomi to respond, but she shrugged and went to the take-out counter.

Moe followed her, still smiling. "Naomi, don't see you much anymore."

"I've been busy, too, Moe," she said, rolling her eyes at Anthony.

"Well look now, don't stop coming here just because you're busy. I'm sure Anthony will find time to see you, so you should make time to see him."

"Is that so?"

"That's so," Moe said with a wicked grin, watching Anthony out of the corner of his eye.

Joe looked up at the ceiling, trying to stifle a laugh, and Chucky placed his hands over his eyes.

Anthony shook his head and said softly, "Y'all ain't worth ten pounds of cow dung."

"Hey, man, take that up with Moe," Albert said softly. "Anyway, we just introduced her to you. The rest was up to you."

Naomi walked back toward Anthony with an exaggerated switch. Her attitude was more conciliatory as she touched him on his shoulder. "I still have the same number."

"I'll call you soon. I promise," Anthony said, rolling his eyes at Moe.

Naomi trailed her hand over his arm. "You better," she said, punching him lightly before walking out, followed by the eyes of every male in the restaurant, including Reverend Riley.

Everyone at the table looked at Anthony, smiling.

"What?" Anthony raised his hands again.

"What? What, is right. What is wrong with her?" Albert asked.

"Not my type."

Chucky snickered. "She was your type a few weeks ago."

Joe shook his head. "How long have we been knowing each other, cousin?"

"A long time, but don't even start." Anthony responded.

Joe ignored him. "Every woman you've ever met, you stay together, what, a month at most?"

Anthony shrugged. "Why are you so worried about me?"

"Because that's what family does," Joe replied.

"Joe, you're my fifth cousin."

Chucky laughed. "Yeah, we're more related than you are."

Unperturbed, Joe continued, "I'm looking out for your welfare. Damn. Albert's been married twice, and you haven't even had a steady relationship. In a few more years you'll be thirty, man. You're good-looking with that Billie Eckstein kind of smile. Women want to be with you. I know you ain't queer, so I'm just trying to get you squared away."

"Like you are with that little horse-faced woman?" Anthony asked.

Everybody screamed.

A slightly hurt Joe threw up his hands. "I'm through with it."

"Damn again," Chucky said resignedly under his breath. Everyone turned as the door opened.

"Hey, Ralph," Albert offered, moving his chair, knowing the latest entry would join them whether they asked or not.

"Hey, y'all. Hey, Anthony. Long time no see."

"Ralph," Anthony acknowledged. Ralph Grayson was not a part of their group, but he wanted to be. He even replaced his overalls with the khaki pants and starched shirts the guys wore for the occasion. Anthony remembered when he first started sitting with them. No amount of verbal abuse could dissuade him. Ralph was the only one of the group who didn't have a college degree, and whenever anyone wanted to pull rank, they would bring it up. Ralph would try to make up for his lack of a degree by discussing subjects that no one else may have heard about. Today was no different.

"I heard there was a killing outside Wynne."

A shudder raced through Anthony, but he said nothing.

Everyone paused to let Ralph go on. No one wanted to encourage him if the story was too farfetched, and he had to be reeled in.

"An old colored man was all shot up and his house burned."

Everyone at the table turned toward him.

"Where'd you hear this?" Donald asked.

"Just came from there, and they were talking about it."

Albert shook his head. "What happened?"

"What I hear, they accused the old man of raping a white lady down the road from where he lived, and the police went after him. Came to his farm, beat him and shot him."

"They didn't shoot him," Anthony offered.

"How do you know?" Ralph asked, upset for being corrected and possibly upstaged.

"We received the body." Anthony rubbed his forehead before running his hand over his face.

"You okay, man?" Chucky asked.

"Yeah."

"But did you know the old man was im...potent?" Ralph asked, stumbling over the word and bringing Anthony back to the present. "He couldn't do anything anyway?"

"How do you know that?" Charles asked.

"His ex-wife told the sheriff that in his defense. That's why they separated."

"So why did they kill him?" Joe asked.

"When he found out they were coming for him, he shot at them. Kept them at bay for five hours before the sheriff got him to surrender, then they beat him half to death. Some townspeople broke into the jail, took him out, and finished the job."

Joe scratched his head. "Man, them Negroes will never learn."

"Learn what?" Albert asked.

"Leave the white man alone. You can't win."

Albert leaned toward his friend. "Is that the way you feel? Just lie down and let them walk all over you like some used rug?"

"All I'm saying is that he was wrong pulling a gun on those folks."

Albert looked exasperated. "I don't believe I heard what you just said. How do you know he did something wrong? You heard what Ralph said."

"Nobody comes after somebody like that unless they did something wrong," Joe shot back.

Donald shook his head. "Man, you're arguing over something Ralph tells you? We don't even know if it happened like he said."

"It happened," Ralph said looking at Anthony for support.

A clearly agitated Albert cut him off. "It doesn't make any difference whether it happened or not, we've heard enough stories. It's inconceivable that all of the Negroes hung down here did something wrong."

"Why not?" Joe asked.

Albert threw up his hands in frustration. "The same reason we're sitting in at Woolworth. The same reason we integrated Central High. The same reason we're protesting a thousand other things because of the inequalities in this country. We aren't the criminals; we're the victims."

"We're only victims if we believe we're victims," Ralph said quietly.

No one appeared to have heard Ralph except Anthony. He looked at Ralph and nodded.

Anthony marveled that such a diverse group of young men could maintain such an enduring friendship. They spanned the full spectrum of civil rights from the aggressive, proactive NAACP member, Albert Gantreau who had worked with Daisy Bates, L.C. Bates, and other civil rights stalwarts, to Donald whose only goal was to meet the standards set by the majority. The only time Anthony remembered Donald being mad at white folks, was when coloreds were denied entrance to see Elvis Presley at the Robinson Auditorium in Little Rock.

Chucky and Joe wavered depending on whose argument was strongest that day. And as his great aunt, Esther, used to say, Anthony usually came down "smack dab in the middle," primarily because civil rights was not his concern at this time. And he didn't know if it would ever be.

Joe turned to Anthony, "Don't you have an opinion on the subject?"

Anthony raised his hands in mock surrender.

Donald answered instead. "I think whether those that have been attacked were wrong is not the question. We have to go another direction. We have all graduated from college,"—Donald glanced at Ralph—"or at least high school. We need to pay more attention to how to make it out here. We need to concentrate on moving up in this world and quit paying so much attention to what's happening to other folks."

"Have white people tried to beat or hang you?" Donald asked, looking at Joe. "Or you, or you?" he questioned, looking around at his friends. "So, why are we discussing something that doesn't concern us? We're above all that."

Albert shook his head, but didn't respond. That ended the conversation. It was obvious to Anthony though, that Albert was disappointed in Donald's answer. It occurred to Anthony that Emmanuel would have been, too.

· Ⅴ ·

The secretary scheduled Anthony's second interview at the paper for Tuesday. Whiting was waiting in the lobby when Anthony arrived. Anthony could tell by Whiting's demeanor that something wasn't right.

"I have some bad news for you, son."

Anthony's heart sunk, but he said nothing, waiting.

"The editor doesn't think it's a good idea to hire a Negro right now, even one with all your skills." Whiting appeared contrite. "Management thinks that it will cause too much turmoil and disrupt the flow we have going on here."

Anthony pursed his lips, looking down, but not saying a word. He had heard all this before in one form or another. This was it. He was tired—tired of rejection, tired of trying to convince people that he was capable, and tired of being colored. "I understand," Anthony said softly as he picked up his hat to head for the door.

"Not so fast, son," Whiting said, scratching his chin in deep thought. "We have one chance left."

Anthony stopped and turned.

"There may be another approach, if you're interested."

"Sure," Anthony said uncertainly.

They sat in Whiting's office talking quietly for more than an hour as he unfolded his plan. Anthony listened carefully.

"What do you think?" Whiting asked.

"It's worth a try, Mr. Whiting," Anthony said hopefully. Anything was worth a try at that point.

"If it doesn't work, at least we tried," Whiting said as he stood patting Anthony on the back.


The assistant managing editor, Carl Morton, asked only a few questions as he looked over Anthony's résumé. The next visit was to Luke Chandler, the managing editor who was cordial, but never smiled during the whole time they were together, as if it was a waste of his time. The editor, Charlie Hargrove, asked the most questions, but he didn't smile either. It wasn't looking good.

Anthony related his accomplishments, but Hargrove didn't seem impressed. Anthony began to feel uncomfortable.

After the questions had ended, Whiting stood and walked slowly with his hands behind his back. "Here's my idea, Charlie." He paused. "If you remember, we talked about this before, but the other reporter left, and we never followed up on it. We have a chance to provide the people of this community with a new perspective. The *Sun* has a circulation of about 89,000—88,920 to be exact. Our competition has about the same. I'm not satisfied with that for a couple of reasons. Number one, the number of two-paper cities is dwindling. There are only about ninety cities that have two newspapers versus more than five hundred in the 1920s. Number two, the *Arkansas Republic* is delivered in the afternoon. Statistics show that those are the newspapers that are dying off, but there is no guarantee. We have an advantage, but we can't be complacent. We need to be aggressive in capturing a significant portion of the *Republic's* market or possibly risk the fate of the few morning papers that folded."

"There are twenty-eight thousand black people in Little Rock alone. Twenty-six thousand of them don't read your newspaper, those that do, buy the *Republic*," Anthony said, reciting the facts and statistics Whiting had given him.

"If we give them a reason to read, you increase circulation. If you increase circulation, you increase advertising. If you increase advertising, you increase revenues and the ability to bury our competitors. It boils down to a matter of survival," Whiting said.

"I don't know," Hargrove said, glancing at Anthony. "What makes you think that Negroes are going to read our paper because we hire one? I don't see how we increase revenue because he's on board. Half of them don't even know how to read."

Whiting ignored the last comment. "Before Jerry, our former reporter, left, I was going over some ideas, some stories that would get folks' attention. I think the time is now, and I'm willing to bet that after six months, you'll see readership pick up in both the black and white community."

"What if it doesn't?" Hargrove asked.

"If we don't see any improvement in six months to a year, then maybe I made a mistake, and I'll take the lumps for it."

Hargrove sat in silence, tapping his pencil in his hand. "Let me talk to Carl and Luke alone, and see what they say."

"I have a better idea, if I may," William Whiting said.

Hargrove nodded.

"Why don't you, I, Carl and Luke meet and talk about my ideas? I'm sure you would want candid feedback on what I see in the future. Let's all get together, and whatever comes from that meeting, is what it is."

"Fine. Let's convene tomorrow afternoon at four o'clock." Hargrove turned to Anthony. "Young man, Mr. Whiting really wants you on board pretty badly. Are you sure you don't have something on him?" It was the first time Hargrove smiled. Even then it appeared more sinister than friendly.

Anthony smiled back. "No, sir, but I would sure hope you decide to agree with him."

"We'll see, young man. We'll see."

The smile had already disappeared.

## · VI ·

It was another month before Anthony heard anything. He was already prepared for the bad news. Someone once said that a lie could travel around the world ten times while the truth was still putting on its shoes. Anthony hoped it was the same for bad and good news.

The phone rang while Anthony was contemplating his future. It was Hannah, the middle-aged receptionist and secretary. "Tony? Is that what you like to be called?"

"No, Miss Dickinson. It's Anthony." The two seconds it took for her to continue seemed like two hours.

"Well, call me Hannah."

"Fine, Hannah." Anthony walked with the phone, careful not to trip over the cord.

"Are you available to meet with Mr. Whiting on Monday?"

Anthony hit the wall with his fist. He turned his face from

the phone. "Yes!" he hissed quietly. "Of course, Hannah," he said politely. "What time?"

That Monday they made him an offer. Anthony accepted immediately and began his search for an apartment in Little Rock.

Anthony started work feeling like a felon pardoned from death row. The curious looks he received, the snubs, even the obvious dislike meant nothing to him. There were a few reporters who welcomed him on board and offered help whenever he needed it. Anthony was thankful for them.

Hannah was the most helpful. "Don't mind some of these people. They would snub you even if you were white. I know because they snubbed me at first."

Anthony smiled. "That's good to know."

"Your mainstay in this place is going to be Mr. Whiting. If you have any questions the staff can't or won't answer for any reason, he'll take care of it. He wanted you here in the worst way, and he plans on making sure you make it."

It felt good knowing that he had that type of backing. If there were doubters, he didn't care. He would work harder and longer than all of them.

Anthony's first reporting assignments were trivial. He worked with one of the veteran reporters, reviewing copy and sitting in on interviews. Anthony then moved to the obit section and eventually covered hospital, then police department news. Even though some incidents stirred the devil and tested his ability to cope, those menial tasks were still exciting because he was home. He absorbed every word the veterans spoke or wrote, sitting quietly as they worked, watching, learning, and waiting until it was his time.

Seven months into his job, Anthony received the call. Whatever Whiting discussed with Hargrove was finally going to happen.

"Anthony, I've been watching you and looking at some of your work. I like your work ethic, and I like how you write," Whiting said, as he motioned Anthony to sit.

Anthony accepted the compliment without comment.

"Are you ready to do some real work?" Whiting asked in his deep, booming voice that reminded Anthony so much of his father's.

"Yes, sir," Anthony said too loudly, doing a bad job of hiding his excitement.

"Good. Here's what I have. As we discussed before, Arkansas has had its share of racial atrocities. Many have gone unsolved. No one to my knowledge has documented all the bad that has happened to Negroes down here. I don't even think the state attorney general has that complete a file.

"What I want you to do is to begin to find as much as you can about all the hangings, shootings, and other foul play that has happened to Negroes in this state. We will pick the most interesting, and you'll write a series of stories to be published once a month. You'll get as much information as you can on the case, go to the area where the offense took place, talk to anyone with any knowledge of the victim, and write a compelling story about the person and the event."

Anthony listened carefully, trying not to show the overwhelming joy he felt. This was it, an assignment that would showcase his talent and tell the stories he always wanted to tell. He could hardly contain himself as he stood to shake Whiting's hand.

"Sir, I know you went through a lot to get me hired, and I can't tell you how much I appreciate it. I can assure you, Mr. Whiting, that you'll not be disappointed."

"I better not be, son. Now get out of here, and let me get some work done. Be in my office tomorrow at eleven, and we'll discuss details. I have some ideas that we need to go over."

Anthony didn't sleep that night for two reasons. There was a party in the apartment next to him that didn't finish until after 2 A.M., and after everyone left, it was obvious that one female stayed. Whatever his neighbor was doing with her lasted another hour. A symphony of grunts, moans, and an occasional high-pitched whine, with a background of squeaky springs and a headboard that recorded every movement, allowed for little sleep.

Victor Carson, the occupant of the apartment, had invited him to the party since they knew each other from Bell High School, but Anthony declined. Nothing was going to interfere with the work he had to do the next day.

He arrived at the office at 6:30 A.M., two hours before he was due for work. The two lovers had started at it again around 5 A.M., so there was no use in him trying to go back to sleep.

Anthony made a mental note to call Naomi that night.

Ideas about his assignment kept running through his mind. As quick as one idea popped up, another replaced it. He recorded all of his thoughts on a yellow pad, making sure that even the dumbest of ideas was on paper. Whiting arrived at 7:30 A.M. He smiled when he saw Anthony. "Come on in, son. I can see you're rarin' to go."

Whiting pulled out a manila envelope with a number of loose papers inside. "Here's the deal. Another reporter had this assignment a couple of years ago, but I shelved it because I didn't think he was the right person for the job. Jerry went to another paper shortly after, but he did do some preliminary work, so I had Hannah compile his notes." Whiting slid the folder across the desk. Several lined yellow legal papers were stacked and paper-clipped according to their date. The notes on them were written in neat but small letters: Anthony chose a few at random. *Manning J. Brown, age 39, hanged and burned by a group of white men, Shelby, Arkansas, 1946. Possible Cause: insolence.* An involuntary shudder raced through Anthony as he continued to read.

Some of the reporter's notes were almost illegible from smudges, but he had no problem piecing together what happened.

Whiting waited while Anthony read a few more cases. "There is one case in particular I want you to check out first, Anthony. Did you get to the doctor yet?"

"No, not yet," he said softly.

"There was a black doctor hung in Evesville about twenty years ago. I think this might be the most interesting of the cases because of his status."

Anthony sifted through the papers until he found it: *Dr. William Elmore Washington, age 42, was hung August 19, 1939, in Evesville.* The notes read that there were rumors he performed an emergency operation on a white woman. Townsmen were mad because he saw her naked.

"I think you should investigate this one first. It should get the readers' attention and make them interested in reading more."

Anthony tried to clear his mind. His head roared and his heart pounded. He gritted his teeth and reached for an aspirin, which he had started carrying after his encounter with the body at the funeral home. Then he touched the folded piece of paper in his jacket pocket. "When do you want me to start?"

"As soon as possible. We have a goal of increasing our readership by at least three percent this year. I think your stories will play a big part in that increase. If they do, you'll have the brightest of futures with this paper. I guarantee it." Whiting stood and walked toward the door. "Go to Evesville and see what you can find out. Interview the doctor's family and anybody else who might have any knowledge of what happened. If Doctor Washington kept a patient list, or if the family knows of any of his other records, ask if you can see them. Be straightforward, and tell them you want to write about the incident; that you want the world to know what happened there. You have six weeks to write the first story. After that, I want a story a month." Whiting's voice sounded as if it was coming from some far-away place.

"I'll start on it today."

Whiting walked out, leaving Anthony behind with the files.

"I forgot something," Whiting said as he reentered.

"Yes, sir?" Anthony answered, removing his hands from his forehead.

"There's a gal named Carla Monroe. She's a history teacher at Philander Smith College here in Little Rock. I understand she wrote a book called *Strange Fruit* about the tragedy of hangings. You might want to check her out. She might have information you can use."

Anthony wrote her name on his yellow pad. The last person he needed to meet right now, he thought, was someone who studied hangings.

It was quiet in the apartment as Anthony, still drowsy, raised his head. Naomi lay on her side, watching him. One hand lay casually on his chest.

"You have a good sleep?" Naomi asked.

"Hmmm? Yeah, I guess I did," Anthony answered.

"You *really* missed me this time, didn't you?" she said, giggling. Her eyes, still dreamy, held remnants of their encounter.

Anthony looked at her and smiled. He had almost been afraid to call her since he had been so negligent about keeping in touch, but she acted like they had just talked the day before. After dinner they came back to his apartment, and she stayed.

After all the time they had known each other, they still began their lovemaking with the uncertainty of strangers, tentatively touching, holding, kissing, and eventually seeking, probing. Trembling turgidity sinking into a soft, undulating, swelling, enveloping warmth, comforting a frantic mental state, searching for relief through connection; each movement created a slowly rising heat that upon exploding, released a thousand demons.

"Yeah, I guess I *really* did."

He ran his hand over his face as he watched her walk to the kitchen. She had put on a few pounds since their days at high school, but it only added to her attractiveness. If her walk through Moe's restaurant was any indication, her body still drew plenty of attention.

"You want some orange juice?" she asked.

"That would be fine."

Naomi returned and sat on the edge of the bed, quiet, looking at Anthony as he drank his juice.

"Yes?"

"This is about as good as it gets, isn't it?"

Anthony waited, knowing what was coming next.

"You feel an urge, you call me. That's been our relationship since we've dated. Is that all I should expect?"

"Naomi...I enjoy you. I enjoy being with you, but—"

"But I'm not your type. I mean, I didn't come from a well-to-do family and I don't have a college education, so I guess I can't expect somebody like you to want to marry me, right?"

Anthony sought the words that would appease her, knowing that the truth lay somewhere else—the fact was that if she had a degree, came from a well-to-do family, and looked like Dorothy Dandridge, he still couldn't marry her. It wasn't something he could do at the moment. He refused to burden someone else with his problem, and he felt badly that he couldn't explain it.

## · VII ·

The next day, Anthony arrived outside the town limits of Evesville about mid-afternoon. It was sweltering hot. Even the trees looked beaten down by the unrelenting rays. The battered sign—EVESVILLE, POP 291—should have been evidence enough. The crumbling barn he passed, the unattended fields, a rusted tractor, half on the road, that looked as though it had been there for years, told him all he needed to know before he even reached the town.

It was abandoned.

Something bad had happened. He sensed it. A rush of anxiety careened through him like a flash flood, before finally slowing to a trickle then dissipating somewhere in the recesses of his stomach.

The blue 1954 Chrysler Imperial turned slowly onto what used to be the main street. The pock-marked road was full of weeds and plants growing from the cracks of the crumbling red bricks that someone laid long ago, no doubt trying to elevate the town's image and at the same time make the street more negotiable.

Anthony's shoes kicked up small clouds of powdery dust as he stepped from the parked car and walked carefully along the street, hoping for some sign of life, but knowing there would be none. Except for the drone of what sounded like a million crickets and the occasional bleating of the only remaining inhabitants that he could see—two goats—there was no other noise but his footsteps.

The air was still. The town was still, as if waiting, like a child would wait, looking at a stranger who first entered her house to see what the visitor would do next. Anthony walked tentatively, looking at the small cluster of buildings on either side of the street, some with doors or windows open. Where they once may have beckoned strangers to enter, they now just stood there, abandoned and forlorn.

There would be no answers in Evesville.

The sheriff's office was easy enough to find among the worn and weathered buildings. An old faded wood shingle with the word "SHE IF" still hung from the roof. Not wanting any surprises, Anthony slowly eased the door open. It whined in protest as the rusted hinges grated against one another. He stopped to look before entering. The wood floor creaked as he hesitantly walked to the nearest desk. Even now, in this empty office that previously serviced those who enforced the law, he felt as if he were trespassing.

Papers were strewn everywhere as if the place had been ransacked. There were only two cell doors in the place, and they both stood wide open. Chairs were knocked over, and one desk had a crack down the middle. What looked like dried blood was splattered on the wall near the desk.

Anthony backed out and walked quickly to his car. He looked around once more before turning the car and driving to the town limit. According to records and newspaper accounts, this was a thriving town in years past. What made everyone leave so quickly? Was there an epidemic? What happened there?

Only when he drove for a few miles did he feel comfortable stopping and pulling out a map. The next town was eighteen miles away. First he would call Whiting, but he knew what his response would be even before he made the call. There was another story there. He felt it. Something bad had happened in this town, and whatever it was could be an entirely different story from the one he was assigned to write.

Anthony called Whiting after entering the town of Wynne.

"So it's abandoned? You mean nobody lives there?"

"Nobody, Mr. Whiting."

"What happened?"

"It's hard to tell. It appears there was a fight of some type in the sheriff's office. Blood was on the walls, and the place was torn up."

Whiting whistled. "I'll be! If something happened in that town, somebody should know something about it. Shoot, I remember having a hamburger at Ryder's Saloon there. Every year, the town used to have a pig roast. They'd have a contest for the fattest hogs, and whichever one won, that was the one the people roasted. Coloreds and whites used to get together for the occasion. People would even travel from other towns to participate.

"If I remember, they used to have a sawmill down by the river there. A large part of the town worked at the place."

The phone was silent. "This might be something, and it might not, but I'm leaning toward the former. Don't forget about

Doctor Washington, but I think you should pursue this, Anthony. I'm going to see if we have anything in our back files, meanwhile you see what you can find in Wynne. See if you can find somebody who was from Evesville, and see what they have to say. I'll get back to you if I find anything here."

"It would be nice if I could get a list of names of families in the town," Anthony suggested.

"Good idea. I'll get somebody on it... and Anthony?"

"Yes?"

"I'm getting a little excited about this."

"Yes, sir. Me too."

## · VIII ·

Wynne was a typical small southern town. It was created when a train derailed, leaving one boxcar without wheels and off the track. The car was placed upright and designated Wynne station in tribute to Captain Jesse Watkins Wynne, a prominent businessman and banker of Forrest City.

The town was larger than Evesville probably because of the railroad that still ran along the side of the town. There was a gin and lumberyard that employed a substantial amount of the 4,900 plus people living there. Front Avenue, the main street, was dirt with a boardwalk. The street contained an inn, a dry goods store, a barbershop, a post office, and a few smaller stores.

Anthony had always been curious about small towns. Each seemed to have its own character. Some were open to strangers and some suspicious of them. As he parked on a side street, he saw colored people in a sizable number walking, working, and socializing. There were the usual "White Only" signs, but from the look of things, there wasn't much tension. That was good, he thought, because folks might be more open to a colored reporter asking questions.

Anthony walked toward the inn to check on accommodations. The sign in the lobby suggested he look elsewhere.

He spotted some colored folk congregating around the dry goods store. He headed that way and nodded to them as he approached. "Good afternoon. Where could I find a room to rent around here?"

The five people nodded in return as they continued whatever they were doing. One of the men pointed northwest of town across the tracks. Anthony looked in that direction to see a cluster of homes. "Any house in particular?" Anthony asked, trying to keep the sarcasm out of his voice.

"They'll tell you when you get there," the man said, blunting Anthony's attempt at any further conversation.

Not very friendly, Anthony thought. Maybe he would have to change his assessment. Anthony drove slowly down the road, trying to steer clear of the ruts and holes. To avoid any damage, he eased the Chrysler across the uneven tracks. It wasn't hard to figure out that his people lived in this part of town. Young colored kids frolicked in the street, only getting out of the way of the slowly moving car at the last minute.

One house stood out from the others because it was the largest house on the street and the only one with a small patch of lawn. Anthony guessed it was the one that took boarders. "They have rooms for rent?" he asked one of the older boys, pointing toward the house.

"Yeah. Mrs. Warner," the boy said without looking up.

Once he got closer, Anthony could tell that the house was well kept by the fresh paint on the fence, the well-manicured lawn, and the spotless windows. There were a few men lounging on the porch, but there was no other activity. Anthony nodded at the three men before knocking. They returned his nod.

The woman who opened the door was small, compact, and about fifty years old. Her movements and gestures suggested she was all business. "You looking for a room?" she asked, her eyebrows raised as she stepped aside to let him in.

"Yes, ma'am," Anthony said, removing his hat.

He followed her into the parlor where she motioned him to sit.

"Where you from?" Mrs. Warner asked, looking at him closely.

"Little Rock, ma'am."

She grunted as if she already knew the answer. "Why you here?"

"Writing a story, ma'am."

Mrs. Warner squinted at him. "By the day or by the week?"

"The day."

"Ain't going to get much writing done in one day, son. It's six dollars a day. You get your own room, breakfast, and a towel a day. For another dollar, you can eat dinner here. I don't fix supper. You pay six dollars as a deposit, and I'll give it back when you return the last towel and I inspect the room."

Anthony already felt comfortable in the house. The parlor was furnished with white cane-bottomed chairs with white tidies. In the living room was a large couch decorated with green, red, and yellow flowers and a matching chair and footstool. Fresh flowers sat on the shiny, wooden, glass-topped coffee table. A large yellow throw rug that matched the yellow curtains covered most of the immaculate wood floor.

The fireplace mantel contained as many pictures that could fit of Mrs. Warner and what appeared to be family and probably friends. There was a slight smell of ammonia as if someone just finished cleaning. The walls appeared freshly painted, and everything had a fresh, clean look. It was obvious that Mrs. Warner was a fastidious housekeeper.

"Can I see the room?"

She pointed toward the stairs. "Second room on the left. The door is open."

Anthony found the room clean and neat as he expected. It was probably better than that flimsy hotel in town anyway.

He came downstairs to a waiting hostess and held out his hand. "My name is Anthony James Andrews, ma'am, and I'll be a good guest."

Mrs. Warner looked at him closely as she shook his hand firmly. "I expect you will."

Dinner was the first real meal Anthony had eaten that day, and it was the best he'd had in a while. There were six other guests at the table. The conversation was light and respectful, probably because of Mrs. Warner, who looked like a mean mother hen watching over her brood.

The guests fed on fried chicken, ham, collard greens, okra, yams, red tomatoes and onions, boiled potatoes, and corn bread. Each of the items was seasoned differently from anything Anthony had ever tasted. His compliments were acknowledged with a slight nod from the hostess.

Mrs. Warner introduced Anthony to the guests. There were the half-brothers Turner Major James and Willie Elder Mason, who were permanent residents in the house. Hanford Ray Collins lived in Forrest City, but moved out of the house because his cousin had contracted tuberculosis. Alvie Parkinson was passing through going north. Carl and Chandler Sutton were two brothers from Mississippi looking for work.

"So I understand you writin' a book," Hanford Collins asked.

"Well, I work for a newspaper, and I'm writing on racial atrocities."

The guests all chuckled. "Atrocities." Alvie Parkinson said it slowly letting the syllables roll out of his mouth one after another as if he were in a spelling bee. "Is that like people doing something bad to other people?"

Anthony nodded. "Exactly."

"I suspect you'll have a job until you is one hundred. There ain't no shortage of them," Parkinson said.

The guests chuckled again.

Anthony smiled. "I guess you're right, because I've just begun, and already my hands are full. I came from Evesville looking for one story, but I ran into a dead end. I was surprised to find the town vacant."

"Town's been vacant for some time. Why you interested in Evesville?" one of the Suttons asked.

The only other side conversation stopped when he mentioned the town. Mrs. Warner appeared at the kitchen door with a ladle in her hand, waiting for his response.

"A doctor was killed there. A Dr. William Washington? That was going to be my first story."

"That was a long time ago," Turner James responded.

"Yeah," Mrs. Warner agreed. "Why are you going back that far? We got stuff that happened this year."

This was going to be easy, Anthony thought. How lucky was it the first people he ran into knew something about Evesville? "Well, first, there are not that many black doctors in the South, and second, this is the first time I ever heard of one being killed. We thought that this story would catch everybody's attention and maybe shed some more evidence on who did it and why."

"Who is we?" Mrs. Warner asked.

"The *Arkansas Sun*. You read the paper?"

"Sometimes. You work for a paper like that?" Mrs. Warner asked suspiciously.

"Yes, ma'am. Been there less than a year."

"And you getting that type of assignment?"

"Yes, ma'am," Anthony said proudly.

"Humph!"

The table was silent for a moment in respect for the owner of the house, but she was through.

"Hell," Turner James said, then bowed his head to Mrs. Warner. "Excuse me, Ma'am."

Mrs. Warner glared at him, but said nothing.

"Most people know why they killed the doctor, and most know who did it," Turner said.

"Are you from there, sir?" Anthony asked.

"I ain't no 'sir,' and the answer is no, but I know people who are."

"Could you tell me what happened?"

"It's simple," Turner replied. "The Negro was getting too big for his britches, so they brought him down. I don't know all the details, but I know folks who do."

"I would certainly like to talk to them about that incident."

The room was silent.

"See," Anthony explained, "the whole reason for the stories is to bring to light all of the bad that has been happening to colored folks over the years. We only hear about the ones they choose to write about—the sharecroppers in Elaine, the Edward Coys, the Henry Smiths and the Edward Perkinses—but there are a whole lot more stories out there, and many are in Arkansas. If we print these stories regularly, it might make more people aware and avoid more of the same. At least that's our hope."

"Our hope?" Mrs. Warner asked skeptically then turned to go back into the kitchen. "You old enough to know about Elaine?" she asked, her back turned as she ladled out more greens.

"Yes, ma'am. I know a lot of good sharecroppers were killed just because they wanted equal pay."

"There were some doctors killed there, too. They were just minding their own business," she countered.

Anthony paused out of respect for the deceased. "I didn't know that, but I'm sure there are other stories that are similar. I'm going to start in Evesville first and see if I can pin that story down, and if I do a good job there will be more."

"Good luck," three of the guests said in unison.


"The person I'm going to introduce you to is Hero Redding," said Turner James. "I'm going to have to get my brother to drive you out to the farm he works on. I don't know how much he's going to want to tell after all he's been through."

Anthony liked James. He seemed the most open of the guests at the house and was also the one who knew people from Evesville. "What happened?"

"Well, Hero started out as a sharecropper and worked fourteen, sometimes sixteen, hours a day for almost ten years until he made enough money to buy a farm. When folks left Evesville, he had to leave the farm behind, and now he's sharecropping again."

"There must have been something mighty dangerous happening for a man to leave behind ten years of work."

"Yeah, well from what I hear, it was."

"But you don't know what?"

"I'll let Hero tell you."

Turner's brother, Willie, was the silent type. He didn't say more than four or five words during the whole trip. Once they reached the road to the farm, they had to take a smaller dirt road to Hero's shack. "It's a damn shame," Willie murmured as they approached in the car.

Hero appeared to be about sixty years of age. He was a tall, proud man. Anthony could see it in his walk. It surprised Anthony to see him coming out of the shack because of his reputation for working, but it was Saturday afternoon, and maybe this was the time he took a break.

"How y'all? Turner, Willie." He smiled as he approached. "Who's your friend?"

"This here's Anthony. He's a newspaper reporter. He wants to write a story about some doctor who was killed in Evesville."

Hero's back stiffened as he looked at Anthony with a solemn stare. It took a few seconds for Hero to offer. "Well don't just sit there in the car, come on in."

The four men walked through a group of clucking chickens that parted only when they were almost stepped on. The shack was a sparsely decorated, one-room, narrow building that recently had an addition built. It was evident based on the different colors of wood. Anthony looked at what it was before Hero enlarged it and wondered how anybody could have lived so cramped up like that. He wondered what Hero lived in when he was in Evesville.

"Y'all hungry?"

"Naw. Thanks," Turner said. "Just ate." Willie shook his head, and Anthony followed suit.

"Well y'all have to eat something. It ain't right if I don't feed you. Don't feel right. My wife, Anna, gonna be right back, and you gonna have to eat some of this stew she made, okay?"

"Hero, if that stew is as good as that chicken she bakes, I guess I got to have a bit," Turner said.

Willie shrugged, and Anthony did the same. "Sure."

Hero pulled out his pipe, filled it, and sat at the table with the men. Looking at Anthony, he asked, "So, what's this you want to know about Evesville?"

Anthony waited until Hero tapped and lit the pipe before he told the story. "Do you remember the incident that took place there?"

"Incident! Wasn't no damn incident. It was a killin', plain and simple."

"Were you there when it happened?"

"Yeah. Nobody saw nothin'. One day a man is treating people for sickness and the next day he hung," Hero said bitterly. "That's all I know."

"You don't know why?"

"Yeah everybody knows why. He was an uppity colored man who was making too much money, and his clothes were too fancy for their taste, that's why."

"I heard it was because he did an emergency operation on a white woman and saw her naked."

Hero leaned over, resting the pipe on the table. "If you know all that much, why you come to see me?"

"We need a story that backs that up. When we put it to print, we want the facts to be right."

Hero leaned back and picked up the pipe again, seemingly satisfied with the explanation. "That's what I heard, too, but that was just an excuse to hold another of us back. What I told you is the real story."

This was a good a time as any to bring up the deserted city, Anthony thought. "What happened that everybody left the town?"

Hero glared at Anthony for a minute before everybody turned to the opening door. "My goodness, Hero, you didn't tell me you were having guests," a woman said.

"Turner and Willie is guests. This man here, I don't know," Hero answered, pointing at Anthony with the pipe.

"Well if they in the house, Hero, they're all guests," she admonished as she took down three bowls for stew. Anthony and the brothers ate the stew quickly and silently.

Turner pushed his bowl toward the center of the table. "Anna, your food gets better every time I eat it." Not waiting for a response, Turner nodded at Hero. "Hero, thank you for your hospitality, but I guess we done stayed long enough. Good to see you both again, and don't work so hard that you can't come to town and visit every now and then."

Hero waved without saying anything as they left.

"Did I say something wrong?" Anthony asked.

"Some people are touchy about that part of the Evesville story. You got to be careful who you're asking." Turner said.

Willie nodded affirmatively. "Yep. You got to be careful."

## · IX ·

As Anthony entered the parlor from his morning run, he overheard Mrs. Warner speaking to one of her cousins. "Word got around town fast about the reporter."

"Yeah," Turner interjected, "everybody in town is talking about him and Evesville now."

That was good, Anthony thought. Maybe somebody with information would come forward.

When Turner came to his room late that morning to tell him he had a white visitor, Anthony didn't know if he was more surprised or concerned. He was jotting down a few more notes about his visit with Hero when his new visitor knocked on the front door. The quick scuffling of Mrs. Warner's feet indicated it was an unusual visit.

From his room, Anthony had watched the man approach the house. He was a scruffy-looking, thin, sandy-haired white man about forty to fifty years of age, but there was something about him that didn't fit his looks. Anthony could tell it in Mrs. Warner's voice and the grudging voices that responded to him from the men sitting on the porch.

"Mrs. Warner, I hear you got a newspaperman here looking for information."

"Seems like it, Mr. Byrd."

"I'd like to speak to him if I could."

"Yes, sir, Mr. Byrd. I'll go get him for you."

Anthony had already started down the stairs. Although the visitor was as short and scruffy as he appeared from the upstairs window, Byrd's most notable feature was his eyes. They were the bluest eyes Anthony had ever seen. It almost seemed he could see through a person. The piercing stare threw Anthony off for a moment.

Byrd was dressed in blue overalls over a pair of work shoes and a shirt with Cummins' Plow on the pocket.

"Bobby Joe Byrd," he said as he offered his hand.

"Anthony. Anthony Andrews, sir."

"Can we go somewhere and talk?" Byrd said glancing sideways at the men gathered on the porch.

For some reason, Anthony was nervous. He didn't know why. If there was a fight, he could take this guy, but then why was he thinking like that? Byrd said nothing that could be considered threatening.

"Sure. Where do you want to go?" Anthony asked carefully.

"Let's just walk." The three men on the porch looked anywhere but at Anthony and Byrd. The strange-looking man didn't say anything else until they had walked for a couple of minutes. "So what you doing in Wynne?"

Anthony hesitated. He tried to be just as direct. "I'm trying to track down what happened to a black doctor who was killed some time ago in Evesville."

"So what you find?" Byrd scratched his head as he talked.

Anthony found it odd the way he used his right hand to scratch the left side of his head. "Not much. You have some information?"

"Well, I suspect you're also curious about why that town is deserted, too, ain't you?" Byrd stopped to look Anthony straight in the eyes.

Anthony looked off into the fields full of ripening cotton. "Yeah, I have to admit, I was surprised."

Byrd nodded. "Several people are interested in what happened in Evesville."

"Oh?" Anthony responded.

"Yeah. I don't know how much you heard, but some people who was in that town plumb disappeared. Some of them boys had relatives, but can't nobody shake loose anything, especially since Sheriff Jefferson was missing too."

Anthony perked up. "So what do you know about what happened there? I haven't been able to make heads or tails out of what I've found out yet. Are the disappearances related to Dr. Washington?"

"I don't know if them missing is related."

"What happened to them?"

"That's what don't nobody know." Byrd bent his head, looking at the ground ahead. "Most of them missing was good ol' boys from in and around town. Used to always get together for some fun most weekends. Suddenly, one weekend, they missing."

"Exactly when did this happen?"

"I'd say 19...48 or thereabouts."

"So when did the town become deserted?"

"Two or three years later, maybe four."

"Was it because of the missing people?"

"Yep. First the white folks moved. That was shortly after they found that the sheriff was missing. Then the Nigras moved."

Anthony tried to overlook Byrd's pronunciation. "The whites moved because the sheriff was missing?"

"Yeah, and them boys. We think it was fourteen of 'em all total."

"Fourteen? And nobody knows what happened?"

"Just suspect. But we're glad to see you looking into it. White folks don't have a clue, and the Nigras ain't talking. "

They turned to go back toward the house. "Look," Byrd said in a conciliatory tone, "I want to help all I can. I got friends who can help you if you need it. You ask for Bobby Joe Byrd at the tavern there, and I'll get to you. I'll be in town for another week before I head back to Little Rock." He hesitated. "I need you to know how important any information you find about the missing men is to some of us. If you find out anything, you let me know now, you hear?"

Byrd's voice remained soft as it had been during their whole conversation, but Anthony sensed that his last statement was more a command than a request.

"I sure will, Mr. Byrd."

Byrd left without another word. Anthony didn't know if he had gained an ally or an adversary, but he suspected the latter.

· X ·

Mrs. Warner looked worried when Anthony returned. Anthony didn't think anything could faze her, but obviously Bobby Joe Byrd did.

"What did he say to you?" she asked, rubbing her hands nervously.

"Nothing much. He wanted to know what I found."

"You be careful of that man. He is an evil, evil man." Her voice quivered as she talked.

Anthony was only slightly surprised at her emotional statement. Byrd did have a sinister way about him. "I will, Mrs. Warner."

"Look, you need to get what you looking for as fast as you can. I know a family named Wright who used to live in Evesville and a white family named Jackson. They may be mad at me for getting you together, but you need to get what you need and keep going. You hear me?"

Anthony smiled slightly. She sounded more like a mother than a landlord.

"This is not funny," she scolded, her hands on her hips.

"I'm sorry. I didn't mean to take you lightly."

"You sure as hell better not, and when you meet these people, you don't go sharing nothing with Byrd. I trust him about as far as I can throw a plow. I don't know what happened in Evesville either. A couple of people from there stayed at my house for a while before moving on. They talked among themselves, but didn't say much to us, and we didn't ask." Mrs. Warner continued, "Ezell Wright, though, he was a talker, and he probably would tell you what went on. His wife is a talker, too, so I'm going to give you their address and the Jackson family's address with a note so you won't be a stranger."

Mrs. Warner smoothed her apron as she talked. "The Jacksons were sharecroppers in Evesville. My daddy and Thaddeus Jackson's daddy were on the chain gang together. My daddy helped old man Jackson a few times. If they know something, they'll probably tell it."

"I appreciate that, Mrs. Warner. I really do."

"What you going to do with that information once you get it?"

"I really don't know yet."

Anthony wasn't being completely truthful. He was superstitious about telling people his business before it was finished. If the stories proved to be anything at all, they were definitely going to press.

The Wrights lived in a cozy house that showed that whoever built it took pride in their work. Anthony felt somewhat comforted by that fact as he walked toward the porch. Ezell Wright opened the door before he could knock. Mr. Wright was a tall man, probably six feet six inches, thin, with a quick smile. Mrs. Wright was as short as he was tall at about four feet three inches, slightly plump, and just as pleasant.

Mrs. Warner was right; Ezell and Edethel Wright were talkers. After they read Mrs. Warner's note, they never asked why he wanted to know about the town. Mrs. Wright poured Anthony some tea.

Everything they said was in a hushed tone as if someone might be listening outside the door. Anthony couldn't figure out if this was the way they always talked, or if it was the subject matter.

"We lived in Evesville for eight years. Was getting enough money together to buy some land when all this stuff started happening," Ezell said.

Anthony waited.

"Yes," Edethel chimed in. "They was big trouble about to brew in that town, so we hurried up and got out with the rest of 'em."

"They hung one of the Coulter boys. At least that's what we hear," Ezell said.

A pounding started in the back of Anthony's head. Ezell's voice sounded like it was coming from a tunnel.

"Next we know, folks trying to find the sheriff, trying to find out what happened to some of the men in town. They was missin'."

"Missing?" Anthony asked, wiping his brow and trying to stay focused. "How many?"

"Eight, nine, or more. They say they went out one night and didn't come back."

Ezell looked to his wife for confirmation.

She nodded. "Uh-huh. But Sheriff Jefferson come up missin' too."

Anthony sighed quietly with relief. The pounding had suddenly stopped.

"Yep, people in town say the doors to his office was wide open. The jail doors was open, and there was blood on the wall like there was a big fight," Ezell chimed in.

Anthony was writing furiously.

"That's when the white folks started leavin'," Edethel said.

"Yep. Like Moses and the Jews."

"One after another."

"One after another."

It was obvious the two had been married for a while, Anthony thought. "Then what happened?"

"We Negroes ran the town for a few years. Had a sheriff and everything," Ezell said proudly. "Never used Sheriff Jefferson's office though. Avoided it like the plague."

"Yup, like the pox. But rumor was they was comin'," Edethel said.

"Who are they?"

"You know." Ezell said even quieter, nodding.

Anthony nodded, too, although he didn't know why.

"They been known to burn down whole towns of Negroes, and we heard we was goin' to be one of them towns."

"So what happened?"

"Well, the Coulters and the Williams family moved with the white people, and they was the strongest of the colored families. If they had stayed, we all might have stayed, but they moved early on, and we didn't feel like we wanted to wait to see what was goin' to happen. We just farmers, you know?" Ezell returned to his normal hushed tone.

"Coulter?" Anthony asked. "Wasn't it a Coulter you say they hung?"

Ezell and Edethel looked at each other like they may have said too much. Neither responded.

"Can I get you some more tea, Mr. Andrews?"

"Thanks, but no thank you. Is there anything else you remember?"

Both shook their heads. It would have been amusing except for the subject matter. The Wrights even shook their heads in unison.

"Where can I find any of the Coulter family?"

"Don't know," they said together.

"Well do you know anything about a black doctor who was killed?"

"Nope. Heard about it, but it was before our time," Ezell responded.

Anthony returned to Mrs. Warner's house that evening. He looked forward to a good meal and rest. Talking to the Wrights and then driving the two hours back was tiring.

"Well?"

It was evident from how quickly she opened the door that Mrs. Warner must have been looking out the window for him. "What they tell you?"

Anthony looked behind Mrs. Warner to see three of her guests sitting in the living room. "I received a lot from them. Thank you for that information."

Mrs. Warner ignored his thanks. "You got enough for your story now?" She still seemed disturbed.

"I'm going to see the Jacksons tomorrow on my way back to Little Rock, unless you have somebody else I can talk to," Anthony said.

"Nope. Sure don't."

Anthony paused as he stepped inside the front door. "Who is this Coulter family the Wrights were talking about?"

Mrs. Warner shrugged.

"All I heard was the Coulter family was a mean bunch. People used to call them the, 'Bad, Bad Coulters.' Didn't nobody mess with them," Turner said as he and Willie came down the stairs.

"But I heard the Klan hung one of the sons," Anthony said.

"Big mistake," Turner said shaking his head.

Anthony pulled out his notes. "What about the Williams family? What do you know about them?"

Turner looked at his brother who had sat on the sofa for help. "All I heard, the Williamses was good people," Willie said quietly. He hesitated. "The Williams and Coulter families was supposed to be close. Maybe related."

"I know some of them people," Carl Sutton chimed in. "Our cousin used to date one of the Williams girls."

"What do you know about them?"

"They were good people like Willie said."

Anthony glanced at Mrs. Warner and caught the end of a fading frown. "Is your cousin around here?"

"No. He lives with some other cousins in Tyronza." Carl kept glancing at Mrs. Warner.

Anthony grimaced. "Tyronza, shoot, that's in the other direction, but maybe I can look him up."

Carl hesitated, still glancing at Mrs. Warner.

"I guess if I get to talk to him, I can move on, otherwise, I might have to stay longer." Anthony saw Mrs. Warner nod out the corner of his eye.

"Name's Toby. Toby Fawcett. Lives with his parents on the old Cheney farm off Pocahontas Road."

Toby Fawcett was a stocky young man approximately twenty years old with a ready smile. Anthony liked him before he said one word. "Yeah, I knew the Williamses. They was somethin' else," Fawcett said. "I had to go through three men in that family before they let me talk to Mary, but they was good people. As straight a people as you'll ever want to meet. When somebody needed help, they were the first ones there."

"What about the Coulters? Did you know them?"

"The Coulters?" Toby hissed. "They wasn't worth a shit!! Always drinkin', fightin'. I had a fight with one of them brothers, and they all came and jumped me. Put me up for a while."

"What did you fight about?"

"A woman."

"If the Coulters were so bad, why would anybody want to mess with their kid?"

"That's a good question. The way I hear it, Hosiah Coulter was out playin', and some white boys came by and started throwin' rocks at him. The boy started throwing back and hit one of the white boys in the head. Split his head wide open."

"Did he die?"

"No. But they went back into town and told everybody they were attacked."

"So then what happened?" Anthony asked as he turned a page in his yellow pad.

"I guess nobody thought too much more about it since some time passed. Then they found little Hosiah hung one day."

Anthony's hand began to tremble, but he had to keep writing. He knew he should ask more questions, but he doubted he would have the strength to continue with that storyline. Anthony stopped and wiped the gathering perspiration from his forehead. It had started again. This was even worse than the last time.

Anthony excused himself to go to the outhouse. It felt like the inside of his head would explode with those horrible childhood images of Emmanuel's hanging. The dank, acrid smells in the small wooden enclosure helped divert his attention for a while.

Gathering himself as best he could, he returned to the house. "Is it true then that white men came up missing after that?" Anthony asked, patting the perspiration still forming on his forehead.

"That's what some folks told my parents. I never believed it, but something happened for all them white folks to leave town like that."

"What do you think happened?"

"Hell if I know. But I know one thing, if they hung a Coulter—"

"Do you know anything about where the Coulters might have gone?"

Toby shrugged. "Can't tell you anything about them. They could all be in hell as far as I know."

"Tell me more about you and the Williamses."

"I don't know. They was strange. Had strange ways, you know? They were always available if any families needed help though. They helped rebuild my uncle's barn after a fire, and I remember going to their farm to go to school when the regular school was closed. That's how I met Mary."

Toby chuckled. "But when you see the family out, you know they meant business. Coloreds and whites respected them. Always armed. Didn't never hear of nobody messin' with them. Just didn't happen. "

Toby leaned back in his chair. "I remember my father telling me that one time a group of white men had this colored man dancin' for 'em in the middle of the street. They was laugh-in' up a storm. Old man Hilton Williams came into town with his nephew Thompson, and they had to walk by these men. Old man Hilton started out, then went back and pulled his shotgun from the carriage as casual as can be. They walked by them men with their heads down, minding their own business. A couple of them boys looked up, but they didn't say a word to those two. Just turned back and kept egging that colored man on."

"What happened to the Williamses after they moved?"

"They all moved out, different places. Mary moved three times, but she wrote."

Toby went to his bedroom and came out holding the letters gently. "I put them under my pillow. That way I can smell her whenever I'm in bed."

Anthony looked at the postmarks. The last one was from Cleveland, Ohio. Anthony waited until he reached the car before he wrote down the address.

The Evesville mystery was becoming a little clearer. Maybe this white family, the Jacksons, could shed more light on the subject.

## · XI ·

The next day Anthony was on his way back to Little Rock after interviewing the Jacksons. He looked out of the car window and leaned back. It was a quiet, peaceful day. The sun was shining. The sounds of singing birds drifted through the air. He was beginning to feel good about life again.

The Jacksons, a white family who once lived in Evesville, were cooperative, but not too helpful, and he was no closer to solving either of the Evesville questions than he was before he met them. The Jacksons moved there long after the tragic death of Dr. Washington.

It was amazing that so many men could be missing, and nobody knew anything. Anthony expressed his observation to Mr. Jackson.

"After two or three days," Mr. Jackson recalled, "I hear some folks went to the sheriff, but they couldn't find him. Must of us was farmers, Mr. Andrews, so we don't get into town that often. All we hear are rumors, and you know how rumors are. They take on a life of their own. Without any bodies or any proof of foul play, and the sheriff missing, it just kind of faded away."

"What about the sheriff? Anybody find out anything else about him?" Anthony asked.

Jackson should his head. "That was the last straw for most of the families. Something was going on in that town, and nobody wanted any part of it. That's why we moved, and that's why a lot of the other families moved. It was everybody for themselves. If it was true that somebody was killing town folk, we didn't want to be next. At first it was just a few families, then a few more. Next thing you knew, there was a stampede."

Anthony had a pile of notes that he would go over at the office. Bits and pieces of information had to be analyzed, but he wasn't too confident that he was any closer than before.

Some time ago, a veteran reporter had told him that the first assignment was always the hardest, and took the longest. Usually a more seasoned reporter would go with a cub reporter like him, but Anthony guessed Whiting had his reasons, and from a purely selfish standpoint, he was glad.

The Chrysler moved slowly along the road as Anthony, watching for stray animals, left the Jackson's farm on his way back to the office. It was a winding, rolling stretch lined by an occasional group of cedar trees that then opened to more fields of cotton. The Jacksons lived a way off the highway, and it was a job finding them. He'd been lucky to meet Mrs. Warner. He smiled as he pictured the smallish woman with her stern face, eyes raised and widened as if she always had a question to ask.

Anthony drove around a corner, slowly moving through another group of trees lining the road when he heard the sound. It was unfamiliar in the quiet surrounding and would have been inconsequential, except for the buzz of something that passed across his windshield and tore a limb off the tree near the passenger side of his car. The sharp crack to his left and the sound of the impact on his right were only milliseconds apart.

Birds squawked at the strange and intrusive noise, and Anthony flinched as he realized that someone had fired a shot.

A second crack followed, and a tree just in front of the car spit bark. Anthony ducked and simultaneously pushed down frantically on the accelerator. There was a third shot, but it was fainter and behind him. The car bounced over a rut before settling down to churn dust as he sped away, almost bouncing out of control, trying to negotiate the dips and the curves.

A few minutes later, his car hit the highway. Tires screeched as they met the asphalt. Head still down, and the car at full throttle, Anthony accelerated to breakneck speed for two or three miles before pulling to the side of the road to recover.

Anthony's hands were shaking, and he was sweating profusely. Thoughts tumbled through his mind faster than he could process them: Were they shooting at him? Why? Was it an accident? Was it hunters? Was it Klansmen, or some white man trying to kill a colored man? Could it have been the Jacksons or someone related?

He took a deep breath to slow himself down. If the shots came from a hunter, they would not have been firing in his direction. Any hunter would know the sound of a car. If it was somebody intent on killing him, either they had poor aim or it was a warning. The sound was close. Whoever the shooter was would have been able to hit him, or at least his car at that distance.

But why?

Bobby Joe Byrd! The name came in a flash. Did he have anything to do with this?

Maybe.

But why?

After settling down, Anthony glanced behind him once more before easing the car back onto the highway for the drive back to Little Rock. He cursed as the car picked up speed. It had started again. The devil was back, pounding at the door with a vengeance this time.

When he arrived in Little Rock, his clothes, including his starched white shirt were completely soaked, and he was weak from exhaustion. He went to his apartment and retrieved the folded piece of paper on his dresser silently promising himself that he would never go anywhere without it again.

Later at his desk in the *Arkansas Sun* building, Anthony thought long and hard about what happened that day. He concluded that somebody was shooting at him, and it was probably connected to Evesville. If so, someone wanted whatever happened in that place to remain a mystery. There was no other reason for those three shots to be that close and not hit him. What was most unnerving, though, was that in the South, warnings like those could quickly turn to serious injury—or even death.

The first letter he wrote to resign the job it had taken him three years to obtain was illegible. Anthony had to wait for his hand to steady before completing it. He read it over, took a deep breath, laid it on his desk, and walked out of the office to clear his mind. After much contemplation, more deep breaths, and a slow walk around the block, Anthony returned.

The letter was gone.

Anthony panicked. "Hannah, what happened to the letter on my desk?"

Hannah peeked around the corner. "It was near your outbox, so I thought you meant for me to deliver it."

Trying to keep his anxiety from showing, Anthony approached her desk. "You still have it?"

"Ummm... yes Anthony. Here it is."

"Did you read it?"

"No. I usually don't read anything but the addressee."

Anthony retrieved the letter and walked back to his desk. He read it three more times before balling it up and throwing it into the trashcan. He took another deep breath. It would take more than a few gunshots to scare him away.

# · XII ·

nthony's run that morning was intense and exhaustive. As hard as he ran, he couldn't shake the lingering effects of the shooting. It probably would do no good to report it. The police would bury it in some file and forget about it. He debated telling Whiting and decided he wouldn't. Not yet. If Whiting thought following this story was dangerous, he could pull Anthony from the assignment. What he was most afraid of was falling into some mental quicksand, but Anthony concluded that he would have to take that chance.

It was after five o'clock in the afternoon when Anthony requested to see Mr. Whiting. A few minutes later Hannah motioned Anthony to go to Whiting's office. Whiting got up to look out his door. "Let me close this first," he said. Anthony pulled out his pad as he waited.

Whiting settled into his chair. "Go ahead, Anthony."

Anthony recounted his trip and interviews.

"Sounds interesting. I'm still surprised nobody in the office has heard anything about Evesville."

"It was a small town, sir. I guess when the sheriff disappeared, there was nobody to follow up on it."

"Can you connect the doctor, the missing men, and the vacant town?"

"Not quite. I need to follow up with the two families and see what actually happened. Right now, the missing men are still a question, although they've been mentioned twice. I don't even know exactly how many, or who they are. I do know the Williamses and Coulters families moved first, and I know where the Williams family lives."

"Where are they, son?"

Maybe it was Anthony's imagination, but Whiting's voice seemed strained. "The Williamses are in Cleveland, Ohio. I'm not sure about the Coulters yet. They may be there, too, since they're supposed to be so close."

"What do you think? You think it's worth a trip?"

"Yes, sir, I do," Anthony said with confidence.

"Let me check. Are you coming in tomorrow?" Whiting asked.

"Eight A.M., sir."

"Good. What about the Monroe girl? Have you talked to her?"

"The professor? No, I haven't. Do you think it's necessary now that we have all this information?"

"It couldn't hurt."


Anthony called the college and made an appointment with Professor Monroe for 5 P.M. the next day. It surprised him that she would see him so quickly, but on the other hand, it didn't. Everything was starting to fall into place. With any luck, he would get to the bottom of the Evesville incident and pen his first story in a few weeks. That would put him ahead of schedule.

At the office, Whiting asked Anthony to brief the editor, Charlie Hargrove. Both of them were encouraged by his progress. Their enthusiasm stoked a fire in Anthony as the three plotted his next move.

"I think Anthony should follow this through to the end," Whiting offered.

Anthony had never seen Hargrove so animated. "I agree." Hargrove couldn't sit down. He waved his hands as he talked. His small head bobbed, providing a visible punctuation to every other word. "We need to follow this story wherever it leads. I think we're on to something." He patted Anthony on his back. "You break this story, and who knows where you end up."

That was all Anthony needed. He would go wherever necessary and do whatever was necessary to solve this puzzle, then write the best story the *Sun* had ever printed. Anthony's temper flared for a second. Bullets be damned.

After meeting with Whiting, Anthony did some research on Professor Monroe. It wasn't as hard as he thought it would be. He found that besides *Strange Fruit*, she had published several articles and had written two other books on different aspects of the colored family's experience in Arkansas. *Strange Fruit* was still available at the college bookstore, but after purchasing it and glancing through it, Anthony laid it aside. The graphic pictures weren't what he needed to see right then.

Anthony waited in the lobby of the administrative building on the campus. As was his habit, he was early. Anthony wasn't able to draw a picture of the professor on the phone. She sounded down to earth, but stern. There were no pleasantries, just point-by-point discussion. Her voice gave no indication of what she looked like. He concluded that she was young, plain, and probably obstinate.

Classes were over, and the traffic was light in the building. The few young students that passed by, so bright and cheerful, caused Anthony to reminisce briefly about his college days. As a professionally dressed woman rounded the corner, he stood as he watched her approach. She walked with the confidence of royalty. The few students in the hallway gave her the same respect Whiting received at the newspaper. Without knowing for sure, he guessed it was Professor Monroe. Except for the young part, none of his other characterizations fit.

Even in heels, her long legs moved effortlessly, as if she were gliding. "Mr. Andrews?"

"Professor Monroe?" He bowed slightly as she approached. It was the first time he ever remembered doing that.

"Carla." She offered her hand as she smiled at the gesture. Her brown eyes twinkled. "I was intrigued by your call."

She was completely different from his first impression. There was a hint of a rose fragrance that briefly permeated the air as she extended her hand. Her grip was gentle but firm.

The professor was maybe a few inches shorter than him. He guessed about five feet ten with a slim but shapely build. Her closely cropped hair framed a burnt-brown face that had the blunt but attractive features of Eartha Kitt. "I'm glad, otherwise, I probably wouldn't have had the pleasure of meeting you."

Although Naomi was the sexiest woman he had ever dated, the professor had that intangible something that was, in her own words, intriguing.

"Did you have a place in mind where we could talk?"

They agreed on a coffee shop off campus. Anthony offered her a ride, but she insisted on driving, with him following.

The shop was on the outskirts of downtown and nondescript, serving coffee, tea, and pastries. There were no other patrons. Carla ordered sassafras tea. Anthony ordered the same.

"So, racial atrocities. That is a subject near and dear to my heart," Carla said as she stirred her tea.

Anthony shrugged, slightly disappointed. She was straight to the point. No small talk. No getting to know you. All business. "I can see based on your many writings. How did you come up with the title of your book, *Strange Fruit?*"

"That was a Billie Holliday song about hangings in the South."

I've heard Billie Holliday records, but I'm not familiar with that particular song," Anthony replied, trying to tap his memory.

Carla grimaced briefly. "If you heard it, you would remember it. In all my twenty-six years, I've never heard a song as haunting as that one."

Jazz got her off the subject for a moment, and the two found that they had a lot in common besides music. Carla was an avid reader as well as a writer. It surprised her to find that Anthony was familiar with most of her work.

"Are you working on another book?" he asked.

"Two actually. The subject matters are related. One is about the black migration from the South, particularly Arkansas. I'm interested in the colored families who migrated, why, where they moved, and for what reasons, and finally, what are they doing now, and whether they feel the move was worthwhile."

"Interesting."

"Did you know that between 1950 and 1960, there were close to one hundred fifty thousand colored families that left the South to go North?" Carla asked.

"I had no idea."

"It's well documented."

"I'm sure. What was your second topic?"

"The second is about families who fought racial discrimination and violence. I'm interested in the circumstances that made them stand up to their aggressors."

"That sounds like where this investigation is headed," Anthony offered.

"I know. That's why I found your call so fascinating. So Evesville is a ghost town now?"

"Yep. I've never heard of towns completely deserted like that, have you?"

Carla hesitated for a moment. "I have. I recall a study I conducted with another colleague about three years ago. If I remember correctly, Arkansas has had about twenty or more places that have become ghost towns."

Anthony looked at Carla incredulously. "For what reason?"

"Many different reasons. I remember a few like Hopefield in Crittenden County. It burned down during the Civil War. The town of Rome in Arkansas County was another one. There was a big dispute about land titles. Most of the townspeople moved to nearby Arkansas Post, which eventually faded, and is now a national historic park. More recently, Graysonia in Clark County along the Antoine River was abandoned. It was a lumber town that if I remember had a population of about seven hundred."

"You have a good memory."

Carla laughed. "Keep in mind, I said there were over twenty towns. I only remembered three."

"So those were the main reasons towns were abandoned?"

"There were other reasons. Some towns were ports, and when the railroads came, some faded. One town I vaguely remember had a smallpox epidemic that started from a ship that docked. They had to burn the whole town down to stop the disease from spreading. You had lumber towns, mining towns, and other towns with a major employer that closed down. When employment dried up, people left."

It was hard for Anthony not to stare at her. "Have you ever heard of a town being abandoned because of fear of violence, like Evesville supposedly was?"

"No. I can't honestly say that I have, but that doesn't mean it couldn't happen." Carla's eyes widened. "You think that's why the town is empty?"

"It appears that way from folks I've talked to so far."

"That is fascinating."

Anthony nodded. "It's scary if you ask me. I was there a few weeks ago. Something bad happened in that town. I could feel it."

"So how far are you going to take your investigation?"

"The city editor told me to solve the mystery, so that's what I'm going to do."

Carla grimaced. "The *Arkansas Sun.* That paper never impressed me. How were you hired?"

"After three years of rejection by every newspaper you could think of, someone finally recognized my talents. I received good grades at the University of North Carolina, was assistant editor of the campus newspaper, and interned for a summer at the *New York Times.*"

Carla laughed lightly. "I received good grades at Spelman, too, but I was a rebel on campus. If there was a march for racial justice, I was in it. Even if I had received a 4.0 grade point average in journalism, I'm sure the *Sun* wouldn't have hired me."

Anthony smiled. "I wasn't a marcher. In fact, one of my first articles was about how unnecessary marching was."

Carla cocked her head. "Is that right? What else did your article say?"

"That racial justice was only going to come when we have elevated ourselves."

She leaned forward, eyes narrowed. "Elevate? Do you mean to their level?"

Anthony raised his hands, palms upward. "I guess I mean that we need to work on our shortcomings, and we would eventually be accepted. I guess you could call it rising to their 'level'."

Carla folded her arms and glared. "Many of us are already at their 'level' and are still not considered equal. I'm not understanding you."

"None of my friends have ever had a racial incident. No one has tried to hurt them, and no one has done anything against them because they were colored. I just believe it's because they've reached a certain status in life," he explained.

"You told me a few minutes ago that it took you three years to land this job you have. How come your *status* didn't help you then?"

"I'm talking about violence."

"Oh, I see. Since no one's hung you yet, everything is fine?"

Anthony could almost see the heat rising from where she sat. "Look, I can tell you're getting upset. Why don't we get back to why I asked to meet with you?"

"Fine." She paused, looking at Anthony. "Don't you feel uncomfortable with this assignment?"

Anthony looked down. "Yeah, but not for the reasons you think."

Carla looked at him closely. Her stare softened. "So where do we go from here?"

"I want to use your expertise in acquiring information."

Carla agreed to look in her files to see if she had anything on Evesville or Dr. Washington. They shook hands, but her coolness was obvious. Anthony breathed a sigh of relief after they parted.

Her rose scent lingered long after she left.

# · XIII ·

Anthony was sitting at his desk thinking about Carla. Even though they had met only twice, there was something that tugged at him when he thought about her. It wasn't the first time he had those feelings, but this was the first time he acknowledged them. There was something else though—something that appealed to him on a deeper level.

He could understand her getting mad. She had obviously experienced a different life than his. Anthony understood prejudice, and he saw it almost every day, but he also believed it could be overcome without putting your life on the line. Marching, chanting, and getting beaten and harassed wouldn't be how he would deal with that situation. He imagined that if he came from a family of farmers, laborers, or such, he would probably be like the Williams family and possibly the Coulter family and carry a gun everywhere he went to protect himself, but he wasn't a farmer or a laborer.

He quickly snapped back from the thoughts roaming around in his head. There were priorities, and right now, Evesville had his complete attention.

Hannah broke his train of thought to notify him that Mr. Whiting wanted him in his office. Whiting was standing when Anthony entered. "Anthony, Hargrove and I talked it over, and we want you to go to Cleveland, get next to this Williams family and see what you can find out about Evesville and the Coulters. We did some research here, and it appears there were some men missing from that town like one of your people said. Nothing's been one hundred percent confirmed, but we found a source that might help us with this."

He sat as he continued. "With your research, Professor Monroe's help, and further discussions with folks in the Evesville area including the Williamses, I feel confident that we can uncover what happened."

"While you're investigating here, would you see what information you have on a Bobby Joe Byrd?"

Whiting hesitated for a brief second. "Sure. Was he a resident?"

"No. I don't think so, but he has a strong interest in what happened in Evesville."

Whiting began to tap his pencil on his desk. The noise was disconcerting as Anthony debated how much he wanted to tell Whiting. "Where did you meet him?" Whiting asked.

"Wynne."

"And what exactly did he say?"

Anthony recounted their discussion, and Mrs. Warner's reaction to him.

The pencil continued its steady rhythm on the desk as

Anthony talked. It was odd. As long as Anthony had known Whiting, this was the first time he appeared nervous.

"Where is he now?"

"I guess he's still in Wynne."

"Anything else?"

After some hesitation, Anthony told Whiting about the shooting.

Whiting sprang out of the seat, startling Anthony for a moment. "They shot at you. My God, Anthony! Why didn't you say something sooner? Jesus! You could have been killed! Who would do something like that?"

It surprised Anthony how cool he was at that moment. "Obviously somebody who's not interested in anyone finding out about Evesville. That's all I could figure."

Whiting threw the pencil on the desk. Anthony watched as it took two bounces before falling to the floor. "Shit!"

The outburst startled Anthony. Cursing was also uncharacteristic for Whiting.

"This is going to be a good time for you to leave town. Whoever shot at you will probably be long gone when you get back. You go ahead and find out what you can in Cleveland. See what that Williams family knows, and see if you can locate that damn Coulter family."

There he goes again, Anthony thought. It was as if he was talking to another person. This wasn't the gruff but pleasant speaking Whiting he knew. Something had him extremely agitated. Either something else was going on in his life, or it was this story.

"You know anybody in Cleveland, son?" Whiting asked as he slowly settled back into his seat for the second time, still sitting on the edge.

"No, but my father does."

"Good. You think a week will allow you to get what you need?"

"I guess so. I'm in unfamiliar territory, Mr. Whiting."

"Well, if it takes longer, don't worry about it. Call me after you get there, and check in every day. If you're making progress, I don't think anybody's going object to you staying longer. Just get the job done, son, and good luck."

Back at his desk, Anthony sat rubbing his forehead. The paper was putting a considerable amount of trust in his ability to get the job done. It was exhilarating and scary. What if he failed? He wouldn't though. This was a make-or-break situation. There was no way he was going to fail. He had come too far.

That night Anthony called Naomi. It was the second time that week. After she left, he jogged five miles then worked out for almost two hours with his favorite jazz musicians providing him with the background rhythm he needed. Only then did his nervous energy begin to fade.

PART II

## · XIV ·

*August 1961*
*Cleveland, Ohio*

T hompson Williams picked up the *Cleveland Press* from the kitchen table and shook his head. Orville Faubus was serving his fourth term in office as governor of Arkansas, and if there were no surprises would probably serve a fifth . The article, like many of the past articles about Faubus, included the story of Central High and the nine Negro children that were turned back by the governor and his national guard before they eventually were able to attend the school. The last of the nine children who had bravely integrated that school in spite of Faubus and the seg-regationists had graduated in 1960. Whether the governor liked it or not, it appeared that throughout history, he and those stu-dents would be joined at the hip.

The segregationists were in almost complete control before then. They wanted nothing to do with colored people in their schools, churches, businesses, or homes, unless they employed them. Thompson had no problem with segregation. He had rarely encountered white people during his life. His father didn't let any of his kids work for whites no matter how much money they offered to pay, so to a young Thompson, whites were at most a curiosity.

There was something to be said for Negroes having their own "village" as Aunt Dahlia used to say, where colored businesses thrived, kids were raised to be responsible citizens, and leaders were developed. Dunbar High, the all colored school where the kids who integrated Central High previously attended, was a highly respected school, so the colored community perceived the integration of Central High as a mixed blessing. But Thompson, like most others, also resented the fact that someone could tell him where to eat, sleep, do business, and go to school, especially when he paid the same taxes as everyone else.

Nine years had passed since his own family had departed Evesville, but now the Williams family was finally together again. Nine long years of separation and anxiety had finally been put to rest.

Thompson was able to relocate all of the families to Cleveland but one, and no one knew where they were. Thompson feared the worst, and had almost given up hope when he received the call he had been waiting for.

"Thompson?"

"Cread?"

"How are you doing, cousin? We haven't talked for a while," Cread said in his deep, slow, monotone voice.

"That's true, cousin." A relieved Thompson sighed.

"Evidently, you got the message though. Everybody's here now but you."

"I hear. Me and the family stayed with the Swansons for a while, but now we're ready to move on."

"The Mississippi Swansons?" Thompson asked.

"Yep. Granddad's second cousins."

Thompson smiled. Leave it to Cread to find the only relatives whom no one remembered to contact.

"How are they doing?"

"Just fine, Thompson. Just fine."

"So... are you heading this way?"

"No place else."

Thompson pictured his cousin, medium height, broad shouldered, with a flinty stare. Cread hardly ever smiled, and wasn't much for words. That was fine with Thompson who was relieved that he had found his cousin. What was most important was that they all be together again. "I need a couple of weeks to get you placed, but you and the family can stay with me until then."

"That's fine. How is it up there in Cleveland, Thompson?"

"It's different, Cread. That's all I can say."

"How's everybody?"

"Everybody's fine, Cread. You probably wouldn't recognize Raymond and Johnny."

"Raymond. I always did like that boy. So he's doing fine?"

"Yes he is. He's smart, just like his Cousin Cread, and hard nosed, just like his Cousin Cread."

Cread chuckled.

"You'd be proud of him. Look, I've saved some money. Do you need anything for traveling?" Thompson asked.

"Naw. I'm fine. Mabel and I saved money from working in the lumberyard down here. Even the kids found jobs."

Cread was like that, proud and self-sufficient. It was just as well because it had cost a lot to get the family to Cleveland. "We have a lot to talk about, Cread. I look forward to seeing you and the family soon."

"Me, too, Thompson. Me too."

Thompson sat back on his sofa, relieved. When the family left Evesville, they were lucky enough to sell the farm to an out-of-town lumber company. Martin Lumber had been after the family to sell for years. He and his uncle Hilton always left their talks open, understanding that circumstances could change for the worse for Negroes overnight. When events required that they leave, the family sold the farm without hesitation. They felt sorry for many of the other residents who owned property. Many left their life's work in that town. Few left with nothing more than their personal belongings to start again somewhere else. The tragedy of it was that their plight was no fault of their own.

Cread arrived five days later, and that night, Thompson had a dream. His father came to him smiling. Behind him was his grandfather and his great-grandfather. They never said a word. The three of them gathered around him, hugged him and then silently walked away.

That night, Thompson slept more peacefully than any other time in his life.

## · XV ·

Thompson walked slowly through the house, humming an old gospel song his mother used to sing to the kids. The family was going to tease him again when he showed up for Sunday dinner wearing the same sport coat he always wore, but at age fifty-one, he did what made him comfortable.

The family had settled in the Glenville area. It was a stable neighborhood with mostly well-kept homes that was populated primarily by working-class people like the Williamses, and a few professional families interspersed.

Most of the Williams family was able to move within blocks of one another. Thompson's brother Deacon, who was having the dinner, lived around the corner. It was such a beautiful day that Thompson decided to walk to Deacon's house. He had to come to love this neighborhood even though it was nothing like the farm where the Willamses mixed with only a few other families.

The neighborhood had taken some getting used to, but the people were friendly, and they looked out for one another. It made him feel at home knowing that his neighbors had some of the same attitudes as their neighbors in the South. But there were differences, too.

Thompson and Hilton noticed it within weeks after they arrived. "Did you see that, Thompson?" Hilton had asked as he watched a young man get out his car, leaving his female companion behind to open her own door.

"I saw it," Thompson had said, "but I've seen even worse. I saw a kid talk back to his mother in public."

Hilton shook his head. "This is a different kind of place. You don't see the respect the families in the South had for their elders. There isn't the common courtesy that you expect. When a guest came to our house, we fed them first. You said 'yes ma'am' and 'yes sir' to anyone your senior. You tipped your hat to a lady and stood and bowed when she approached. You only cursed on rare occasions, but never in front of your family, elders, or kids, and you always took care of your younger brothers, sisters, cousins, and anyone sick or elderly."

Thompson nodded. "I see some of it, but not enough. Not like we did. It doesn't seem like this city living agrees with all colored folks."

Hilton continued, "In school, learning was a must. Remember one year the city closed the colored school, and your father paid a colored teacher to come to the farm to teach our kids, and any other child who wanted to come? Every last one of them came. Kids up here though seem to take education for granted."

Thompson nodded again and thought about the children in the Williams family. Some excelled in sports or music. All excelled in academics.

Although Thompson couldn't show favoritism, his nephew Raymond was his favorite. Since his wife, Maryann, and their unborn baby had passed in the maternity ward of the hospital, Raymond was the son Thompson never had. Watching Raymond grow was gratifying. Sometimes when the elders got together, Raymond was the only kid who would sit silently listening to every word.

It didn't seem like there was anything that Raymond couldn't do. At six feet and 180 pounds, he lettered in track, basketball, and football. He played the saxophone, and had a 3.5 grade average. Raymond also had other talents.

Thompson remembered receiving a call from his sister-in-law one Saturday evening, upset because she found several coins in Raymond's pocket. Unable to lie to his mother, he told her he won them shooting pool with the counselors at the YMCA.

"Gambling, Thompson. They let them gamble at the Young Men's Christian Association! What should I do? I need to put a stop to this right now."

Thompson remembered muffling a laugh. "How much did he win, Ludie?"

"What difference does it make, Thompson? He was gambling."

"I understand, Ludie, but how much was it anyway?"

"Seventy cents!"

Thompson laughed out loud. "Ludie, I wouldn't worry over the boy winning seventy cents. It's not like he stole it. Anyway, boys will be boys. You have to let them grow."

"You men are all alike. That's what Hopson used to say."

They both were silent for a while. Ludie's husband and Thompson's brother had committed suicide shortly after they moved from Evesville. It devastated Thompson because he was closer to Hopson than anyone. No one talked about why he did it, but they all had an idea. Hilton called it, "pressures from the past." It was as apt a description as any. Almost every colored family in the South was affected by events that had taken place in their past. It was inevitable. The Williams family was no different in that respect, but in another, they were. Not many families had experienced what their family had.

It was up to one of the other men in the family to assume Hopson's role as father to Raymond and his sister, Lanny. Thompson's brothers Ransom and Deacon were willing, but Thompson did it without hesitation. He loved both of the kids as if they were his anyway. "I'm sure Raymond knows you're upset, and I bet you won't find that kind of money on him anymore," Thompson said.

If Raymond were as smart about that as he was about most things, he would hide his winnings the next time, Thompson thought to himself.

## · XVI ·

They hated him. He could sense it. He could feel their stares when he wasn't looking. The feeling was mutual. This wasn't about winning friends. It was about conquest and money. Everything else was secondary. Raymond Williams scanned the pool table, focusing on the task at hand. There were only six balls left. Running all the balls off the table would be easy except for one shot, but that wasn't the main problem he faced that night in Riley's poolroom.

Riley's was located near the corner of East 105$^{th}$ Street and Massie Avenue on the east side of town. This busy street Raymond found early on was affectionately called The Five by folks who lived on and around it. Although Riley's had no aesthetic value, he loved the place. It was a plain, drab building that sat between the Café Tia Juana and Abbott's Bar-B-Q. There was only one thing that stood out on the building: its dirty windows.

The dirt served two purposes. Mr. Riley used to say that folks inside weren't interested in being seen from the outside and folks outside didn't want to know what was going on inside, therefore the windows were never washed.

The place smelled of incense, probably to cover the smells of old age and bad plumbing. The billiard table was located at the entrance. Walk up a few steps and there were the regular pool tables. Benches and high-backed chairs were located along the walls. The worn floors were hardwood, and there were six-foot fluorescent lights over each of the tables. These were the only source of light. The tables were solid oak with green felt. The wood glowed from the lights above. The tables were the centerpieces of the room. They stood out like fine pieces of furniture in a dreary antique shop.

Over time, Raymond noticed a certain traffic pattern. The people who frequented Riley's varied from folks of the most questionable character to recreational players who stopped in only on occasion. Everybody had their hours, though. Recreational players came early and were eventually replaced by the night folk, generally after 9 P.M.

Listening to the regulars, Raymond found the poolroom had seen enough drama to fill five books—shootings, fights, robberies, thousand-dollar games, police brutality, scams, numbers running, major dope deals, and even a birth. Raymond noticed that anyone visiting for the first time usually sat or stood quietly, slowly absorbing the atmosphere, otherwise they would have been overwhelmed by it.

The hustle was the main business inside and outside of the poolroom. Those, like Raymond, who were in the game, appreciated the hustle the most. The squares who had some inkling that it was going on could only watch and learn. Of all the psychological ploys, diversions, and sleights of hand—which were sometimes magical—the pool hustle was the most beautiful of all. It required skill, finesse, artistry, and a little juju. To take a square's money one time was nothing. To take it continuously was a work of art, and Raymond was the game's most avid student.

Riley's was Raymond's second home. On weekends he was there when it opened and didn't leave until it was almost closed. On weekdays, he tried to make Riley's at least twice. The weekends were when the money flowed though, and this weekend was going to be a big payday, if he played it right.

Nine Ball was a sucker's game. Of the nine balls on the table, all you had to do was pocket the nine ball to win. Money was won when the nine fell on the break; was pocketed after hitting one of the other eight balls, numbered from one to eight, as long as they were hit in numerical order; or if a person made all the balls in order and then pocketed the nine as the last ball on the table. Many people played it because it was easy to learn. You could also get lucky, but what escaped most was that in its purist form, the game was hard to master. That's what made it a sucker's game.

Raymond was playing Nine Ball with G'Money, and G'Money was running out of dough. G'Money's main man, Roach, had come in and was heading toward the table. He was a better shooter and probably had a lot more cash. Raymond's problem was making sure he didn't scare Roach away before he busted the fool he was playing.

"You might think you down with this game, but you ain't," G'Money said loudly, standing with about four of his friends who were cheering him on. "Ain't no college-bound punk going to out-hustle G'Money. You ain't got enough heart."

There were another eight or nine observers sitting and standing around the table. "Talk to him, G," one of the men said. "Show him what's happening out here on the street."

"Yeah, school him, G," an older man shouted. "School him like college never will."

Raymond looked at G'Money and smiled.

Roach sat silently, glaring at Raymond.

G'Money was a wannabe hood, short, slight of build, and he sauntered with an exaggerated pimp walk. When he was excited, he stuttered. G'Money bragged that he had held up more drugstores than anybody in Cleveland. At least that's what he said.

He was ten years older than Raymond and had been around the street for years. Like many of the other guys who drifted in and out of the poolroom, he called the street his home.

Raymond could care less. He concentrated on one thing: two things actually—busting G'Money and then busting his boy, Roach. Who in the hell would name themselves G'Money any damn way? He could never get over these names. Whatever happened to Frank, John, Robert, and Charles? Who in the hell would want to be called Roach?

Although G'Money was always packing and tried his best to be hard, Roach was the protector. Roach was a small-time dope dealer, but he always had a stash. He was an ex-boxer, but always looked like he had just left the gym. Roach was about the same size as Raymond, but he was compact with muscles rippling from his short-sleeved shirt whenever he made the slightest move. His bald head and drooping mustache gave him an even more imposing image.

The few times he had seen Roach, Raymond never saw him smile. Word on the street was that he had killed two people in his lifetime over an unpaid debt and had spent some time in the joint. G'Money was like his baby brother. Roach and his boys protected G'Money whenever anything funky went down. That's why Raymond knew that if he played G'Money right, Roach would try him. They had that kind of relationship.

Raymond leaned over the table, looking at the crowd. "I would appreciate you all keeping the noise down. I'm trying to think."

"Ain't no thinking to be done, chump. Play the game," G'Money replied.

Raymond looked at the balls again. The six and the eight balls were frozen together against the upper rail. He could break them up, but it would take a great shot to do it. Besides the six and eight, the three, four, five, and nine balls were left, and they were at the opposite end of the table.

In a flash of brilliance Raymond decided what he would do. He remembered overhearing a hustler named Bugs from Chicago, one of the best one-pocket players in the world, telling another hustler, "The difference between a good shooter and a great shooter is creativity." Raymond walked slowly to the table, studied the layout, and shot the three ball into the side pocket. He then ran the four ball the length of the table, giving him the angle he needed. The five ball was in the right front pocket, the nine ball in the left front pocket. Instead of shooting to break up the six and eight, Raymond hit the five with high right english, making the cue ball slam into the object ball, jump back, then dip toward the nine, knocking it into the pocket.

All that practice was paying off. The way he shot the ball, a novice would think he had tried to break up the six and eight, but got lucky and pocketed the nine. The small crowd groaned. Game and match. G'Money turned and threw his cue into the rack. He had no more cash. He was busted, just as Raymond figured.

"You lucky mu..mu..mu..mmmm."

Raymond smiled as he pocketed the money. "Thanks for the game and the money, brother man," he said mockingly. "Come back when you get some more."

G'Money glared at Raymond, then shrugged and turned his back, ignoring the outstretched hand.

"Rack man, come get this black man!" one of the watchers in the crowd yelled. Raymond pulled down the stake money from under the light, counted and then pocketed it, deliberately keeping his back to G'Money's friends.

There was a few seconds of silence followed by movement toward the table. "Come on. I'll try you."

"Yes," Raymond said to himself as he turned toward Roach. "How much we playin' for?"


That night Raymond strolled down Massie Avenue to his house with three hundred and sixty dollars of Roach and G'Money's cash tucked in his sock. He placed the winnings there, not so much to avoid being robbed, as to avoid his mother's scrutiny. Since the YMCA, Raymond was careful about leaving any evidence of his gambling. If his mother was upset about the dimes he made when he first started playing, she would have a blue-faced fit now.

At the age of twenty, Raymond was a predator. He didn't know when and how he made the transformation from a decent, churchgoing kid to a pool hustler. Nothing in his personality would have foretold it. He kept to himself, and his family was straitlaced. They didn't drink, smoke, or curse, but with all those good habits in his background, he still ended up in Riley's smoke-filled poolroom among alcoholics, addicts, and drug dealers, hustling the hustlers.

Playing as well as he did that night gave him a rush that was better than any drug or alcohol high. The pockets seemed a foot wide, and the power he commanded over the game and the players was like one hustler said, "The best feeling I ever experienced with my clothes still on." It wasn't just about the money either. It was about playing that almost perfect game, where your only real competition was yourself. It was about making inanimate balls come to life and do your bidding.

Neither his mother nor the rest of the family would understand. His gambling went against everything he was taught. If they found out, it would probably result in one of those "family meetings" where problems were ironed out. As his uncle Hilton always said, "The action of one person in this family affects the reputation of all of us." Gambling was up there with drunkenness and dope as far as Raymond's family was concerned, and they would consider what he did a disgrace.

Even his friends didn't understand.

"Why do you spend so much time in a place that probably has more criminals in it than Mansfield Penitentiary?" His best friend Drew asked one day.

"I'm good, man. What can I tell you?" Raymond thought that at least Drew would understand. An athlete as good as Drew knew how it felt when they were at the top of their game and in full control of the outcome. "The best part though, man, is that I can be even better."

"Yeah, but at what cost, Raymond?"

"It's cool, man." How could he explain that he was addicted? That he took his first "hit" when a friend invited him to play a game and he saw the art of the hustle, watching the players and learning after a while that he was just as good as they were, if not better. If he had lost the first few times, he might have quit, but he didn't.

Like a junkie, one fix led to another. Every win was a validation of his skills. That was what satisfied him most. Sometimes he approached the game like a rabid, ravenous dog. Other times he tiptoed up on it like a heroin junkie. The goal was the same.

He needed that high, and the only way he was going to achieve it was to find a victim, and for the brief time they played, feed on his soul.

It was only 10:30 at night, but as usual, Mom was waiting for him. She never went to sleep until he came home. It didn't matter how late it was, she was always up, waiting. Never saying anything, just looking at him closely before going to bed. He guessed she was checking to see if he was drunk or on drugs.

His mother was like that. She made sure that her children were growing up right—church on Sunday without fail, social clubs, piano lessons, skate lessons, etc. All the things they never were able to do on the farm back in Evesville. Then there were uncles and aunts who always pried into your business: Who are you dating? How are you doing in school? Are you still working at Bonds clothing store?

Damn!

Raymond found out about G'Money later that day. The money he lost to Raymond wasn't his, so he tried to rob a drugstore on Hough Avenue to replace it. It was his first robbery, folks on the street said. He pulled his gun, but froze trying to say "Stick up!" The owner and his son both shot him.

Everybody was talking about it when Roach walked in. The crowd parted expectantly. Without hesitation he walked up to Raymond and punched him in the side of the head. It was a hard punch that left Raymond stumbling and his head ringing. Raymond recoiled, then gaining his balance, coiled. The guys in the poolroom moved backward, laughing softly, but respectfully. A firm hand on his shoulder kept Raymond from retaliating. He turned to look at Mr. Ambrose, one of the elders who always seemed to be around. "It's not worth it, son. Let it go," he said softly.

Raymond spun back around, but Roach was walking toward the door. Without turning, Roach warned, "Watch your back, bitch."

## · XVII ·

Raymond was shaken but he tried not to show it. Everybody in Riley's was looking at him. He had to be cool, even while he was churning on the inside. It was there that he borrowed and smoked a cigarette for the first time in his life. It was a Lucky Strike, and it burnt his throat, but he didn't show it.

The guys in Riley's told Golly the rack man that Roach was steaming when he found out about his friend. Golly relayed the story to Raymond. Roach believed it was Raymond's fault. If G'Money hadn't lost all that cash, he would still be alive.

Roach had always said he had never liked Raymond from the first time he saw him. He wasn't from there. He didn't need any money. He thought he was better than them anyway with his college-bound ass. Roach told his guys the punk didn't know it, but his ass was grass. He would learn who to mess with out there. He would learn who to respect.

"You need to watch yourself, kid. This ain't nothin' to play with," Golly told Raymond in parting.

Raymond thanked Golly, but thought little about it. He could handle whatever came up. There were very few things that scared Raymond in life, and another person wasn't one of them. As a matter of fact, Raymond couldn't think of anything that he was afraid of. He was sure there was something out there, but he hadn't met it yet.

That same weekend, Raymond learned about "The Bench." The few times he heard it mentioned, it was as if the guys at Riley's were talking about some mystical place. He never paid that much attention because whenever he looked over to the bench that was reserved for certain people, all he saw was a bunch of old men sitting up high with nothing to do but watch the players and talk among themselves. They reminded him of old crows on a fence. In his mind they were nothing but fixtures like the bench itself.

When Mr. Ambrose stopped him from rushing Roach, Raymond told Trey that he almost blasted him. Trey was the one who called the rack man on G'Money. Raymond thought it was funny that he almost hit an old man. Trey didn't. Trey was in his mid-thirties, about six-one, wiry thin with smooth blue-black skin. His mouth was always twisted in a perpetually wicked-looking smile, even when there was nothing funny.

He grew up two doors down from Riley's. Although he wasn't that good a shooter, he knew how to make money. He also knew everything that was happening on the street.

"If any of them get off the Bench to talk to you, that means they watchin' you," Trey confided.

"Watchin' me for what?" Raymond asked.

"Watchin' your game!"

"For what, man? For what? Why are those old farts so inter- ested in my game?"

Trey hit his forehead with his open palm in exasperation. "You really don't know, do you? Let me explain somethin' to you. Ain't but four dudes in this poolroom ever been invited to the Bench. *Four.* You know how many brothers been in and out this place? Thousands, and that's since I been here."

Raymond still didn't get it. Trey was probably high again. He sure wasn't making much sense.

"You know who those four brothers were? Huh?" Trey con- tinued, running off their names: "Playboy, Deuce, Dandy, and Dead Man. You ever heard of any them dudes? Huh?" Trey's voice kept rising. "They're world champions, fool. World cham- pions! Dandy been on TV. Dead Man beat Minnesota Fats out of four thousand dollars in five hours one time. Deuce moved to New York and rules from Ames's Billiard Parlor, and Playboy travels the country makin' big money. Bad dudes, man. All of 'em been to the Bench."

"So what you're telling me is that if I get invited to the Bench, I'm going to be a star?"

"Naw, fool. You got to already be a star when you get there; you a world champion when you leave there. Them old men got more knowledge in they little fingers than you got in your whole body. Mr. Ambrose was a world champion three-rail billiard player. Mr. Campbell was Fast Eddie Perkins's personal rack man. Mr. Jenkins backed five-thousand-dollar games in his time. Never lost a major bet. These dudes know the game!"

Raymond looked at Trey, trying to see if he was just talking crazy. Trey never broke his gaze. He was looking at Raymond as if *he* were crazy. "Dumb ass. Don't know shit!"

Raymond didn't go into Riley's during the week. He was going to give Roach a chance to cool out. Trey would tell him if he had been around and what type of attitude he had. Raymond wasn't scared, but he was going to be cautious. If Roach had already killed two people like they said, he wasn't going to be the third, and Raymond surely didn't want to kill anybody himself.

On Thursday, Trey called Raymond to give him the low-down. "Roach was in Wednesday. He said he had somethin' for you. I think he going to sneak this dude in to play and bust you. They'll probably be at Playboys poolroom up the street sometime next weekend."

Raymond was relieved. If that was all Roach had in mind, bring it on. He figured that if the dude had a major rep, it would get him that much closer to the Bench.


Too much was happening too quick in Raymond's life not to share it with someone. Uncle Thompson—Raymond called him Uncle T for short—was always a good listener, but what's more, he was closer to Raymond and his sister, Lanny, than any of his other relatives. Raymond figured if anybody would understand, it would be Uncle Thompson. Raymond needed direction. He wasn't stupid enough to believe he had everything figured out. Uncle Thompson told him once before to come see him if he needed anything. It seemed that everybody in the family came to Uncle Thompson at one time or another.

Uncle Thompson was the coolest of all the family members and the oldest of Raymond's father's brothers and sisters. At fifty-plus years old, he looked a lot younger. Only the graying hair gave him away. Unlike many men his age, he was still in good physical shape. Raymond liked him because he never asked many questions.

Word was that he was part of the street for a short time. Although he had only graduated from the ninth grade, he was intellectually equal to any college graduate Raymond knew. He heard enough discussion between his uncles and other elders to know this for a fact. Uncle Thompson was the kind of man he wanted to be.

His uncle was mowing his lawn when Raymond approached. Raymond remembered that he was scared of his uncle when he was young. Anytime Uncle Thompson came near him, he would start crying. That lasted until he was almost seven, according to his parents.

As he watched his uncle walk back and forth across the lawn in long, purposeful strides, it dawned on Raymond why he was probably afraid of him. Uncle Thompson had a presence that was almost menacing. His close-cropped hair and thick mustache, which drooped below the corners of his mouth, gave him the appearance of someone who carried a constant grudge. Coupled with his six-foot-three muscular stature, a normal person would cross the street at night if they saw him. What was funny was that everybody thought Raymond, without the mustache, was a carbon copy of his uncle in looks and manner.

"Hey, youngblood. What's happening?"

"Hey, Uncle T. Nothing."

"What brings you over this way?"

"Just decided to drop by. How are you doing?"

"Good. I'm always happy to see my favorite nephew. You want some iced tea?"

"Yeah. That's cool."

Thompson placed the mower against the house and went inside to get a pitcher of tea. They both settled on the front porch. "School okay?"

"Yep."

"Work?"

"Okay."

"You still seeing Myra?"

"Yep."

Thompson paused, then with a twinkle in his eye said, "So then how's your game?"

Raymond froze. "What game?"

Thompson chuckled. "Your pool game, young man. They tell me it's pretty strong. I hear you have the potential to be one of the best. That true?"

Knowing he would be chastised, Raymond tried being vague. "How did you hear about all that?"

"I got connections. I knew the first time you stepped your little green ass inside Riley's doors. I heard about you and G'Money and Roach, and I heard about the Bench."

Raymond shook his head in amazement. He should have known.

"So it's true about the Bench?"

"Yep. Everybody who got their counsel became world champions. I've heard of each one of them."

Raymond looked at his uncle. "So, I have a chance if I keep winning?"

Thompson paused for a minute. He looked into space like he did when he used to argue with Raymond's father, Hopson, and was about to throw out some heavy stuff. "Winning is not your problem, Raymond. Your problem is deciding what path you're going to travel. I've watched you grow up. You're good at several things. You're a good athlete. You're good at this pool thing. You're smart. You have common sense. You're a fine, caring young man. I'm telling you this because you need to decide what world you're going to live in. You go to the Bench; you'll probably become a bona fide hustler. In a year or two, you could be a world champion, but you have to go through the streets to get there, and you're not from the streets."

Thompson paused. "You have any real friends in the pool-room?"

Raymond thought of Trey. "Nope."

"You have any friends on the street?"

"No."

"Let me ask you another question. You take care of G'Money after you beat him?"

Raymond looked puzzled. "What?"

Thompson looked exasperated. "That's the kind of stuff I'm talking about. You always give your man something to take with him. It saves him face because he walks out with something in his pocket. If you treat him right, he is more inclined to play you again. It's also a respect thing. You understand that, Raymond?"

Raymond gave him the slightest of nods.

"See," Thompson said kindly, "that just goes to show that their world is not your world. You don't know anything about the street. You have no respect for it. You know how to hustle, but barely. You got no foundation, no history, no references, no backup. You know what I mean? You're bringing one dimension to deal with a multidimensional situation. Part of the hustle—hell, part of living—is controlling your environment. You control with knowledge—knowledge of history, knowledge of the present, knowledge of everything around you. Nobody is telling you jack in that place but slow-ass Trey. You didn't even know about the Bench, and you almost sleep in that place."

Raymond ran his hand through his close-cut hair, surprised that he was having this long of a conversation with his uncle. Like most of the men in the family, none of them talked much, so when they did, everyone listened. "So what are you sayin' Unc? You don't think I can make it?"

"I'm saying, Raymond, that you're a doberman pinscher, but you're in a wolf's den. Your future is going to college and being a square. Take what little you learned from hustling and apply it to the rest of your life. With what you learned, you're already one step ahead of most people. Anyway, I have some other things planned for you, family things."

It was the first Raymond had heard about "family things." Like most of the men in his family, he didn't ask many questions. He learned some time ago that if you listened long enough, everything would be revealed in time.

Raymond left his uncle's house with an even greater appreciation of him. He was thankful to have an uncle like Thompson. Not that Raymond agreed with him completely. No, he didn't have any friends in the poolroom, and he had no connections, but he had skills, and his skills would make a way. Winning a chump's money was the way. Becoming a world champion was the way. School and all that middle-class B.S. were secondary—at least at that moment.

## · XVIII ·

You're doing it again, Raymond."

"Hey, Myra. Hold on one second." Raymond knew he was about to get scolded so he carried the phone to his room and closed the door. "Hey. How you doing?"

"Like you care."

"Okay, I know I haven't called you in a few days, but I've been moving fast. I apologize, baby."

"What would it hurt for you to pick up the phone and call me every few days?"

Raymond started to reply there was a dialer on her end, too, but he didn't. She was upset, and she did deserve better. "Look, next weekend I'm taking you out to dinner downtown and to Leo's Casino. The Temptations are going to be there. I'm going to make it up to you, okay?"

Myra sighed, "Okay."

Raymond figured he had said something right—at least this time. There was so much to learn. He didn't know if he would ever understand women, but Myra was cool. She didn't press him, and she wasn't selfish. She worked harder than he did, so she understood. Her job as a nurse's assistant at Mt. Sinai Hospital kept her going for twelve hours at a time. All he had to do was talk to her and let her know what he was doing. They saw each other every weekend, but she wanted to hear from him during the week and that wasn't too much to ask. He just had to do it.

"You still trying to hustle pool?"

"Trying?"

"Yeah, trying. You aren't that good, or are you?" Myra teased.

"You better hope I am, or else you won't be getting that dinner."

"You better find a way to make that happen, man, whether you win or lose."

Raymond laughed with Myra. He had met her in the tenth grade. She was five-foot-seven, built like a model with short hair, a beautiful dark brown pixie-like face, and a quick temper. Quiet as it was kept, she could beat most of the boys in track and basketball. Plus, she could also kick most of their butts in a fight.

When he first met her, she was the leader of a gang of girls. She challenged him to a fight one day because he had beat up her smartmouthed brother after a pickup basketball game at Cory Church. Myra and her girlfriends came on his street and called him out of the house. Raymond knew right then that the girl was out of her mind.

Their fight lasted about a minute. To the surprise of everybody but Raymond, a new kid on the block then, she was no match for him. Raymond was ruthless in the fight, and although he didn't hurt her too badly, he did knock her into a garbage can and kick it down the street. It was a message to her and anybody else who thought they could come on *his* street and punk him out.

His biggest worry was that one of the women in the family would see him not only fighting a girl, but humiliating her like that. It was a rule in the family. Boys did not hit girls much less knock them into garbage cans. The Williams women would have killed him, without a doubt.

It was another five months before they would even speak to each other. Myra was steamed that she hadn't won that fight and had lost a little of her rep in the process. One day at canteen, though, Raymond asked her to dance, and to his surprise she said yes. Raymond apologized for the fight, and Myra reluctantly accepted. Her girls were flabbergasted since all she had talked about was revenge.

They became friends first, then boyfriend and girlfriend. She continued to challenge him, and they constantly went at it, racing, playing one-on-one in basketball, wrestling, and competing in anything else they could think of, including who would get the best grades. Raymond was her first boyfriend, and based on almost everyone's opinion at school, they were a perfect match.

"A big game is coming up this weekend, and I'll have plenty of money after that."

Myra sighed. "Just be careful, Raymond. I know some of those guys, and they aren't anything to play with. They almost killed my brother who was messing with some other guy's woman down the street at Scatters, so be careful, please?"

"Myra, I'm cool. It's just a game."

"It's more than a game to some of them, Raymond. That's what you don't understand. Some of those guys try to make a living doing what you're doing for fun. You take somebody's money like that and they're going to be mad. Why don't you take Drew and Skeet with you?"

"They have better things to do than to sit around and watch me shoot pool."

"Have you asked them?"

"Myra, everything will be fine. I promise. I can take care of myself." As an afterthought Raymond offered half jokingly, "You're beginning to sound like my Uncle T."

"Yeah? Well then you heard it twice, and twice should be enough."

## · XIX ·

The bus ride wasn't that bad, but Anthony was still worried. With all the stopovers, it took more than twenty hours to get to Cleveland. Besides his salary, he was only being compensated for the room and food while he was in the city, and only for a week. He had to get busy.

There were a few leads. Carla Monroe was able to track the Williams family through some of her resources at the college. Anthony's interview with an ex-boyfriend, Toby Fawcett of Tyronza, provided him with the address for Mary Williams, and he found a real estate broker through one of his father's connections who sold and rented several houses to the family.

Anthony was able to find a third floor for rent through the same broker. The owners were looking for permanent tenants, but when Anthony told them he would only be a week or two at most, they let him have it anyway at eight dollars a week. The residence was located on Drexel Avenue off East 105<sup>th</sup> Street, not far from the Williams family. It was a well-kept house that reminded him of Mrs. Warner's place in Wynne.

The space was cramped with only a bedroom, bathroom, and small kitchen, but he was glad to have found it rather than renting some hotel room. One redeeming feature was the view. He could see almost the whole street from the dormer, which jutted over the front of the home. His ability to see what was going on would help acclimate him to the area.

Staying in touch with the office wouldn't be a problem. The owners said he could use their phone and pay for his calls as he made them.

So far, things were working out.

The real estate broker's office was on East 105<sup>th</sup> near Hampton Avenue. Mr. Homer Johnson was a talker. He reminded Anthony of Ezell Wright. Johnson was glad to share what information he had with Anthony. "Yeah, man. They just kept coming. I sold them three houses and rented them four more. I made a killing off that family."

"So where do they all live?"

"Let me think now. Two families live on Massie Avenue. One lives on Parkwood Drive. One lives on Pasadena Avenue. Two live on Adams Avenue, and one lives on Kempton Avenue. They all live within a few blocks of one another. Nicest people you ever want to meet, too, but it was strange how they all came to live together. I've been selling real estate for thirty years, and I've never seen anything like that before."

"I would guess not. Tell me, who did you deal with the most?"

"Thompson Williams. He was the first one here and arranged everything. Whenever one would be on the way, he would call."

"What type of man is he? You think he would talk to a stranger?"

"About what?"

"I'm writing this story about black families who migrate from the South and why."

"I don't know why not."

"You talk or deal with anyone else?" Anthony asked.

"I dealt with one of the young men. When Thompson wasn't around, he told me to talk to the boy. He's smart as a whip too. I had to show him six houses before he would accept the one I was trying to rent for one of his uncles. He was a pain, but I could appreciate his concern.

"One day he asked me to meet him at Riley's poolroom because he said he didn't want to miss playing this guy. The guy didn't show, so I played him a few games. I didn't know he was a pool hustler until he took me for twenty dollars before I could say my name."

Anthony perked up. "One of the family members is a pool hustler?"

"You telling me. I happen to shoot a little pool, but, man, this kid could shoot the lights out. I would never have thought that any of that family would have anything to do with gambling."

"Why not?"

"They seem so straitlaced. So decent and respectful, like good churchgoing folks, you know?"

Anthony nodded. "What was the young man's name?"

The broker thought for a moment. "Raymond. Yeah Raymond. As slick as they come."

*That's good, it might be an opening*, Anthony thought as he remembered his college days. He was a pretty good pool shooter himself. Although he never gambled, he could hold his own. This might be his best bet, because if Thompson Williams was the head of the family and told him no, he probably wouldn't get to speak to any other family member.

"You ever hear of a family called Coulter?"

Johnson thought for a minute. "Nope. Can't say that I have."

Anthony nodded. That was one piece of the puzzle that continued to elude him.

That evening Anthony put on some casual clothes and walked toward East 105$^{th}$. He could hear the buzz before he could see it. The street was busy. It was nine o'clock, but all the stores were open. People of all types were out that night. An older man walked a small black dog past a tall, processed-hair pimp in a bright red suit. A mother, father, and two children were turning off the street, to go home, he imagined.

A group of men stood on one corner arguing about a basketball game and whether any school could ever beat East Tech in basketball. Cars honked as the drivers acknowledged someone they knew on the sidewalk. One of Anthony's favorite songs, John Coltrane's *Naima*, wafted from one of the bars.

The combination of the sounds of music, conversation, laughter, cars, pets, and the smells of cooking food swirled around and over Anthony like playful birds in flight. The drifting sounds reminded him of an orchestra tuning up before a concert. But as distinctive as the clangs of symbols among the dissonant musical notes were in an orchestra, the click of pool balls provided a unique accompaniment to the collective music of the streets.

It didn't take but a second for Anthony to find the source. The most traffic was around Riley's poolroom. Some men were standing outside the door, but there was also a steady flow of people entering and leaving. Anthony eased past the group on the outside and walked straight to the back. He felt uncomfortable in this setting, but it was part of the job. This is what investigative reporters did.

"Want to play some, dude?"

"No thanks, I'm waiting for somebody," Anthony responded to the request without turning his head.

"Give you eight and nine."

"Maybe another time," Anthony said.

"No problem. I'll be here. I ain't going nowhere."

Anthony glanced at the hustler as he turned away. He was a nondescript-looking older guy with coveralls. Anthony got a little upset. The man must have thought he was a chump or something. Did he look that much out of place?

And if this guy was a hustler, Anthony thought, he sure didn't dress the part.

Anthony sat at the back of the room watching two men playing Bank, where they had to drive a ball to the rail before it could go into the pocket they would call. Both were good. Anthony admired their skill at making two and three consecutive shots. He didn't want to be too obvious and ask if they knew Raymond Williams, so he waited, hoping that either Raymond was already in the room or that someone would mention his name.

The two players weren't saying too much, so Anthony moved closer to the middle of the room. Three players were playing Rotation at a table nearer to the front door, a game where balls were hit in succession according to their numbers. The conversation, led by the tallest of the three, was going a mile a minute.

Anthony sat quietly, as did a few other observers, watching.

"You leave that ball sittin' in the pocket again, and I'm going to think you playin' 'two friends and a stranger'," said the taller man as he turned the bill of his cap to the rear.

"Don't nobody have to play together to take your money, chump," a player wearing all black responded.

"Yeah, fool. If you would quit missin', there wouldn't be no balls hung up in the pocket," the third man with a scar running the length of his arm said.

The conversation stopped suddenly as a young man entered.

"Anybody up for a game?"

There was silence before one of the men sitting said, "Ain't nobody here going to play you, slick. Can't get no game here today."

"I'm giving up a spot," the young man offered.

Nobody said anything. Even the man in the overalls looked down at the floor. The young man looked around, glanced at the would-be hustler in overalls for a minute, sucked his teeth, turned, and walked out.

The men paused in their game. "He better be worried about Roach and his boys rather than gettin' a game," the tall man said softly.

Anthony sat up straight, trying to hear every word.

"Yeah, Roach ain't nobody to fool with," the man in black said.

"That young fool about to get wasted, and he don't even know it," the man with the scarred arm added.

"Yeah, I wouldn't shoot with that dude if he gave me every ball on the table. That would be the time Roach and them come in here spraying lead," the tall man said as he turned his cap around once more.

"Who was that guy?" Anthony asked, hoping that they wouldn't think he was intruding.

The man with the scarred arm looked over at Anthony, sizing him up. "Raymond."

"And he a dead man," the tall man said solemnly to the other players.

The players returned to the game.

"A good kid, too, but he hustled the wrong dude," the man in black said.

Tall man nodded. "Got him killed."

The man in black nodded. "And now Roach about to get some payback."

Anthony just listened.

"Yeah, it could be any day now," the tall man said as he ran three balls.

Anthony could barely hear as the two men playing Bank on the other table started arguing. He thought he heard the word *Playboys* but had no idea what it meant unless it concerned Raymond.

"Yep, that's the word," scarred arm said softly.

The conversation turned to another subject. Not hearing anything else of interest, Anthony left.

The next day was Wednesday. He missed his running, and made a mental note to find a place he could work out. First things first though, he thought, so he decided to try the poolroom one more day. He pulled out a few extra bills from under the loose tile in the bedroom closet ceiling in case he had to play. He didn't want to stand out too much. If he had to lose a few dollars playing, so be it. Then again, he wouldn't be a walk over. He could very well win.

Anthony showered, changed shirts, and went looking for a breakfast spot. A small restaurant called Three Sisters was a few blocks away. The place was noisy with shouts from the diners and the waitress. Bobby Blue Bland played much too loudly for Anthony's taste from a jukebox at the back of the restaurant.

Everybody seemed to know everybody else, but it was nothing like Moe's restaurant.

The food was surprisingly good. Anthony sat at the counter near the back and ordered scrambled eggs with cheese, grits, sausage, and biscuits. He ate in silence, watching and trying to get used to the way folks up North acted.

After he finished, he decided to walk past Riley's. He was surprised to see the poolroom open at 11 A.M. There were only a few men lounging around. Anthony sat near the front, this time watching a three-rail billiard game.

He sat there for a while with little happening before renting a table to knock a few balls around.

"From out of town, huh?" the old man who gave him the balls asked.

"Yeah," Anthony answered. "How did you know?"

"I know almost nearly everything, son. My name's Golly."

"Anthony."

"Welcome to Riley's, Anthony. Enjoy yourself," Golly said as he laid chalk on the balls he had given Anthony.

Anthony shot for close to a half-hour before he began to feel his game coming back. Just as he was getting some rhythm, his concentration was broken by a familiar voice.

"Want to try some?"

## · XX ·

Raymond was going to devote all of his time to working out at
Riley's before making the trip to Playboys. Hopefully he
would find a few games before then so he wouldn't have to
put up as much of his own money. It was strange that nobody
approached him about staking him. Most of the good players had
a backer when big money was on the line. It didn't matter
though; he had five hundred dollars saved from his past winnings. That should be enough.

The first dude Raymond asked for a nine ball game that day
agreed. He wouldn't even have to give up a spot, which was even
better. Usually an opponent wanted an advantage like being able
to win if they pocketed the nine or the eight ball instead of just
the nine ball, and usually Raymond gave it, but he wasn't giving
it if the other player didn't ask for it.

"How much we playing for?" Raymond asked.

"Let's play for a few dollars," Anthony responded.

"A few dollars? Let's do at least five." Raymond knew from looking at him that this guy wasn't a gambler. Nothing about him said much for his skills. "You new around here?"

"Yeah. Just in for a while."

"So, how much are we playing for?"

"Three."

Although the guy had some game, he was no match. After dropping eighteen dollars in a half hour, the guy quit. Raymond peeled off two dollars to give back to him. "What's your name?"

Anthony extended his hand. "Anthony, Anthony Andrews."

"Raymond. Raymond Williams."

"What's this for?" Anthony asked as he accepted the money.

"Just don't want to leave you broke."

Anthony pocketed the money. "Quiet around here."

"Golly," Raymond called out to the rack man, "I'm going to keep the table."

"Your money, your time."

Raymond threw some balls on the table, answering Anthony without turning. "It gets crowded in the afternoon."

Anthony watched as Raymond made ball after ball. "So I was in here last night and heard that you're supposed to have some big game tonight."

"Yeah. This guy is setting something up for a big match."

"I would be careful if I were you."

Raymond stopped shooting. "What do you mean?"

"I mean how can you be sure that everything is on the up and up?"

Raymond looked at Anthony for a long while. "For somebody who just got in town, you sure know a lot about other people's business."

"It's what I do."

"What do you mean, it's what you do?"

"I'm a reporter."

Raymond perked up. "Oh yeah, college graduate and everything?"

"Yeah. University of North Carolina."

"So what are you doing up here?"

"Writing a story about black families who have migrated from the South."

"Where's the story in that?"

"Families come to the North for different reasons. I want to find out what they are."

"So why are you so concerned with my game?"

"Well, these guys were talking about this guy Roach and that you need to be careful."

Raymond was becoming ticked off. He didn't know if he was madder at this guy or Roach. "Look, I'm a pool player, not some damn detective. You come in here with some mysterious crap about being careful. How can you know anything? You just got here."

Anthony shrugged. "I'm just telling you what I hear."

Raymond didn't know what this guy's motive was and didn't care. Being a reporter, maybe he was trying to create a story. Raymond, however, was ready to play. Beating a world-class player would take him over the top. This guy didn't know what was going on. Anyway, if there was any stuff going down, he could handle it.

Later that day at Riley's Raymond finally heard from Trey that everything was set. Raymond was hyped. He left Riley's to get something to eat at Dearing's restaurant across the street, but not before some parting words from Golly. "You be careful with yourself, youngblood."

Golly always said that whenever Raymond got ready to play. "No problem Golly. I'm going to take care of business tonight."

It was funny that no one was on the Bench while he was in Riley's. *They're probably at Playboys sitting on that bench, waiting for the big game,* Raymond thought as he weaved through a group of young men singing on the corner. Trey said he should be at Playboys around eight. Raymond would be there before nine. He wanted the other player to sit and think a little bit.

Instead of taking a bus, Raymond walked the nine blocks to Playboys. If Riley's was like the local meeting place, Playboys was like Grand Central Station. At various times, the poolroom hosted hustlers from around the city and sometimes out of state. Any given day, one might find some of the premier players lounging around, waiting for a game. Raymond visited Playboys early in his career, but was intimidated by all the good shooters. Now though, he knew he could play with the best of them. The only reason he didn't come to Playboys that often was because he didn't know anybody there who would have his back. At least at Riley's he wasn't that far from home.

It was beginning to darken, but it was a beautiful day. Somewhere near the lake he could hear the faint clap of thunder. The news predicted rain, but so far, even though the air was heavy, the weather was fine. The street was unusually quiet, but Raymond never gave it a second thought. He approached the poolroom, preoccupied with the game, concentrating on how he was going to win, pumping himself up mentally.

Walking with his head down, he didn't pay much attention to the small crowd at the front of the building nor to the flurry of movement at the rear. One of the guys directed him around back. It seemed strange to enter from the rear, but Raymond didn't think much about it since this was only the second time he had shot at Playboys. Lost in thought, he turned the corner to open the back door.

Raymond turned at a sound just in time to see Roach come out from the shadows. "Watch your back, bitch. Always watch your back!"

Everything after that happened in slow motion. Raymond watched Roach raise his arm like in a dream; people scattered. Raymond stepped sideways, quickly ducking into the back door. The sound from the shot seemed like it was two miles away. Two more followed. Brick and wood chips flew as the bullets missed Raymond by inches. Another shot that sounded different and even farther away was the last noise he heard from outside as he closed and tried to barricade the door.

## · XXI ·

Cread cursed as he left his car and ran toward Playboys. Thompson gave him an assignment, and he was about to blow it. That damn kid had plenty of balls, but no brains. He prayed he wasn't late.

The sound of shots made his heart sink as he ran up the driveway in a lot adjacent to the poolroom. He couldn't go back to the family having failed to protect his young cousin. Even if the family were to forgive him, which they probably would, he couldn't face them knowing he failed. A second shot quickly rang out. Cread looked across the bushes at Roach who had his gun pointed at a closed door. He only needed one shot before Roach fell to the ground writhing in pain.

The crowd that had gathered behind Roach scattered again as Cread dashed into the back of the poolroom, gun out, and dragged Raymond to the car.

"Cousin Cread! Where'd you come from?"

"Just got in town, boy, and the first thing I have to do is to save your sorry little ass!"

Cread glanced at Roach on the ground before pushing Raymond across the yard and into the car. Raymond sat quietly, still shaken as Cread burned rubber, leaving a gathering crowd behind.

"Your uncle found out about the setup and sent me down here to protect you. You're lucky that dude couldn't shoot that well."

"Man, Cread. All I wanted to do was shoot some pool," Raymond answered, his voice quivering.

Cread drove for a while, making sure no one had followed them. At a red light he settled back into the car seat looking at Raymond. "Your uncle told me about your conversation. Didn't anything sink in? What did he tell you about these streets? This is not you. You don't know these people like you think you do. How are you going to graduate from college with a bullet up your butt? How are you going to take care of the family if you're dead?"

A chill ran through Raymond as the reality of the incident sunk in. Roach could have killed him. The thought caused a tremor that knifed through Raymond's body and settled in his shaking hands. When Roach raised the gun back there, he saw nothing but blackness, a dark nothingness that tried to engulf him. The darkness scared him more than Roach did because it seemed so final and so removed from all he loved and cared for.

Cread drove straight to Thompson's house. The whole family was waiting. His aunt Esther and his mother looked as if they had been crying. None of them said a word. Thompson came forward and put his arms around Raymond. "You okay?"

"Yeah, Uncle T. I'm okay," Raymond said, trying to sound

nonchalant, but failing. "Thanks."

"Well, you're okay because you have this young man here to thank." Thompson pointed to Anthony at the back of the crowd of family. "He found out where I lived somehow and told me the story." Thompson looked at Anthony appreciatively. "I'm glad he found me."

Raymond looked at Anthony with a mixture of surprise and relief. "Thanks, man."

"No problem. I just happened to be in the right place at the right time."

Thompson looked closer at Raymond. "You sure you're okay?" he asked softly.

Raymond nodded and took a deep breath, hoping the tremor that still lay inside his body somewhere didn't show in his voice. "I apologize for putting you all through this," he said to the family. "It won't happen again."

Thompson turned to Anthony. "Look, I don't know what you have planned, but we're having a family dinner and cele-bration on Sunday; we would appreciate it if you would come as our guest."

The family stayed together until early evening, then began to leave. No one said much during the time they were together. Thompson comforted his sister Ludie while Raymond's Aunt Dahlia kept him close, holding and patting his hand. "We didn't come all this way for you to get killed doing something stupid, boy," she said quietly. "You got to be more careful." Ludie left last, hugging her son tight. "You coming home now?"

"Naw, Mom. I'm going to stay here with Uncle T and Cousin Cread for a while, if you don't mind."

She nodded, squeezed his hand, and left. Aunt Dahlia went

inside the house leaving Thompson, Cread, Anthony, and Raymond on the porch. They sat there for more than a half an hour without anyone saying a word.

Raymond stood. A nervous energy had replaced the lingering dread. "I need to take a walk, Uncle T."

Thompson's quick look and nod let Raymond know he understood. Raymond had been challenged, and as scary as the shooting was, he was intent on reappearing in public and not running for some hole like a scared rabbit.

Cread stood, but sat again as Thompson waved him off. "Why don't you take Anthony with you?" Thompson said.

Raymond wanted this time to himself, but couldn't refuse under the circumstances. He knew that his uncle Thompson wanted someone who would keep an eye on him. Raymond looked back as he started down the street with Anthony and watched his uncle lean back in his chair. His uncle's calmness meant a lot to Raymond. It meant that he had confidence in him. As terrifying as his confrontation with Roach was, it wasn't going to take his heart.

## · XXII ·

It was about 9 P.M. and Massie Avenue was unusually quiet for that time of the evening. Raymond walked slowly down the street, deep in thought. Anthony walked quietly beside him. They turned the corner on 105$^{th}$ toward Riley's poolroom, but instead of going in, Raymond walked past Riley's to the Café Tia Juana. He barely responded to several people who spoke to him as he made his way to the far corner of the bar.

"You want something to drink, Raymond?" Anthony asked.

"Yeah, I'll have a Coke, but they have a waitress. Have a seat." Anthony sat, looking at the crowd. The jukebox was playing James Brown's, *Think*.

"Hey, youngblood. What's happenin'?"

Raymond looked up at an older gentleman with a walking stick, dressed in all black except for a pink hanky in his suit pocket. A girl who had the pasty, goat's milk skin of someone who purposely avoided the sun, trailed behind looking out of place in the all-black bar. "Pinky, everything's all right."

"Heard about that thing down the way. Glad you okay," Pinky said.

Raymond looked at Pinky and smiled briefly. "Thanks." Raymond turned away. "I'm always going to be okay," he said softly to no one in particular.

The waitress appeared and poured their drinks. "Raymond, right?"

"Yeah," he said looking up. "Do I know you?"

"No. I'm Sheila. I heard about you from my brother."

"Who's your brother?"

"Rodger Franklin."

Raymond hesitated. "I don't think I know him."

"They call him Pea."

Raymond brightened, "Oh yeah. Pea."

"He says you are the best around," she said brushing her apron with her hand.

"Thanks. Tell Pea I owe him for the compliment."

"You here later, maybe when I get off, I'll keep you company for a while?" she asked.

Anthony glanced at Sheila. She was nice looking. Actually she was very nice looking.

"You know, I appreciate the offer, but I'm waiting for somebody," Raymond answered.

"Oh. Maybe another time?"

"I would love to, but I have a girlfriend."

"Oh. Okay."

Anthony smiled. He noticed that others in the bar wanted to approach Raymond but didn't. They probably saw that he wasn't interested in small talk, but Anthony decided to make some anyway.

"You ever date a white woman?" Anthony asked looking at Pinky's lady.

Raymond looked at Anthony curiously. "Nope."

"Why not?"

"Never had an interest."

"I mean, you're a good-looking guy, haven't any white girls ever approached you?"

Raymond turned to Anthony. "Where's this going?"

"Just curious."

Raymond turned back around to look over the crowd. "You haven't met my girlfriend."

"No, I haven't had the pleasure."

"You'll never meet a girl, black or white, who is even close to being like Myra. Does that answer your question?"

"Yep."

Anthony laughed to himself. He figured that if the Williamses were as close as everyone said, dating outside the race was not an option. Raymond seemed a little irritated by the question, and Anthony understood. They had just met, but here he was already getting personal. It was Anthony's curiosity that took over though. He wanted to know everything he could about this family.

Undaunted by the sharp response, Anthony continued. "Things change though, Raymond. You'll be going to college soon, and I've seen a few couples break up because of the distance. Plus you'll have a college education, and she won't."

Raymond looked at Anthony and smiled. "With or without a college education, Myra is one of the most intelligent people I know. She knows people. She knows about life, and she's at peace with herself. They can't teach you that in college. Anyway, you can't fault somebody because their parents couldn't afford college."

Raymond leaned back, looking into space. Anthony said nothing as he watched in fascination as the people in the bar swirled around them talking, laughing, and drinking.

"All I wanted to be was the best pool shooter there ever was."

Anthony turned back to Raymond and thought for a moment, "Maybe the Creator has other plans for you."

Raymond glanced at Anthony but said nothing.

"You ever regret leaving the South?"

"Yeah, I do. It was peaceful there. All of our families were together. Everybody helping each other." Raymond leaned back in his seat. "I didn't know many people outside the family, but family was all we needed."

Raymond settled back. "I miss Junior Wilson Wells, though. He was my best friend. Junior cried when he found out I was leaving. When we first met, we fought like cats and dogs, but we eventually became the best of friends."

"That was the last time you saw him?"

"Yeah. I hear he moved to Chicago and joined a gang."

Anthony responded. "That was stupid."

Raymond put both hands on the table before leaning forward. "What's stupid if that's all you know? He moved into an area where you had to be in a gang. Plus, his father was an alcoholic and beat his mother and the kids. All Junior knew was violence. What do you expect?"

Raymond's answer made sense, but Anthony continued. "I would expect that he would find a better way."

Raymond shook his head. "You didn't turn out that way, and you lived in the same town," Anthony said.

"But I didn't live in the same household," Raymond said, pointing at Anthony. "If I lived under the same conditions he did, I might have done the same."

Anthony continued, marveling at the young man's awareness, "I doubt it. You're too intelligent."

Raymond sighed. "You haven't been out here in the streets too long, so let me clue you to something. Intelligence alone is not going to guarantee your future. There are a lot of intelligent people out here." Raymond waved his arm at the crowd. "All you have to do is talk to some of these people and you would know that."

Raymond continued. "Some of them are pimps, hustlers, gangsters, stickup artists, alcoholics, and drug addicts. If they had grown up in a different environment, with the information and opportunity that is available to other folk, they could be police chiefs, managers, business owners, preachers, and teachers." Raymond looked around the room and smiled slightly. "They might still be drug addicts or alcoholics. They might still beat their wives, but at least they would appear respectable."

"So if you grew up in a different family for instance, you might be different?" Anthony asked.

"Yes, and so would you. Aren't you influenced by your family? How they think, how they act?"

Anthony said nothing. Raymond was right of course. What was it that causes a son to always try to please his father even when they disagree on so many things?

"It's all about family. It's all about your environment." Raymond said as he tapped the table with his finger, emphasizing each word. "Where you live and how you live is a matter of luck. We don't get to choose. All we can do is react to our individual situations. I can't make a wrong move without somebody straightening me out. Even when I hustled pool, somebody was watching out for me. What if I could do anything I wanted to because nobody cared? What if everything I did wrong was okay as long as I brought some money home? What if I lived in a family that was not used to anybody achieving anything in life? What if there were no expectations? What do you think I would be? What do you think you would be?"

Anthony smiled inwardly. Raymond was insightful beyond his years. It was apparent that he was a student of human nature. No wonder he was so good at hustling. Anthony would have loved to have had Raymond as a little brother.

Activity in the bar was slow, even languid except for the flash of movement that burst through the door and rushed over to the two men engaged in conversation.

"Raymond!" Anthony could hear the anguish in the woman's voice.

He watched as the woman grabbed Raymond when he stood and hugged him with all of her strength.

Tears welled up in her eyes as she stepped back. She was oblivious to the crowd that had stopped to see who was in trouble. Raymond looked embarrassed. "I'm fine, Myra," he said quietly as he brushed a drop forming in her eye.

Then she hit him in the chest. Not a hard punch, but one that reflected her frustration. "If you ever put yourself in that type of situation again, I'll kill you myself!"

Raymond smiled at the irony of her statement. "I'm fine, baby. I'm fine," he said softly, trying to calm her.

Myra turned to Anthony. "Are you Anthony?"

Anthony, slightly self-conscious, nodded.

"I heard what you did, and I want to thank you from the bottom of my heart."

"It was nothing," Anthony answered. "I was lucky enough to be in the right place at the right time." He couldn't help admiring the woman. Even when she was upset, there was a warmness about her.

"Well, at least somebody around here has some sense!"

Raymond pulled out a chair for Myra, but she remained standing. "I have to go to work now, remember? I wanted to see you before I went though. Call me tomorrow, Raymond. You're not off the hook yet." She punched him again before turning to leave.

Anthony watched as Myra headed for the door. She left like she came, a baby whirlwind with a purpose.

"She's beautiful!"

"Yeah, she is."

"She must love you a lot."

"Yeah, she's good people. I love her too."

Anthony was envious. It was apparent that this was one subject on which the two could agree. Anthony was also glad to talk about something less confrontational. "How long have you two been seeing each other?"

"Four years."

"Do you think you two will get married?"

Raymond raised his eyebrows at Anthony, but didn't answer him.

Anthony leaned back in his chair. If that was Raymond's way of saying he was asking too many questions, so be it.

Raymond sipped his drink deep in thought, then responded, "We probably will."

Raymond looked over at Anthony's empty glass. "You ready to go? It's getting late, and I don't want my mom sitting up worrying about me."

"Yes, I'm ready," Anthony answered, although he wasn't. Questions about the family would go unanswered that night.

"I'll walk you to your house, and then I'm headed home."

Anthony was a little perturbed that Raymond thought he needed protection. "I can make it to the house by myself."

Raymond ignored Anthony and headed for the door.

It was after 11 P.M., and the street was quieter except for an occasional car or two that slowly rolled down the Five, highlighted by the lamp poles they drove under. There was a slight drizzle, but the warm rain felt good.

Anthony said nothing as he and Raymond turned the corner to the dimly lit, quiet street where all he could hear was the faint, faded sounds of soft music coming from someone's house interrupted occasionally by a dog's bark. Neither said anything as they walked. Except for the slight hiss of the rain falling through the trees, the quietness enveloped them.

Anthony saw them first. The stirrings in his stomach served as a warning sign. It was as if the men appeared out of nowhere. There were three of them (on the sidewalk that he and Raymond had to pass) standing approximately four houses away from where he was staying. At first he thought of Roach, and a chill passed through him. Raymond noticed them seconds later, and without hesitation, stepped in front as they approached the men. There was the slightest change in Raymond as Anthony, prepared for a confrontation, observed from behind. Watching Raymond was like watching a lion prepare for battle without the benefit of sound.

"How you brothers doin'?" Raymond asked as he approached.

Raymond's head was high. He slowed for a moment, apparently to look each one in the eye. Two of them mumbled some type of response. Anthony, following directly behind, tense but ready. The three parted as they walked past.

When Raymond and Anthony walked up the drive to the side door, Anthony turned to look at the three men. They argued quietly as one of the men put an object back in his pocket. Anthony let out a silent whistle. "They were going to rob us."

"Probably, but they didn't see any victims," Raymond said

as he turned to walk back down the drive. "Check you tomor-row."

Anthony nodded in response. The near confrontation brought to mind a bedtime story his great-grandmother had once recited about a certain tribe of Africans trained as children to be able to walk among a pit of poisonous snakes without being bit-ten. They were called snake walkers. He never found out if the story was true, but Anthony grew to envy them anyway, just as he envied Raymond now.

He stood at the door and watched as Raymond headed back toward 105$^{th}$ Street.

The street was quiet.

The rain had stopped.

The three men were gone.

## · XXIII ·

I'm in, Carla."

"What do you mean, you're in?"

"I had a meeting with the family, and I've been invited to Sunday dinner."

"How did you pull that off?"

Anthony told her about the poolroom incident.

"Anthony, you could have been hurt!"

Anthony smiled. "Don't worry, I was nowhere around when they started shooting."

"What happened to the guy Cread?"

"Nothing. He left with Raymond before any police arrived. Anyway, he's new in town, so nobody knew him." Anthony hesitated. "That Cread is nobody to mess with."

"It sounds like it. You be careful with that family, Anthony. If they had anything to do with those missing men, the same could happen to you."

"If you met them, you would know they didn't. They're the nicest people you ever want to meet."

"Be careful, Anthony."

Anthony smiled again. "I will."

"So you've been in one of their houses?"

"Yes, and they have some strange ways Carla."

"Like what?"

"I happened to get there when they were eating dinner. When they all get together the oldest in the family prays. Her name is Aunt Dahlia, everybody calls her aunt, even people outside the family, and she's eighty-seven. She reminds me so much of my grandmother, Bertha Rae, it's amazing. She prays to their ancestors, naming each one of them. When they eat, they line up. The oldest is served first. Then when they sit down to eat, everybody takes a piece of a flat, round bread and dips into this bowl to get greens. After that everybody eats off their own plate."

"That's very interesting, Anthony."

"I asked them about it. They said it was something they had done for generations. Aunt Dahlia says that it was passed down from their slave days, and probably goes farther back than that."

"Did you talk to them about the Coulters and Arkansas?" Carla asked.

"Not a lot. I didn't want to appear eager. Thompson Williams did ask me what I did, and I told him I was a reporter writing about colored families who have migrated to the North. He looked at me, nodded then changed the subject, so I dropped it. I was also invited to meet with him tomorrow."

"About what?"

"Thompson, Cread and Raymond were talking about Martin Luther King, Jr. and the marches, so we started discussing strategy and how we should confront racism.

Carla sighed. "What did you say, Anthony?"

"I said that I didn't think we needed to march. We will get

what we want in due time. I said that eventually a colored person will be okay if he or she kept working hard and stopped trying to force ourselves on people. That's all."

"Anthony. What did they say?"

"Thompson Williams gave me this strange look. Cread walked out of the room, and Raymond shook his head. That's when Thompson Williams asked me to come back and see him. He wanted to talk to me more about that. That's when I'll bring up Arkansas."

"Anthony, you and I had this conversation before. I already know what they're going to say, and you do too. I suggest you be quiet and listen. You might learn something. If you get them mad at you, you won't get any information."

"I just believe that's the way to go. What's so wrong about that?"

"What's wrong with thinking the people who enslaved us, fought a war to keep us in bondage, treated us like dirt, and thought we were less than human are suddenly going to say, 'I'm sorry. It was all a terrible mistake. Let's make amends and give you that forty acres and a mule we promised you.' What's wrong with that? Is that what you're asking?"

"Not all of them are bad. Some fought for our freedom."

"Why should there have been a need to, Anthony?"

Anthony decided to shut up. He could tell Carla was getting upset with him again. Anyway, the subject wasn't as important to him as it obviously was to the Williamses, Carla, and others. It certainly wasn't worth arguing over. He had more important goals. The whole issue of whites versus the Negro would work itself out on its own.

Anthony was becoming more familiar with how Carla thought. She was a fighter. After their second meeting on campus, she warmed up a little bit, but still did not give an inch in her convictions. He admired the fierceness she showed, though, whenever she felt strongly about something.

"Carla, I have an idea!"

"I'm listening."

"Why don't you come up here and meet the Williamses yourself? Don't you need to talk to people like them as part of your research?"

"I'm not sure I want to be a part of this charade, Anthony."

"What better type family to meet than these people who probably migrated for reasons different from most? Anyway, I need to find this Coulter family, and by all accounts, they're a mean bunch, so the Williamses will serve as a resource and a buffer."

The silence on the Carla's end was encouraging. At least she was thinking about it.


Raymond looked at his uncle. It always amazed him how calm his uncle was. "What do you think about Anthony, Uncle T?"

Thompson looked at Raymond and smiled. "That young man Anthony has book knowledge, but he doesn't understand this country any better than you understood the streets."

Raymond winced.

"You know, Harriet Tubman once said 'I would have freed more slaves if they'd known they was slaves,' " Thompson recited.

Cread chuckled.

Thompson continued, "I've seen his type before. He's smart and seems to be a good kid, but some of us think we can go it alone, thinking that if we just play by their rules, everything will be okay. But after we make the improvements, get educated, get a good job, and are still faced with discrimination, we wonder what went wrong. Others who see us in this dilemma and are so used to believing all that they read and hear from the majority, begin to make excuses for the perpetrators, and blame the victims." Thompson sighed. "Some folks believe there must be something Negroes are doing wrong to receive so much grief, and that if they'd only improve themselves, they wouldn't have these problems. You soon find out though that it was never about self-improvement for them because they never had our best interest in mind to begin with."

"Amen," Cread said as he left the room to go to the kitchen. He came back with a pitcher of iced tea.

Thompson paused, smiling slightly. "That young man is interesting. We don't get a chance to meet people who think like him too often. I look forward to talking to him more."

"For what?" Cread asked.

"For everyone's benefit." Thompson leaned back in the chair. "The young man is right in one respect: We can't blame other folks for all of our shortcomings. There's a lot we do have to do for ourselves. Aunt Dahlia has this inside-out theory and I believe she's right."

Raymond remembered his great aunt lecturing him on any number of subjects but not this one. "What is that, Uncle T?"

"She believes that our fate lies with us, and that anything we get is because we first lift ourselves, our family, and our community."

"That's what Anthony said though, isn't it?"

"There's one big difference though, son," Thompson said. "He stopped with himself. We're all connected Raymond, and we aren't going anywhere unless we help one another. Our progress will be measured by how the least of us has fared."

"That boy bears watching," Cread said quietly.

"Anthony? He's okay, Cousin Cread."

Cread looked at Raymond. "I ain't going to say it twice."


That was all Cread had to say, but it wasn't all he was thinking. Cread saw something in Anthony's eyes. Anthony hadn't been completely truthful about himself. Cread sensed it. Besides the dishonesty though, there was something else in Anthony that would probably create a kinship between the two if not for the mistrust he provoked. When Cread came home from France, it wasn't hard to identify men who were in battle. He became sensitized toward those who had been to hell and back. Somewhere, somehow, this boy Anthony had been there too.

# · XXIV ·

Carla was coming to Cleveland. Anthony felt elated, anxious, and something else he couldn't describe. There was something about Carla that kept him thinking about her all the time. She was different. If he were ever in an argument or a fight, he would want her on his side.

Chucky's deep-throated laughter exploded through the phone as Anthony related his experience with Carla. Anthony wondered out loud how she got along with her students, her parents, and her friends in light of the way the two of them interacted. "It sounds to me that both of you have your opinions, and if neither one of you backs down, you won't have to worry about her being any more than an acquaintance."

Anthony laughed too. "This is a long-distance call, so I'm not going to argue with you on that point, but she's different from any other woman I've ever known."

"Does she have a boyfriend?"

"I don't even know, Chucky. I never asked. There was no ring on her finger though, so I assume she's not married."

"Well, I wouldn't put much hope in her being anymore than a resource, man. Even if she isn't married and doesn't have a boyfriend, it doesn't look that good for you. You're like the Lone Ranger, and she likes to ride in a posse. You would probably ignore situations that she would charge into. You know what I mean?"

Anthony thought about that. He used to be that way, but what was the use? What was the use in fighting other people's battles when you hadn't won your own?

"Yeah, you're probably right. I seem to bring out the worst in her. As many times as I've discussed these issues, no one has been as passionate as Carla. The most I would get out of any of my other woman friends is a sigh and an 'Oh, Anthony', so they at least agreed with some of what I said."

"Not necessarily, my friend. It depends on what position you all were in when you brought up the subject." They both laughed, then hung up.

What's the use? Anthony thought. It was clear she didn't like him. Plus, she seemed like the type of woman who would want to settle down. That wasn't in his plans. Not even for someone like her. But then who knew for sure where this might go? Maybe she wasn't interested in settling down either. That was possible, but who was he fooling?

It was easier convincing Carla to come to Cleveland than he anticipated. They had talked again, later that day, and he brought up the subject one more time.

"I don't know. It's so sudden."

"I know, but I think you could benefit from talking to these people, and they think like you." Anthony was also thinking that they might say things to Carla that they wouldn't say to him.

"How would I get there?"

"How do you want to get here?"

"Plane. I don't like to ride buses if I don't have to. They take too long."

Anthony had mentally counted his money. "That's fine, Carla. You want to make the arrangements, and I pay you back?"

"I'll make the arrangements, Anthony, and I'll pay for the trip. My budget can handle it. It will be a working vacation for me."

"I'm willing to pay, Carla. It was my idea."

"No. If everything works right, I'll see you in another day or so. I'll call you with the details. Where will I stay?"

Anthony had hesitated. "You could stay with me," he had said hopefully.

"No, again. Are there any hotels in the area?"

"I have plenty of room," Anthony had said, even though he knew the third floor was almost too small for two people.

"If I come, I'll stay in a hotel."

Anthony had sighed under his breath. "I'll make a call to this real estate guy. He'll know a place you can rent."

"Good. Call me with the information." Carla had paused. "I almost forgot. I did get some information on the family for you. The dinner ritual is African. That ceremony they perform with the bowl and praying to their ancestors? Several African tribes do that in one form or another. I also was able to trace some of their history. I'm not through with my research, but the family is originally from Mississippi, and according to some archived records, they were in Mississippi from the time their great-great-grandfather was brought there as a slave."

"The rituals are African?"

"Yes."

Anthony paused, "Anything else?"

"Not yet, Anthony. I'm still researching."

"That's good, Carla. Keep searching, please. I want as much information as I can get."

"I'll do my best."

"Thanks. I can't tell you how grateful I am." Anthony had hung up, elated for the little information he had received. This was going to work out fine. Carla was right, though. If he was going to get any information, he needed to talk less and listen more. It was hard listening to someone less educated trying to lecture him, though. Nobody in that family had graduated from college, and he overheard that Thompson only had a ninth-grade education. Anthony's father and his friends were successful businessmen and college graduates. So if he were to follow anybody's line of thinking, it would be theirs.

Anthony remembered that he finally saw the hint of a smile on Carla's face when they last met, and although she didn't laugh outright at something silly he had said, the corners of her eyes crinkled. The way they lit up and her mouth puckered, was satisfaction enough that he could elicit a response other than a rebuke. After she left him, he watched her walk back to the administration building on campus. It was inappropriate, but he couldn't turn away. The sway of her hips was in direct contrast to her stern demeanor and hinted there might be another person residing somewhere in that body.

Anthony chastised himself for daydreaming. He needed to call his boss and keep him up to date. There was a lot to report these last couple of days. Fate was on his side so far. The next few days though would require him to use all of his investigative skills.

"Anthony, what's happening?" Whiting asked.

"Well, Mr. Whiting, I've gained the trust of the family, and I'll be meeting with the head of the family tomorrow."

"Great! What kind of man is he, Anthony?"

"He's a good enough person. Not too educated, though. The family has some strange ways, but they're close, and it's possible they might know something. They mistrust strangers."

"Did they mention anything about the Coulters?"

"No, sir, but I'll bring it up tomorrow."

"The first question I would ask is why they left Arkansas. Listen carefully to his answer, Anthony, because it could tell you a lot. What's more, watch the speaker closely. Sometimes the person's body movement, or the person's eyes give them away. If he answers you and is doing something out of the ordinary—squinting, shifting, even tapping the table—make note of it. If he looks anywhere but at you, make note of it. You understand what I'm saying?"

"Yes, sir."

"Then, in an offhand way, you might mention the Coulters and the list of other names I sent you. Tell this person that you remember being impressed after meeting a guy with that name, and ask him if he knew any Coulters. If he says yes, tell him that you want to get in touch with them along with the others, because you want to write their stories too."

"Okay, I will. Hopefully within the next day or two, I'll have something to go on."

"Keep up the good work, son."

"Thanks, Mr. Whiting."

"Oh, by the way that Bobby Joe Byrd called you and left a message."

"Yes?" Anthony said quietly.

"Hannah took it. He wanted you to know that he was available if you needed him. We haven't found out much about him yet, but we'll keep digging."

"Good. I'm leery of that guy."

"I understand. If you need us to do anything more on this end, let me know."

"I would appreciate you digging deeper on this guy. I would like to know more about him."

"We plan on it."

"I would appreciate it, sir."

"Oh, by the way. There was a letter here for you. I forwarded it your Cleveland address. I hope you don't mind."

"No, not at all."

Who would be writing him? Anthony wondered. He was in touch with everybody who knew he was at the paper.

The phone rang as soon as he hung up.

"Hey, Mom, Dad."

"Anthony," his father responded.

"How are you doing up there?" his mother asked.

"Trying to wrap it up. I've made some headway, and hopefully I'll finish in a week or so."

"I understand you're living on somebody's third floor. Is that the best you can do?" His dad asked. "Didn't the paper provide you with money for better accommodations?"

"They did, Dad, but it's better to be near the subject. I was able to talk to them because I saved one of them from harm." Anthony related the story once again.

"Anthony, you're dealing with an element that is dangerous and unpredictable. I suggest you stay out of those poolrooms and limit your time in those streets to a minimum. Those gangsters could rob or even kill you."

Anthony sighed. "Right, Dad."

"Look, I know those type of people. You don't. Just

because they're your color doesn't mean they're your kind. You be careful."

"Anthony?"

"Yes, Mom?"

"Anthony, are you taking good care of yourself?"

"Yes, Mom."

"Be careful."

"Don't worry, Mom, nothing is going to happen to me that hasn't happened already."

"What do you mean?" she asked.

"Nothing, just talking."

## · XXV ·

Raymond was on his way down Massie Avenue to catch the bus for work when Trey appeared. He had not seen Trey since the second run-in with Roach. It embarrassed Raymond seeing Trey. Somehow, he should have been able to handle the incident at Playboys better instead of running from Roach and having his uncle save him.

Trey could be recognized a mile away. He had an exaggerated walk that made it look like he had bad feet. The most distinguishable feature on him was his smile though. His grin reminded Raymond of a hyena who knew something nobody else did. It fit his character. It seemed Trey's mission in life was to pass on information. If anyone wanted to know what was happening on the street, Trey was the man.

Most of his information came from his constant presence. Since he had no job, he assumed the position of town crier. He knew every pimp, hustler, and gangster in the area, and he always had up-to-date news on who was doing what to whom, where, how, when, and why.

"Raymond, my man."

"What's happenin', Trey?"

"Everything is okay. You all right?"

Raymond grunted. "Yeah, everything is cool."

"Man, who was the dude who took out Roach? One shot, and the shit was over."

"A friend of the family who happened to be in the area."

"Yeah? Well you're one lucky dude," Trey said as he walked with Raymond.

"Yeah."

"They say Roach supposed to be out of the hospital soon. Your dude shot him in the ass. Just a flesh wound."

Raymond had mixed emotions about that. If Roach died, there would be no more problems, but then if he had been killed, Cread would be in trouble. "Yeah well, I can't worry about his ass, can I?"

"Ha. No. I guess not." Trey laughed in a high-pitched voice.

"You talk to him?" Raymond asked.

"No. Just hearing around."

Raymond tried to forget the incident, but talking to Trey bought it all to the forefront again.

Trey turned toward Raymond. "How did your man know what was going down?"

Raymond was lost in thought. "Hmm?"

"How did the dude who shot Roach know?"

"Got lucky. Some folks heard some buzz and told a few people. Those people told my people. They happened to get there on time." Raymond was intentionally vague. Knowing Trey's reputation, whatever he told him would be on the street in five minutes. Raymond had probably told him too much as it was.

"Some folks, huh? The gods are looking out for you, my man."

It struck Raymond that if Trey knew everything...

"So Roach is doing all right, huh?"

"Yeah. He'll be out of Mt. Sinai tomorrow."

Raymond nodded. "He still mad about G'Money?"

"Naw. He willin' to let it go."

Raymond looked at Trey as he walked beside him, and at that moment knew everything he needed to know. Trey was closer to Roach than he let on.

"Yeah well, here comes my bus. Got to run."

"Okay, my man. Be careful."

"You too, Trey. You be careful too."

# · XXVI ·

The next day, Anthony awoke at five in the morning. Carla wasn't due in until six that evening, but he couldn't sleep. He pulled out the manila folder Whiting had given him when he first started on the assignment, and read the cryptic notes written by the other reporter. When he reached the last page he found a note from the reporter to Whiting.

> *Mr. Whiting,*
>
> *Here are my notes. If you're really interested in doing some good, read them closely, then maybe you'll begin to understand.*
>
> *Jerry*

The note seemed odd. It occurred to Anthony that he would like to meet this Jerry. He wondered what effect, if any, the information had on the former reporter. It seemed that the reporter felt something about the brutal incidents based on the tone of the note. What was going through this white reporter's mind?

The broker had found a single home for Carla that was closer than any hotel. The owners had moved out of town and were glad to have someone rent it if only on a weekly basis. It was located on Pierpont Avenue and within walking distance of Anthony's place.

Anthony rented a car to meet Carla. Although she didn't arrive until six, Anthony was at the airport by four. They went directly to her house. Carla was pleased with the living arrangement. The street was quiet like his. Most importantly, she had the whole house to herself. He smiled, picturing himself in a bathrobe smoking a pipe while she sat with her trim legs folded beneath her, reading one of her many books.

"Now tell me what you think," he said as she unpacked. "I'm going to call Thompson Williams to tell him that I would like to bring you along as my girlfriend."

Carla cocked her head as she glanced at Anthony.

Anthony was accustomed to that gesture. It was the same one she made anytime they disagreed.

Carla sighed. "If you say so. You need to know though that the only reason I'm here is to continue my research."

Anthony made the call when he arrived back at his place.

Picking up Carla almost felt like a date. She was as beautiful as ever, but nervous. Anthony could tell by the way she pulled at her skirt. Thompson greeted them at the door. Raymond was there and smiled at him as they entered the living room. Cread was in the kitchen. He came out when Thompson called, barely waved, then disappeared back into the kitchen.

Aunt Dahlia was sitting at the table. Anthony was disappointed that none of the other women were there for Carla to meet.

Thompson's house looked more like a headquarters with a long table in a dining room that seemed more like a conference room than a place for eating. There were at least twenty to thirty folding chairs stacked or open scattered randomly around both the living and dining rooms.

Anthony decided that he would take Carla's advice and listen. Thompson already knew how he felt. Hopefully their previous discussion wouldn't be the topic of conversation.

"How are you, Anthony?" Thompson asked as he motioned for them to have a seat. Then turning to Carla, he asked, "And who is this beautiful young lady?"

"Mr. Williams, this is Carla Draper...my girlfriend." No one but Anthony seemed to notice the slight shrug of her shoulders as she turned toward Thompson Williams.

Thompson bowed slightly and shook her hand. "Carla, this is my Aunt Dahlia and my nephew Raymond."

Raymond stood to shake Carla's hand. Aunt Dahlia greeted her with a "Hello, dear."

"Miss Dahlia," Carla said as she extended her hand.

"Aunt Dahlia, dear," Dahlia said as she patted Carla's hand. "Everybody calls me Aunt Dahlia."

"Cread is making some iced tea. I hope that's fine with the both of you," Thompson said as he waited for Carla to sit, then sat on one of the folding chairs.

Both Carla and Anthony nodded.

Thompson looked at Carla. "So I know Anthony works for a newspaper. Do you work with him?"

"No. I am a professor at Philander Smith College."

"Outstanding. What subject?"

"History."

"You study their version or ours?" Aunt Dahlia asked in a raspy voice as she leaned forward to hear Carla's answer.

"Both, ma'am."

Aunt Dahlia leaned back seemingly satisfied.

"How do you like working for the school?" Thompson asked.

"It has its benefits, and its liabilities," Carla responded, smiling. Thompson and Aunt Dahlia smiled back.

Anthony could see they were already drawn to Carla. There was something about her that made you respect her. It was becoming more and more apparent to Anthony that she was special.

"I guess Anthony told you what happened," Thompson said, looking at Carla.

"Yes, he did," Carla said, glaring at Anthony. "For somebody that has led such a quiet life, he sure has been out of character up here."

"It hasn't been that quiet," Anthony said.

"You know what I mean."

Anthony smiled. Her tone was that of a mother fuming over her wayward child.

Carla looked at Raymond. "I'm just glad no one was hurt."

Cread brought iced tea for everyone and sat in a corner of the room, legs and arms crossed.

"Now I remember you saying that you were only going to be here a little while. Is that right?" Thompson asked Anthony.

"Yes. Maybe a week or so at most. As I told you before, I'm writing about colored families migrating to the North."

Thompson nodded.

"Would you be interested in telling us your story?"

Thompson leaned back, his lips pursed. "Isn't that much to tell. We felt it was time to move, so we did."

"But it's so interesting that all of you moved together, and that after you moved, the other colored families in town moved also."

Thompson stiffened. "Where did you hear that?" He looked intently at Anthony for his answer.

Anthony hesitated. He had said too much.

"I started talking to people, and this story came out about the town."

"You were in Evesville?"

"No." Anthony shifted slightly in his seat. "I was in Wynne interviewing people, and they told me about Evesville."

Thompson grunted. "So, last time we talked, you had some interesting ideas. Tell me what you think colored folks should be doing about white folks and how they treat us. We seem to have a different opinion about that subject."

Anthony felt Carla staring at him again, but he responded anyway. It was a relief that Thompson changed the subject. One lie was enough for the night. Lying was uncomfortable to Anthony and he had never become good at it. "I think that we need to quit worrying about how other people treat some of us, and place a priority on improving ourselves."

"So you would ignore the atrocities and concentrate on self-improvement. Something like Booker T. Washington's approach?" Thompson asked.

"Yes, I guess so," Anthony responded. Carla stood to look out the window. Anthony glanced at her, but she gave no hint of what she was thinking. "I think that much of what happens to us is our own fault because we haven't progressed far enough intellectually or financially. Once we have, we'll experience less problems."

Aunt Dahlia grunted. Raymond shook his head.

Thompson talked to Anthony as if he were a young student. "If you knew our history, you would know that we have intelligence. Our history didn't start with slavery; we created the first civilizations and have been contributing ever since, even while enslaved. It's not intelligence that's holding us back."

Thompson turned to Carla who was studiously avoiding the conversation. "Do you feel the same as Anthony, Carla?"

"No." Carla said tersely as she continued to look out the window. "Anthony and I have had these conversations before."

Thompson looked approvingly at Carla. "How long have you two been dating?"

Carla looked at Anthony to answer.

"Several years," Anthony responded.

The slightest hint of a smile crossed Thompson's face. "That's interesting."

During the whole conversation, Cread never said a word. He sat quietly looking at Anthony, while Thompson and Anthony talked.

Anthony felt the same way he did when he first interviewed for the reporter's job. He wished his father were here instead of him. He would know what to say.

Thompson continued. "The goal of white society in the South has been to subordinate the Negro race. Almost everything that is done to the Negro is a result of their unwarranted animosity toward us. In no other country in the world except probably Germany has their been such an open defiance of law to degrade a people. They would love to hear that you bought into their intellectual inferiority theory. It would help to assuage their guilt.

"Through the 1890s to the 1940s, Tuskegee Institute recorded more than 3,400 lynchings of Negroes in the South. Those are the ones recorded. And you want to ignore that?" Thompson continued, "The most comfortable feeling I have is that I know who I am, and where I came from, and I'm proud of what my ancestors did for me to be able to stand before you today. I wouldn't be anybody else for love or money."

Anthony nodded grudgingly. What Thompson said did make sense. Until Carla and the Williamses, Anthony had not heard their position presented so forcefully. He wasn't ready to concede his viewpoint completely, after having heard it repeatedly from his father and his father's friends, but he would consider what Carla and the Williamses said, another time. Right now his focus was on getting information.

"Anthony, on Sunday you'll meet the whole family. We're having a special celebration. Marcia, my cousins Winston and Dee's daughter, was accepted to Fisk University. Dinner will be at my sister Ludie's house. Everybody will be there. I don't want to discuss this with you all night. It would not be good manners. I want you and Carla to meet everybody and have some fun. We owe you that."

"Sure, that would be fine. Is it okay with you, Carla?" Anthony asked, relieved that Thompson had changed the subject once again.

"Of course, Anthony. I would love to meet the rest of the family."

"Good. I'm sorry I hogged up all the conversation," Thompson said, looking at Raymond, then Cread and Aunt Dahlia, "but you'll get to talk to everybody Sunday."

"I'm looking forward to it, Mr. Thompson," Anthony said as he and Carla walked out the door.

\*\*\*

"Well what do you think?" Anthony asked Carla as he walked her to her house.

"I think that Mr. Williams is a smart man to only have had a ninth-grade education."

"Yeah, I guess I would have to agree. I kind of like him and the family. Growing up like I did, I didn't have a chance to meet a lot of people like them. Thompson is interesting."

"Interesting?" Carla responded. "He is more than interesting. In the short time I heard him talk, he has a wealth of knowledge. Mr. Williams is also patient."

"What do you mean, patient?"

"He was very kind to you, Anthony."

As they approached East 105$^{th}$ Street, the hum of activity increased. This street was so interesting to Anthony. It reminded him of West 9$^{th}$ Street in Little Rock, a place the residents called "Little Rock's Harlem." There were goings-on both day and night, but East 105$^{th}$ Street in Cleveland was different. The street had a character all its own. Where southern men and women dressed up to visit West 9$^{th}$ Street and its establishments, residents on 105$^{th}$ Street wore more casual attire. To Anthony, the clothes represented something less noticeable. Unlike 105$^{th}$ Street, there was an underlying tension on West 9$^{th}$ that accompanied the outward formality of its visitors.

As they turned the corner Carla stopped. It was her first time on the street at night.

Anthony watched as she tried to soak in the atmosphere, looking like a tourist as she watched people walk back and forth. Johnny "Guitar" Watson singing the blues drifted out of one bar, and Smokey Robinson could be heard from a second-floor apartment. Some of the people walked along the street with a purpose, and some loitered, either by themselves or in groups. Some talked quietly, and some spoke at a higher volume, either trying to get somebody's attention or arguing a point.

Two men standing outside of a clothing store were louder than the others and commanded some notice from the folks in the street. One was an older, well-dressed man. The other was a thin, rat-faced young man who might have been twenty years old.

"Where's my money, Junior?" the older man asked.

"I told you I'll pay you when I get it, Monk."

"That was a month ago."

"Well, I still ain't got it."

A crowd gathered.

The older man grabbed the younger one by the collar and pushed him up against a door as the crowd surged forward. "You have one more day to mess with me, dude. One more day."

"And then what?"

The older man's hands moved only slightly, but just enough to produce a razor, which he pressed against the other man's neck. "You don't want to know."

The crowd shifted backward. Carla and Anthony were the closest when the crowd formed and were now no more than three or four feet from the two men. Anthony pushed backward, trying to squeeze through, but Carla stood there mesmerized.

"Come on, Carla."

She snapped out of it only when Anthony pulled her arm. "Anthony, that hurts."

"I'm sorry, but you could get cut—or worse. One of them might have a gun."

"I wanted to see."

Anthony shook his head. "You're something else."

As they walked back toward her street, Carla slowed them both down as they passed one of the bars. There was live entertainment, and the level of noise suggested everybody was having a good time.

Anthony noticed her interest and asked, "So do you and your boyfriend get out a lot back home?"

Carla looked away. "I don't have a boyfriend right now."

"Why not?"

"My husband died two years ago in a car accident, and I've only dated once since then. It didn't work out."

"I'm sorry. I didn't know."

"It's okay now. It was painful for a while, but I recently accepted the fact that he's gone and that I have to move on with my life."

"Any children?"

"No." She turned. "What about you?"

"What about me?" he asked guardedly.

"Were you ever married?"

"No."

"Any reason why not?" Carla asked.

Anthony ran his hand over his chin. "I haven't felt that close to anybody enough to want to get married."

"Girlfriend?" she asked.

"No. Not really."

"Uncommitted," Carla said under her breath. "That figures."

Anthony let the comment go without a response.

East 105th was quieter after they passed the bar and turned onto Pierpont Avenue. The last time it was that quiet was when he was with Raymond. Suddenly he became concerned. It was getting dark. Anthony walked carefully, alert to every sound. Carla, on the other hand, didn't seem to have a care in the world.

"Hey, pretty momma."

A chill ran down Anthony's back as he stopped and turned to see two drunk, middle-aged men sharing a wine bottle under a streetlight.

Anthony bristled. "Excuse me?"

"Hey, man, we was just complimenting the lady. Don't lose your cool."

Carla squeezed Anthony's hand and pulled him toward her as he turned toward the men. She wasn't strong enough though, and he took a few more steps toward them.

"That wasn't a compliment. That was disrespectful."

"Come on, Anthony. They're drunk."

"Hey, dude. Didn't mean no harm," the man with the bottle said as he raised it in a salute. His partner watched the bottle carefully.

Anthony wondered if anyone could hear his heart thumping as he turned to walk down the street with Carla. As they approached her house, Anthony tried to gather his thoughts. Should he wait until she invited him in, or should he invite himself?

Carla answered the question. She opened the door, shook his hand and stepped inside. "Thanks, Anthony. I'll see you tomorrow."

Anthony stood outside the door as she closed it gently.

There was always another day.

Walking back, the street seemed less dark and ominous. The encounter with the men emboldened him. Anthony felt like he had won a minor skirmish.

The drunks were still there, but paid him no attention. He walked casually by the men. His heart was still drumming, but at a slower rate.

When he entered his apartment, Anthony found a letter slid under the door. Based on its postmark, he figured it was the one Whiting had forwarded. He was tired and it was late, but he was curious. Anthony ripped the envelope open, wondering who would be writing him at the newspaper. The note was in bold, underlined, typewritten letters:

IT IS IMPORTANT FOR YOU AND
YOUR LOVED ONES THAT YOUR
EVESVILLE INVESTIGATION BRINGS
POSITIVE RESULTS.

Anthony stared at the paper. What was this? Why was anyone threatening him? Anthony was as anxious to finish as anyone. What was the point? He read the letter again, trying to make sense of its intent. Who would write a letter like that? Who else knew about his investigation and who else had an interest in its outcome?

Even though he was dead tired, Anthony slept fitfully that night.

At 9 A.M. the next day, Anthony called to make Whiting aware of the note.

"That's strange, Anthony. Not that many people outside the paper even know that you're working on that story."

"Should I call the police?"

"You can, but I don't think that's necessary. After all, you're going to have positive results, so the threat is meaningless."

"But what if for some reason I don't succeed?"

"You will, Anthony. I have faith in you."

The conversation did nothing to console him. If somebody wanted this case solved, why didn't they go to the police? Why put this burden on him?

An hour later, the phone rang.

"Anthony?"

It was Whiting again. Maybe he had some information. "Yes, sir?"

"Just after you hung up, the Monroe County sheriff paid us a visit. Seems he found out about the story of these missing men and wants to ask some questions."

"Fine. I should be back in less than a week," Anthony responded.

"I don't think he wants to wait that long, Anthony."

Anthony shrugged. "There's not much I can tell him."

"I know, but he's walking around like he's got this stick up his rear end since he found out that something like that happened without his knowledge. He wants to talk to you as soon as possible. How fast can you get back down here?" Whiting asked.

Anthony sighed to himself. "I guess by tomorrow afternoon." Anthony was upset since everything seemed to be moving in the right direction. The return would slow up his investigation. "Are you sure this isn't something we could do over the phone?"

"No, son. He was adamant about talking to you in person."

"Okay," Anthony responded. "I'll call you when I get there."

Anthony called Carla to explain the situation. Hopefully whatever the sheriff wanted wouldn't take more than a day.

The plane ride back took forever. Anthony did a mental review of all the information he had obtained. Since the interview wasn't until the next day, he took a cab from the Little Rock airport to his apartment to get his car, then drove straight to Pine Bluff to surprise his parents. It was a dreary day, but Anthony felt good coming home. He hadn't been gone that long but being around familiar surroundings was great for the soul.

He parked his car on the street so his parents wouldn't hear him coming. The wind blew in brief gusts as he walked up the drive. The noise coming from the house surprised him.

The voices were loud. At least one voice was. It sounded vaguely like his mother, but Anthony knew it couldn't be because she hardly ever raised her voice. There was someone else in their house.

"Where is the money?" a female voice asked.

"I'll have it in a while," a male voice answered.

The voice sounded like his father, but that couldn't be either. He was never that soft spoken in his life.

"My father worked for over fifty years to provide a home and money for us, and now it's all gone? How could you? He loaned you that money on good faith, thinking that you were going to build another funeral home, and you blew it?" the female voice continued.

"I didn't blow it, Mildred. Don't forget, Anthony went to school with some of it."

"That was not how we were supposed to be paying for his education, and besides, his education is still not paid for completely. I read the bill from the university. We still owe them, too, and you didn't even tell me."

"I meant to. Times were hard right then."

"Times have never been hard, Randall. You're the biggest colored mortician in this town. Everybody comes to you. How could times be hard?"

Anthony waited outside the door, but heard nothing for a minute.

His mother's voice, a lot softer, but still on edge asked, "Was it the gambling or that floozy that works in your office?"

"Mildred!"

"Don't Mildred me," his mother said in an even but low tone. "Answer the question, Randall. How did you blow twenty thousand dollars of my father's hard-earned money?"

Shaken, Anthony quietly backed away from the porch. His mother could only be talking about Liz the secretary. Anthony had sometimes wondered about her relationship with his father but never dwelled on it.

He walked away, trying to make some sense out of what he just heard. Self-made man, huh? A moral pillar of Negro society?

Anthony decided to drive back to his apartment in Little Rock. He needed the time to think.

As soon as he arrived, he called his parents, trying to keep the disappointment from his voice. "Hey, Mom. I'm in Little Rock."

"Hi, Anthony. When did you arrive?"

"Not long ago."

"What are you doing back so soon?"

"I have a meeting tomorrow with the county sheriff. He wants to talk to me about Evesville. If I get some time after that, I'll drop by."

"I would hope so," his mother said in a tone Anthony didn't recognize. He could tell there was still tension in her voice. She was usually a lot happier to hear from him, and unlike the past conversations, his mother never called his father to the phone.

## · XXVII ·

Anthony arrived at the *Sun* a half hour early. He went to his desk noticing that Whiting's door was closed, but not enough to mute a spirited conversation between two men. When Hannah knocked to notify Whiting that he was there, the discussion ended abruptly.

Hannah motioned for Anthony to go in where he was introduced to the county sheriff. Alfred A. Cottingham was almost as big as William Whiting. As a matter of fact, they could pass for brothers. They had the same build, the same gruff voices, and the same ruddy complexion.

"Anthony," Cottingham said as he held out his oversized hand, "I've heard a lot about you. How are you doing?"

"Fine, sir."

Whiting motioned for Anthony to sit. "Anthony, Cottingham has been on my tail to get you in here to talk about Evesville. I'm sorry I had to pull you away from your investigation, but this old coot wouldn't let me rest until I got you two together."

"I understand," Anthony responded. "I'll help in anyway I can."

"Good, Anthony," Cottingham said, patting Anthony on his shoulder, "so tell me, what have you found out so far?"

Anthony related the interviews he had conducted and his conversation with the Williamses. He also told Cottingham about the shooting outside the Jackson farm, and the letter. Cottingham didn't seem that interested in those incidents. "So who do you think might be involved, Anthony?"

"I'm not sure, sir. The Williamses did take off out of Evesville kind of fast, but so did a lot of other families. The whereabouts of the Coulters is still unknown. I'm going to have to dig a lot deeper to find out what happened."

Cottingham scratched his chest and frowned. "I have to say I'm a little disappointed. I was hoping for something a little more concrete."

Whiting interrupted, "I told you to let him finish his investigation, Alfred. You got me wasting good money to call him back here in order to tell you that?"

Cottingham ignored Whiting. "Tell me more about the Williams family, son."

Anthony told Cottingham all he knew, except for the conversations he had with Thompson Williams about race.

"What about these Coulters. Anything?"

"Nothing, sir."

Cottingham turned to Whiting. "I've got some men at the Williamses and Coulter's old places in Evesville checking to see if there's any evidence. I also have some people on the trail of these Coulters." He turned to Anthony. "I'll let you know if we find anything on this end."

"Good, sir." Anthony responded.

Son, if it's true what happened to those men, and I believe it is, it would be a most grievous sin, a murder. You understand."

Anthony nodded.

"If you hear anything at all. Anything," Cottingham emphasized, "I want you to get on the phone to me immediately, you hear?"

"Yes, sir."

"You know all about withholding evidence, I'm sure."

Anthony glanced at Whiting. "Yes sir. That would never happen."

"Good. I'm sorry you had to come all the way back here, but I was hoping you would have at least turned up some kind of clues about this thing. You go on back up to Cleveland and finish up this job. I'll be waiting to hear from you."

Anthony barely nodded while he stared at the sheriff's back as he lumbered out of Whiting's office.

Anthony stayed at his desk writing for a while before he got back on the road to Pine Bluff. As much as he thought about it, he couldn't for the life of him figure out why he was called back to Little Rock.

His mother was at the door when he arrived.

Anthony looked at her closely, trying to see how she was holding up. He knew she would never volunteer that information. "Where's Dad?"

"He stepped out," she said tersely.

The way she responded answered his unasked question, but Anthony was at a loss as to what he could do. His mother picked up his overnight bag and put it on the landing. "Now sit down and tell me everything about your job. How is your assignment going?"

After bringing his mother up to date, eating a good meal, and providing her with a few laughs, Anthony watched as his mother became quiet and stared off into space. Anthony finally retired. He was unable to sleep well, so he was awake when his father came in late that evening. His parents murmured something to each other, then there was complete silence.

With all that was going on in his life, the welfare of his mother was foremost. Anthony leaned toward doing nothing, but that was becoming passé in his life. He sighed, yet another dilemma that required a solution, he thought to himself as he drifted off.

# · XXVIII ·

Late the next morning Anthony met with Whiting. His plane didn't leave until the next day. He wanted to learn more about why the sheriff had called him to Little Rock, but Whiting was unable to shed any more light on the subject.

"Oh, by the way, that Bobby Joe Byrd called again. He left a number for you to call him."

Anthony hesitated. He waited a minute to gather himself. "Did you find out anything about him?"

"No. We asked around, but nothing came up on him."

Whiting's answer was too casual for Anthony, but he let it pass. Anthony had completely forgotten about Byrd, or he would have mentioned it to the sheriff. With the way he responded to the Jackson farm shooting and the note though, Anthony doubted that Mr. Whiting's response to Byrd would be any different.

He called Bobby Joe Byrd around noon.

"Yeah."

"Mr. Byrd?"

"Anthony? How you doin'?"

Byrd, recognizing Anthony's voice immediately, gave Anthony more reason for concern. "Okay."

"Look, I'm going to cut to the chase. There's a man in Colt who knew the two families pretty well. I'm sure he will want to share some information with you. It seems him and that Williams family didn't hit it off too well. Everybody else coming out of that town has been so tight, but he might be the man you're looking for. I told him you might be calling on him. I got his address and everything. When do you think you're going to see him?"

Anthony paused to think. "I'll stop by there tomorrow after-noon. I plan to leave here the day after, so I'll have enough time to hear what he has to say," Anthony lied.

"Good. Let me know how it turns out."

Anthony suspected that Byrd already knew how it was going to turn out. If he headed out to talk to Byrd's man now, he could avoid running into Byrd who might try to meet him out there.

Because the information was from Byrd, Anthony's enthusi-asm for this possible break was dampened. The sound of the bul-lets flying past his car was still fresh in his memory. He also remembered Mrs. Warner's warning at the boardinghouse in Wynne. Whatever Byrd's motives were, they probably weren't in Anthony's best interest.

Anthony debated long and hard about the pros and the cons of visiting the new source of information. What if it was a setup? What if there was no source? Whoever shot at him before would have a good chance of finishing the job if that was their goal. Sweat began to bead on his forehead as he considered the con-sequences. The small thuds he felt in his temples signaled the beginning of a headache. Maybe he should quit and go back to the funeral home. Reaching for an aspirin, he dwelled on that thought for only a minute before rejecting it.

First, he didn't know for sure that Byrd was the shooter. Second, if the shooter wanted to kill him, he probably would have done it. Third, if he took off for the place now, it would catch everybody off guard, and he could find out Byrd's real intentions.

His mind wandered to the snake walker story. How did the young men prepare themselves to control their fear?

Crawford Reardon's place was twelve miles outside the town of Colt. The dirt road leading to his place looked like it hadn't been traveled in years. Red dust swirled around his car, signaling to anyone within miles that he was on the way. That was disconcerting. No telling who could see him coming. He slouched in his seat so he was less of a target.

Unlike most of the other people Anthony interviewed, Crawford Reardon was straight out inhospitable. When Anthony knocked on the door of the shack, it opened without anyone saying a word.

"Hello?" Anthony said.

"Door's open. Why you still outside?"

Anthony walked slowly into the dark dwelling. "Mr. Reardon?"

"Yeah. Who else?"

"Just checking. How are you, sir?" Anthony asked.

"You didn't come to see about my health. What do you want?" Reardon replied.

The place smelled of stale food and body odor. Dust was everywhere. The two windows were covered with some type of dark plastic. "Mr. Byrd..." Reardon spit in the corner, startling Anthony and throwing him off guard. He composed himself and resumed. "Mr. Byrd said you might have some information on the Coulter and the Williams families," Anthony said as he moved to the opposite side of the room, afraid to sit on one of the two bare wooden chairs.

"The high-and-mighty Williamses. Yeah, I got some information. What you want to know?" Reardon walked slowly toward the kitchen table before turning and looking at Anthony.

"I'm trying to find out what happened in Evesville and why it became deserted. I understand that town had some problems."

"Town ain't had no problems 'til them fools started actin' up."

"What do you mean?"

"We had a nice, peaceful town. Everybody knew their place. Didn't nobody try to be somethin' they weren't except for them folks in them two families." Reardon spit again. "If it weren't for them Williamses and them damn Coulters, Evesville would still be a town. They was the cause of that whole mess."

"What happened, Mr. Reardon?" Anthony pulled out his pad and pencil.

Reardon sat on a stool that looked like it might fall apart at any second. "Way I heard, two little black kids, Johnny and Hosiah got into a rock fight with some of the white kids."

"There were two kids involved in the rock fight?" Anthony asked. When he interviewed Ezell and Edethel Wright, Anthony was under the impression that only one kid was involved.

The stool squeaked at Reardon's slightest movement. "Yep, from what I hear. One of the rocks busted the white kid's head wide open."

Anthony wasn't sure, but he thought he detected a hint of admiration in Reardon's voice.

"When somethin' like that happens, the kids got to go. You got to ship them out. But no, them two high-and-mighty families don't think they have to do anything. They going around actin' like nothin' happened, knowing full well somebody was comin' after them."

Anthony knew the answer, but asked anyway. "Who is somebody?"

"The same people who come after any wayward Negro. The same people who keep all them Negroes in line."

Anthony looked up from his notebook to look at Reardon.

"Next I know, there is some whisperin' about them boys being taken care of. You know?"

Anthony nodded.

"Days went by though without nothin' happenin'. Everybody wondered when it gon' happen, but it never did." Reardon spit again. The stool squeaked once more.

Anthony was hoping that he was near the end. He wondered if he could catch something from all that spittle flying around.

"One day, Hosiah Coulter ended up missin'. Some kids found his body a few days later."

"Excuse me," Anthony said as he stepped outside.

Reardon stood. "You okay, boy?"

Anthony nodded.

Anthony took a few deep breaths and wiped the sweat from his forehead. The droning noise somewhere in the back of his head was steady. The pain was not. It visited him in spurts. Knowing it wasn't going away anytime soon, Anthony swallowed three aspirin without water and reentered the shack.

Reardon continued as if he had never left. "The Williamses, they going on about their lives like nothin' happened."

Anthony stopped writing. "Why wouldn't they?"

Crawford looked at Anthony as if he should have known the

answer, "Because the other boy was little Johnny Williams. They probably comin' after him next."

Anthony started writing again.

"A few days pass and some of the white townspeople, they missin': Old Mr. George the piano player at the saloon, Mr. Harvey, Mr. Tyson...the sheriff, he missin' too. White folks get scared. All types of rumors start floatin' around about some escapees from prison, some black renegades from Mississippi, some band of cutthroat Indians or maybe just somebody after revenge."

"What about this sheriff? Could he have been Klan too?"

Crawford cleared his throat. "I don't think so. He was good to colored folks. Treated folks equally. I doubt he was a part of that group."

Anthony looked up. "Didn't anybody question whether the Coulter family was involved?"

"Yeah, white folks talked about it, but you got to understand, the Coulters was the meanest family I know, but most of them took off the same day they buried the boy."

"Took off?"

"Yeah. It surprised everybody. You would have thought that with one of the boys bein' hung, somebody was going to pay, but they left meek as lambs."

"What about the Williamses?"

"The Williamses, they standoffish people. Never bother nobody and never been out of line, so nobody 'spect they did nothing, even though they was probably comin' after their boy next. Didn't nobody see or hear about the Klan comin' around their farm so..." Reardon threw up his hands as a question. "Anyway, I think most white folks was scared of that family 'cause they wasn't somebody you just haul off and mess with, plus they all carried guns. You didn't see one of them men without a rifle, shotgun, or somethin'. Most important though, the main people who would have gone after them is missin'."

Anthony nodded again. "So what do you think happened?"

Reardon's voice lowered as he sat back down on the stool. "That Saturday night, there was a storm. You could hear the thunder rollin' in the back hills. A couple of Negroes heard what they thought was a lot of gunshots. Now I wouldn't give a cow's ass for what Charlie Matthews say, but ol' Mr. Johnson, he say he hear gunshots, he hear gunshots.

"Right after that, I hear Hilton and his nephew Thompson Williams done sold the family farm to some lumber company. When the white people move out, the Williamses was right behind 'em. Wasn't right."

"What wasn't right?"

"A couple other families had land, too, but nobody wanted to buy they land because everybody so scared. They can't get nothin' but pennies on the dollar if that. After while, rumor is that white folks goin' to burn down the town."

Anthony noted that this was the second time he was hearing some of this, which helped confirm the story. His head was clearing up, and the pain and dizziness were receding. "Why? Why would they want to burn it down?"

Reardon started to spit again, but jerked his head up like Anthony had suddenly appeared in his shack for the first time. "Boy, I know you ain't that stupid."

Anthony raised his hands. He still didn't get it.

"That town was runnin' all right with Negroes in charge. We elected a sheriff and town council. One of the families ran the feed store and another the general store. We was already runnin' the mill, so we kept that goin'. The blacksmith was already a Negro. We had that town hummin'."

"I still don't understand."

Reardon finally spit again, sighed then stood to talk to Anthony like he would a little child. "You ever hear of Tulsa, Oklahoma? They used to call it the black Wall Street?"

"No."

"What about Rosewood, Florida?"

"No."

"Springfield, Illinois?"

Anthony shook his head.

"You an educated man, ain't you? At least you sound like it."

"I have a degree."

" 'I have a degree'." Reardon said mockingly. "You ain't learnt no history though have you, boy?" Reardon answered his own question. "Naw, because if you had, you would know that white folks burnt them colored towns down just because they was running fine on their own. Tulsa was downright prosperous, I hear. It was like no other town in that state. That's the only reason. Now if they burn them towns down, what you think was going to happen to ours?"

"You said it was a rumor."

"That's all you need, boy, is a rumor, and some scared folks. Next thing you know, you got a stampede." Reardon shook his head. "Colored folks left that town in droves. The ones who wanted to stay couldn't. Wasn't enough folks left to run the mill and make it a town."

"But nobody ever came to burn the town down."

"It didn't make no difference then. Ain't no use in burnin' an empty town. That's like deliverin' mail to a vacant house. Ain't nobody there to get the message."

"So you think the Williamses were involved?" Anthony asked trying to keep the skepticism from his voice.

"I don't know for sure, but unless somebody from the outside came in, the Williamses the only ones who coulda done somethin' like that. They the only ones who had a reason to do somethin' like that. Wasn't no strange Negroes around to do it. Wasn't no renegade Indians around to do it."

"Did anybody else think the same as you?"

"Didn't nobody want to talk about it 'less some white people overhear."

Anthony changed the subject. It was obvious Mr. Reardon had a motive.

"So how do you know Bobby Joe Byrd?"

"He done my family a favor. Saved my son from gettin' hurt. I owe him."

That was strange that Byrd would do a colored man a favor Anthony thought, and filed it away in his mind. He looked around the room again. There was no evidence that anybody else lived there with him. Surely a lady wouldn't put up with the condition of this place and all of that spitting.

"Where's your son now?"

Reardon hung his head. "Out west. They got after him for somethin' else. Broke Corine's heart that he left. She moved north with her sister."

Anthony was sure that wasn't the entire story, but he wasn't going to stay around and hear the rest. He stood to shake Crawford Reardon's hand. "Mr. Reardon, I want to thank you for that information. Can I call on you again if I have any more questions?"

"I told you all I know."

"Thanks again."

Anthony took a rag out of the trunk of his car and wrapped it around the steering wheel. As soon as he approached the pond he'd passed on the way to Crawford Reardon's house, he exited the car to wash his hands, and threw the rag away.

He touched the folded piece of paper in the breast pocket of his shirt briefly, then slouched in his seat again as he drove back along the dusty road.

## · XXIX ·

Anthony called Carla the next morning. The story was coming together. Reardon had shed more light on Evesville, but it was obvious he was jealous of the Williams family. Somehow the Coulters had come back to exact revenge. All he had to do was find out how, when, and where, but he had to find them first. He had to talk to the Williamses as soon as he could.

Anthony sat back on his sofa. Once he found out though, how would he get somebody to confess something without concrete proof? The Coulters probably wouldn't be as hospitable as the Williamses, and why would they confess it to him anyway? Even if he confronted the Williams family with the information he had gathered, and they knew what happened to the missing men, the Williamses could still deny knowing anything about them without anyone to counter their claim.

Anthony made one more trip to the *Sun* before going to the airport. The newsroom looked different. There were some changes. His desk was missing. Hannah had to direct Anthony to his new workspace. It was larger and had a window.

"Mr. Whiting is in a meeting, but he told me to tell you that he was anxious to talk to you. He should be with you in about a half hour."

"Thanks, Hannah. When did all this take place?" Anthony asked, waving his hand.

"Yesterday. Everybody in management is waiting to see how this story you're working on is going to turn out."

"Everybody in management?"

"Yep. Mr. Whiting has already convinced people that this is going to be a blockbuster, so they moved you so you could be more comfortable," Hannah whispered in a conspiratorial tone. "I have to tell you, Anthony, some of the veteran reporters are upset. They think you're getting too much attention for something that hasn't happened yet."

"I can understand, but it's not my fault that everybody's putting so much weight on this. What can you do when you stumble on something like this story? I told Mr. Whiting, and he told me to run with it. How management responds to the story's potential is not my fault."

"No, it isn't, Anthony," Whiting said as he walked toward Anthony's desk, grinning, "but don't feel like you're under too much pressure here. Based on what you've told us so far, Charlie Hargrove and I think there's almost enough information to print a story about the disappearance of the men and the vacated town, but if you were to break this open and find the culprits, we think it will be a national news item. Management here is looking forward to a briefing, once you feel you have enough of a story to develop."

"I feel like I'm a lot closer, Mr. Whiting. A few more days in Cleveland, and I think I'll know for sure."

Whiting smiled and patted Anthony on his back. "Keep at it, son. Good stories are not made overnight, and we know this is a hard nut to crack, but management has faith in you, Anthony. You've been a good reporter. Break this story, and you'll be a great reporter."

Anthony smiled.

Whiting left, and Anthony sat at his desk for a while planning his next move. "By the way, Hannah, where did the reporter, Jerry, who worked here before me go?"

Hannah looked at Anthony with an odd expression. "Jerry? I think the *Washington Post*, why?"

"I don't know. I thought it might be good at some point to talk to him once I get back to Cleveland."

"Don't you have his notes?"

"Yes, but there's nothing like talking to someone who had the project before I did."

"I knew Jerry, and I don't think he can tell you anymore than what he wrote."

It seemed strange to Anthony that Hannah in a roundabout way appeared to be discouraging him from talking to the former reporter.

"Did he leave here under the best of circumstances?"

"I guess so, although I don't think he was that enthusiastic about the project."

"Why not?"

"No one ever knew. One day he was working here, and the next day he resigned."

Anthony suspected that if he asked why, he wouldn't get the whole story, but he asked anyway. "Why was that? Was there a disagreement or something, or was his work not up to par?"

"Anthony, I don't think anyone here knows why. As far as I know, his writing was fine, and he worked well with everybody. He just left."

Based on Hannah's responses, Anthony really became curious, but decided to drop the subject. He would revisit it later.

# · XXX ·

Raymond was in a dilemma. He hated to get so close to the top without making it. The incident with Roach checked his game like no pool player could. He wasn't worried so much about himself as he was about embarrassing the family again. Raymond felt badly having to have Cread rescue him and his aunts and mother crying because they thought they had lost him. He should have been able to take care of himself better than that.

If he were more careful, more observant, the ambush wouldn't have happened. He learned two valuable lessons: One, don't get so focused on something so intensely that you don't pay attention to what's happening around you. Two, don't ever trust people you don't know, especially in the streets.

The major question for him though was whether he should continue to try to take his game to the next level or whether he should cool out and prepare for college. Summer would be over soon. He was accepted to the only two schools to which he had applied, Lincoln University in Pennsylvania, and Howard University in Washington, D.C., and he had to make a decision.

Raymond decided to stop at Riley's one more time to hit the balls around. There wouldn't be a lot of people there at eleven in the morning, and he could practice without interruption. Golly, the rack man, greeted him like nothing had happened. There were only two other people in the poolroom. He went to the back and spread the balls out on the table. The two young men who were shooting stopped to watch as he ran ball after ball with machinelike precision. After a few minutes, they both approached him.

"Raymond?" A thin, young man about sixteen or seventeen years of age with a Cleveland Indians cap approached him. The young man's friend, approximately the same age, shorter, but built like a football lineman, was directly behind him.

"Yeah?" Raymond said guardedly.

"Ummm, we been watching you, and we want to tell you that we think your game is really strong."

"You're one of the best," the shorter one chimed in.

"Thanks. I've seen you guys in here before. What are your names?"

"Jimmy."

"Roland."

"Right." Raymond shook their hands and turned back to the table.

Roland scraped the floor with the toe of his shoe. "We don't want to bother you, but we were hoping that you could teach us how to hustle like you."

Raymond stopped shooting, put down his stick, and leaned against the table and looked at the two young men. "So you want to be hustlers?"

They both nodded.

Raymond paused a moment, gathering his thoughts. He knew he should be flattered, but he had heard the compliments before. It was about their age when he learned he had skills. Roland, he remembered, had a pretty strong game, and Jimmy was right behind him. Both were good kids. He remembered them to be quiet and respectful, but always hanging around like they had no other life than running the streets. How long could that last? If they stayed in the streets, where would they be five years from now? What would he have told himself if he knew what he knew now? What would Uncle T tell them?

Raymond rested his hands on the table's rail and leaned over. "You know what the real hustle in this world is? You know what's going to get you over out here?"

The two young men waited.

"An education. Go back to school. Get a legitimate skill. If you can't go to college, be an electrician, a bus driver, anything, but you need to stop hanging out in these poolrooms. Thinking you're going to be able to take somebody's money enough times to make it out here is bogus. This life is nothing, man. It's glamorous sometimes. You see me taking down the cash, but you don't see the hassles you got to deal with. You stay out here long enough and it will eat your little asses up. There's a better way of living, man. You're both intelligent young men. Don't let the streets pull you down."

He looked at the two as they fidgeted like they were caught stealing. Raymond smiled. "Both of you are pretty good players. I like the way you handle yourselves. That's going to be important as you get older. If you have the intelligence to make money on the street, you have the intelligence to make it anywhere. Don't waste it on this nickel and dime bullshit."

Raymond could tell they were disappointed, but he didn't care. Hopefully some of what he said would sink in.

During his lecture, he also made up his mind about his future. "This fall, I am going to college. I am going to hit the books, get a degree, and be a square for the rest of my life. I'm going to make my money slow and steady and sleep at night. If you have any sense, you'll do the same."

## · XXXI ·

Anthony's dad kept a low profile while Anthony was in town. There was none of the arrogance Anthony usually noted, especially when someone or something disagreed with him. It did flare up when he mentioned his conversation with Thompson Williams. His father was ready to give Thompson some grudging respect even though he was a farmer, until he found that Thompson had only finished the ninth grade. "The man is uneducated. How can he tell anyone anything?" With that one sentence, his father permanently relegated Thompson to the lower rungs of society.

"A lot of what he says makes sense though, Dad. Just because a person didn't have the opportunity to go to college, doesn't mean he isn't intelligent."

"So you go up North, listen to the ramblings of some man with a blue-collar job and no education, then come back down here to enlighten me? How can you even begin to listen to someone like that? I thought I taught you to think for yourself." His father's voice rose with each word until it was booming like a cannon. Words ricocheted off the walls like oversized stray bullets. The wolf was in full force once again.

Anthony's first inclination was to duck, retreat, and get out of the line of fire, but instead he stood, arms crossed, and shook his head slowly. The bullying, the stare, used to work, but not this time. The cub had grown. "No, Dad. You taught me to think like you."

Anthony watched as his father's eyes widened as if he had seen his son for the first time, then he turned away, not saying another word, but Anthony wasn't finished.

"And whatever's wrong between you and Mom, you need to straighten it out, because she deserves that." Anthony took a deep breath. "As much as she's done for us, she deserves at least that."

His father never turned, but Anthony saw his father's head nod. It was hardly noticeable, but it was a nod.


Anthony had become restless during the flight from Little Rock to Cleveland. He was feeling pressure to bring this investigation to a head. There was so much that depended on him developing a plausible, certifiable story. He could always suggest the Coulter family had the most to gain from the death of those men. The article could also include the accounts of the people he had interviewed, especially the account about the Williamses and the Coulter kids' run-in with the white kids. In addition, there was the fact that the Williams family left Evesville so quickly, then dispersed and reconnected in Cleveland. And even though they may not have been directly involved in what happened to the missing men, they probably knew.

Their departure was not all that unusual for Arkansans in those days though. Anthony recalled Carla's statistics about the mass exodus of blacks from the state because of the lack of jobs and discrimination.

Despite the fact that all trails led to the Coulter family, he would feel a lot better if there were one piece of evidence or one eyewitness who would confirm their involvement. The difference could mean everything.

The plane didn't arrived until 6:45 P.M. Luckily he was able to get one of the few cabs left. It took him an hour to get to East 105<sup>th</sup> Street. Anthony instructed the cabdriver to stop at the corner of Massie Avenue and East 105<sup>th</sup>. If Raymond were in Riley's he would stop in and say hello.

Raymond wasn't there, so Anthony headed toward the house to change clothes. He would find a good restaurant, possibly downtown so he could spend a quiet evening with a woman who made him feel more different than he ever felt.

The Five was alive as usual. Folks were getting off work, and mingling with the regulars as they went about their business.

Anthony was stopped by a voice as he exited the poolroom.

"Hey, my man."

Anthony turned to see a guy who looked vaguely familiar approaching him. He had the strangest walk, Anthony thought, like his feet were hurting him, and that crooked smile...

"You lookin' for Raymond?" he asked as he ambled toward Anthony.

"Yes. I was. Have you seen him?" Anthony questioned as he slowed his pace.

"Not today. I know he's not in the poolroom; I just came from there. " He stopped Anthony with a light hand on the shoulder. "You the guy from out of town, right?"

Anthony stopped. "Right."

"Yeah. I saw you and Raymond in the Café Tia Juana the other day. Then I saw you and your lady passing by the Café Society."

The wary look on Anthony's face probably prompted the man to introduce himself. "I'm sorry, man, my name is Trey. I'm a friend of Raymond's."

This brought some relief to Anthony, but not much. A smile like Trey's didn't give him much comfort. "Anthony."

"Anthony. All right. Yeah, I seen you around here the last couple of days, and thought I would try and meet you."

Anthony started walking again with Trey beside him. "Raymond ain't getting out like he used to. He okay, ain't he?"

The way Anthony figured it, if this man were a friend he would know that.

Trey looked at Anthony. "Raymond was lucky to have you around."

"What do you mean?"

"Letting him know what was going down and all."

Anthony paused to say something, but then continued to walk.

"It's cool, my man. We all friends." Trey tapped Anthony on the shoulder again before moving off.


The restaurant was quiet, and Anthony was happy for that. It fit his mood. He was happy to see Carla, but there was a heightened level of anxiety because of Evesville and it was gnawing at him. They ate in silence as Carla occasionally glanced at Anthony. "I want to wrap this up in the next few days. If I don't find the Coulters, it doesn't seem like I'm going to find a smoking gun, so I'm going to have to build my case based on motivation, secondhand testimony, and deduction."

"You sure you want to do that, Anthony?"

"Why not? I don't have any other choice."

"You have a choice to not write anything."

Anthony looked at Carla, but said nothing.

"Are you going to include the Williamses in your story?" she asked.

"Of course."

"Do you know what happens to this family if you write a story like that?"

"This is an Arkansas paper, Carla. They live in Cleveland."

"How long do you think it will take for the news of a Cleveland family possibly being involved in a killing in Arkansas to reach the Cleveland papers? A day? A week? The fact is, Anthony, it will happen fairly quickly. I would bet on that."

"Why are you so concerned about somebody you just met and hardly know?"

"They're people, Anthony, and they'll be guilty by association. A story that links a colored family to a crime by even the thinnest evidence, is like saying they did it. You go on with your life, but they have to live with that shadow over them for the rest of theirs."

"What if they know? What if they know what happened to those men?"

"You know, Anthony, even if they do know, based on the information you shared with me, I wouldn't write the story. If somebody were to come to your house, kill someone in your family and you know they would get away with it, but you could take the assailant's life, what would you do?"

"I don't know."

"I know what I would do."

"You would kill?"

"If I had to. If I had the nerve to." Carla paused. "It's been done before."

Anthony looked at Carla as if it was the first time he had met her.

"Too much depends on me writing this story Carla." Anthony considered telling her about the note, but decided not to. "Succeeding in this business is all I've ever wanted to do for most of my life and I've been through too much to go back now."

Carla looked disappointed, but shrugged. "It's your life, and it's your conscience."

## · XXXII ·

The party for Raymond's cousin Marcia was at Raymond's mother's house because she had the biggest backyard. It was like a family reunion. Relatives from around the country came to celebrate. There were at least forty cousins and other relatives from out of town. They had not been together since the Williams family moved from Arkansas. Since Raymond hadn't notified the family that he was going to enroll, Marcia would officially be the first to attend college. Anyway, there was no way Raymond wanted all that attention.

"The family is everything," Thompson's brother, Ransom, said to no one in particular as he looked out the kitchen window into the backyard where everyone gathered.

"The family is everything," Thompson's other brother Deacon, and his cousin Cread echoed solemnly.

Anthony and Carla arrived, and Raymond met them at the

door. Anthony seemed distant, but Raymond dismissed it. He was probably having a bad day.

He introduced the two to as many of his family as he could to make them feel comfortable. "Food's going to be served in about an hour, so you can either stand out here and talk, or come inside."

"We'll stand out here and talk," Anthony said, glancing at Carla. "There sure are a lot of people."

"Haven't seen most of them since we moved," Raymond said as he looked around. Raymond excused himself as Myra walked up to him.

"I like her."

Raymond turned to her in surprise. "Who are you talking about?"

"That lady with Anthony." Myra motioned.

"Good. Maybe you two will get to know each other better as time goes by." Raymond slipped one arm around her waist. "How about you? You okay? Can I get you anything?"

"No. I'm enjoying myself. There are so many wonderful people here. When I tell them I'm with you, they give me all the attention in the world. Why is that, Raymond?"

"I have no idea, Myra. Just enjoy yourself."

There was the faint sound of a cowbell near the house. Raymond smiled. His Aunt Dahlia had summoned the family with that same cowbell for more than sixty years. Conversation stopped immediately as everybody gathered around her with Thompson standing behind her.

"Today is another important day in our family history. Marcia, Winston and Dee's daughter, will attend Fisk University this fall," Aunt Dahlia announced. Everybody clapped and whistled. "This is the first of our family to get a higher education, but it won't be the last." Aunt Dahlia's gaze wandered around the crowd until she found Raymond. She nodded briefly before continuing as she wrapped her hand around Marcia's waist. "We want to give you our blessings for a successful journey, and let you know that you can call on any one of us for anything at anytime."

There was a chorus of amens as the guests clapped again. Several members of the family came up to tell Marcia how proud they were of her and to pledge their support. Most slipped her an envelope with money. Her eyes filled with tears from the love and comfort the family offered. She thanked everybody and promised everyone she would make them proud. Raymond watched from a distance. He was already proud of her.

The second cowbell signaled the gathering for dinner. Each member held the hand of another as they formed a circle around Aunt Dahlia. As soon as the circle was formed, Aunt Dahlia produced a gourd filled with a liquid that she spilled on the ground. She then called upon a long line of ancestors by name to continue to look over them on their individual and collective journeys. As soon as she finished, each of the members of the family lined up according to age with oldest first to eat. Anthony, Carla and Myra, as guests, were in line directly after Aunt Dahlia.

Raymond watched the two as they entered the house. He then looked around at his relatives. He was blessed to have been born into this family.

Aunt Dahlia settled in at the head of the table to watch the procession move around the table. Anthony and Carla performed their ceremony with the greens, got their food and moved back to the backyard. They ate at the long table reserved for Aunt Dahlia and the oldest family members. "Son," she said. "You ain't got enough food on that plate. You're going to need seconds."

"I'm fine, Aunt Dahlia. Thank you," Anthony said. Her comments more than anything else, made him feel at home.

After dinner, each of the kids recited their accomplishments and then the adults. Anthony marveled at the group gathered in Ludie's backyard. Without exception, all the kids were doing well in school. The adults held different jobs or owned their own businesses, but each was successful in their own right. Their recitation about their careers was obviously for the kids to see what their elders had accomplished.

Anthony's mind wandered to the few family reunions he attended on his father's side. At each reunion, there was at least one or two of the family missing because of imprisonment, drugs, or some similar mishap. One uncle was even in jail for embezzlement, which elicited a twisted sense of pride in some of the family since it was a white-collar crime. So much for the family of echelons, he thought.

What stood out most in Anthony's mind, and one of the reasons his immediate family had not attended that many reunions, was how his father was received. Boisterous and boastful at times, his father would hold court, talking about his success in business and bragging about the money he had made. What Anthony found, as he grew up though, was the rest of the family didn't like his dad. He would notice some of his uncles and cousins whispering and snickering when Randall would start rambling in his booming voice about what it took to be a success.

One summer, however, it became painfully clear why, when one of Anthony's favorite cousins whispered to another, not knowing that Anthony was standing behind her. Anthony's father was holding court as usual, oblivious to his relatives' inattentiveness. "He thinks he's white," his cousin had said.

The words stung Anthony, and he backed away without saying anything. He never told his father, but he suspected that

Randall already knew he wasn't a favorite at these gatherings. Even his mother mentioned that she had argued with one of Anthony's aunts, his father's sister, but Anthony never found out what that was about except that his mother was trying to defend his dad. Whatever it was, she never mentioned it again.

As Anthony looked around the Williams reunion, he felt a warmness that he had never experienced in his family. The children were well mannered. The adults were respectful of one another, and no one in the family sought any special attention. When the kids introduced themselves, the adults clapped and whistled like the child had won a million dollars. It was apparent that these kids had the support and love of every adult in the family.

"Come here, young man," an elder commanded as a young boy who was introduced to Anthony walked away. "Let's do this introduction again."

The boy understood exactly what his elder expected and approached Anthony again, looked him in the eye, and gave him a firm handshake. "Hello, Mr. Andrews. It's a pleasure to meet you, sir." The elder, one of the young boys' uncles, said nothing but patted him on his back as he walked away for the second time.

The cowbell rang again, and everyone turned to Aunt Dahlia. "Has everyone finished eating?" She waited as family members responded, "Yes, ma'am." "As you know some of our kids have special talents. What we want to do now is to present each one for your entertainment."

The family gathered around an open space. One after another, the children played musical instruments, quoted excerpts from popular plays, recited poems and Bible quotations, and sang. Again the adults showed their appreciation as if they were listening to Marian Anderson, Langston Hughes, or Paul Robeson.

Thompson Williams remained low-keyed, but somehow still held a dominating presence among his kin. Anthony watched him closely. There was no question that he was the head of the family. Thompson's goal it seemed that day, despite being surrounded by relatives he hadn't seen in years, was to make sure that Anthony and Carla felt comfortable. They were introduced to each person as a friend of Raymond's although everyone knew the circumstances of them being there. It was a strange feeling, but Anthony felt he belonged. He spent time talking to most of the family members and they accepted him without question.

It was difficult to find a time when he could ask questions. Anthony was able to mention the Coulters only a few times, but the family members he talked to only had secondhand information and no knowledge of the Coulters' whereabouts. One of the men in the group offered that Detroit would be a logical place since they had the most family there.

Everybody was moving around, talking in small groups about family matters and friends, too many questions about the Coulters would be rude and intrusive in this atmosphere. Maybe later would be a good time when everybody had settled down a bit.

Raymond and his cousin Johnny were like brothers as they wandered around the yard together laughing and hugging children and elders alike. Anthony wondered if Johnny even knew what happened after he and Hosiah threw those rocks.

After another hour or so, the cowbell rang again. All the family gathered in a big circle holding hands with Aunt Dahlia sitting in the middle. She began to sing an old Negro spiritual, *Walk With Me Lord*, and the family joined in. Anthony held Carla's hand tightly as they swayed with the others. His eyes became moist as a wave of emotion overcame him. He looked around, marveling at the voices singing as one, the group swaying as one, the family bound as one.

Raymond offered to walk them home, but Anthony declined. "We'll be all right, Raymond. Make sure you tell Thompson how much we appreciate being included. I couldn't find him when we were leaving."

"I will. You two take care."

Myra stood next to Raymond, and smiled as she waved at both of them.

Detroit, Anthony thought. Detroit was a big place. He needed to do some more research before could go back to Whiting with that information.

Carla was quiet as they walked down the street. Anthony glanced at her. For some reason, she seemed tense. "Didn't you enjoy yourself?" Anthony asked.

"Yes, I did. Very much so."

"You don't act like it. Is there something on your mind?"

Carla sighed. "I don't know if I should even tell you this." Looking as if she was about to cry, she stopped walking to turn to Anthony. "They might have been involved, Anthony."

"Who's they? Been involved in what?"

"The Williams might have been involved with the men missing in Evesville."

"How do you know that?" he snapped.

Carla flinched, startled at his outburst. "Isn't this what you came up here to find out?"

"I'm sorry, Carla. How did you find this out?" Anthony asked more calmly.

"One of the older cousins who still lived in Mississippi asked if the others had heard any more about the incident in the woods. Another of the cousins answered no. Then I thought I heard them say something about someone doing a good job."

"That doesn't mean anything. They said this in front of you?" Anthony asked unbelievingly.

"No. I was sitting on the grass on the other side of the big tree resting when they started their conversation."

"Did they ever find out you were there?"

Carla shook her head. "No. They were walking in the other direction as they talked."

"What else did they say?" Anthony asked.

"Something about Cread, and his army training."

"Anything else?"

"No. After that they moved out of my range."

Anthony shook his head as they began to walk again. Both were silent as they approached Carla's house. Anthony was absorbed in his thoughts. When they reached the house, he reached for her hand and squeezed it. "Bye, Carla. I'll see you tomorrow."

"Are you okay, Anthony?"

"Yeah," he said quietly as he walked slowly down the driveway.

# · XXXIII ·

C read was a better soldier than he was a civilian. He had developed the capacity for killing, but not for its consequences. He served in the 371$^{st}$ Infantry, where colored soldiers fought with the 157$^{th}$ French Division under General Goybet. The regiment, with its division, was responsible for the taking of Cote 188, Bussy Ferme, Ardeuil, Montfauxelles, and Trieres Ferme near Montbois.

A young Cread had watched in horror as limbs were torn, heads exploded, and guts were spilled. The regiment lost almost half its men in the first three days. The terror, blood, and fear he experienced as an eighteen-year-old in some of the fiercest battles of the campaign eventually ate their way through every nerve in his body then lodged there like a semi-dormant cancer.

The cancer didn't surface when he quietly sat around with his family. It hadn't when he had to protect his family. It usually waited until he was asleep before it would slowly creep out and take over, filling him with violent visions, bringing forth sweat and a deep sense of rage. He never slept much during those bouts, and was grateful they came so rarely. When they did though, the surging fury within him would carry over into his waking hours, and it took everything he had not to direct it toward someone else.

He would shudder violently, sometimes when he and his wife, Mabel, argued. The arguments were minor, but Cread had to fight to subdue the fierce urge to strike out. It drained him trying to take control of a need for violence that lurked inside.

At Ford Motor Company, he was a good worker. He had friends of all races. It was only luck that enabled him to stay out of arguments. Coworkers would have been surprised if they had known his history.

The only thing that stopped the rage in its tracks was the force of his family. It was stronger than any disease. He was blessed that he was surrounded by so much love. Cread credited Thompson, Deacon and Aunt Dahlia who were always there for him, checking on him, making sure he was all right. He and Thompson would have long talks into the night, and Thompson would let him pour out his heart to him without judgment. Every talk ended the same way. Thompson would always tell him that the family was there for him, and that the sacrifices he made for them would never be forgotten.

Cread was the only one to go off to war. He had wanted to be a teacher. Everyone said he was the smartest of the kids. School was easy for him. Arithmetic, English, history were no problem. The plan was to graduate and go to a private school for his high school diploma, be the first to attend college, and then come back and open a school.

When the war started, out of a sense of duty and a sense of bravado, he joined.

When he came back, people treated him differently. Cread understood, because he had become different. The studious, bright young man who left, came back transformed. The rage was only a part of it. His take on life was different. Some things weren't so important anymore. Some things, though, became very important.

He heard about a few of his buddies snapping. Trent George was with him in Champagne in the trenches. He was the only other man in the army he knew who was from around Little Rock. Trent moved to Altus, Mississippi, and ended up being shot and killed there three months later because he struck a white man for calling him a nigger. Trent's brother told Cread that Trent was confused, then distraught. In France, they were treated like heroes. When they entered the cities they captured, the people loved them. Women flocked to them. Men fought to shake their hands and kiss their cheeks. When he arrived home, it was as if he never left. His uniform meant nothing, and his service to his country meant nothing. Only his color meant something. German war prisoners were treated better than he was.

Cread understood. At least he accepted that. No one gave you respect in the South unless it was out of fear. No one gave up power without a fight. He had seen that firsthand.

He knew that he couldn't save himself. How many times did he wish he could take some potion that would reach inside his body and wrench out whatever poison resided within him? Cread was determined to save his family though. He would save them from those who would destroy them from without. If need be, he would even save them from himself.

Now it was possible another life would be taken. Cread knew it would have to happen before anyone. He had watched the boy, Anthony. Although Cread felt a certain bond with him, he still distrusted him. The smell of deceit rose off that boy as powerful as the stench of death in the fields the day after a battle.

At the reunion, Cread had watched Anthony and his girlfriend closely. When Bostic, Travis, and Walter were talking, he saw her listening. It was the look on her face that alarmed him. The men confirmed that they had talked about the incident, knowing that it was a family secret that no one was to discuss.

Cread knew what had to happen next. What he didn't know was when or who. Who would be the one to do it? Cread hoped to God it wasn't him. Cread also knew that he was the logical choice. Why not him? His soul was already dead.

# · XXXIV ·

Cread relayed what he found to Thompson, and a saddened and disappointed Thompson called Ludie. He never questioned Cread's instincts.

"I need you to check on this boy, Anthony. He might have found out information that could harm our family. He's a reporter with the *Sun*, and I'm not sure what he would do if he found out what happened that night." Thompson stopped to think, trying to recall past conversations he had had with Anthony. "He said he was in Wynne, Ludie. Check around and see what questions he's been asking."

It only took one day for Ludie to find out all Thompson needed to know. Thompson was sick to his stomach. Ludie had eventually talked to Ms. Martin who owned the boardinghouse in Wynne and found out that Anthony's primary interest was the Williamses, the Coulters, the missing men, and the deserted town

235

of Evesville. In the back of his mind he suspected that Anthony wasn't being truthful, but he had no idea he would be dredging up information on an incident that took place more than ten years ago—and for what purpose?

He sat down heavily, head in his hand. It had to be the newspaper that he was working for that put him up to it. Why else after all this time?

He looked at Cread and sighed. "I thought it was over. I thought we could live normal lives now and move on, but what happened back then has been haunting us ever since."

Cread shrugged. "We aren't guaranteed peace, Thompson, and because of who we are in this country, I don't know if we will ever get it, but we were given the ability to deal with it. Maybe that's our legacy."

"Lord, I hope not. I hope you're wrong."

Cread shrugged.

Thompson placed one hand on Cread's shoulder as he often did when things were serious. "We need to have an emergency family meeting."

Cread knew exactly what that meant. Only the adults were to come to this meeting, and the urgency of it meant that everyone had to attend. "Let me check with Aunt Dahlia first though," Thompson said. "I need to get her blessing on this."


The sky was overcast as Raymond entered his uncle Thompson's house. Even though it was after one in the afternoon, there was a slight chill in the air. Raymond was ticked about attending a meeting on his only day off. He had a lot to do that day and none of his business had to do with family.

Uncle Thompson's place never changed. He called the house "functional." Today only the elders were present, and

Raymond greeted them with a quiet hello. They silently acknowledged him. Even talkative Ransom was solemn. Raymond wondered why he was the only non-elder in the house and why everyone was so serious. Was it about him? He tried to recall something he had done or said. It couldn't be about his hustling. Everyone knew about that now.

Thompson nodded at everyone as they entered.

Thompson ushered the elders into the room. "We'll be with you shortly, Raymond," he said as he slowly closed the door.

Whatever it was, it must be damn important, Raymond thought, still hoping he wouldn't be there all day. He tried to listen to the discussion coming from the other side of the door, but could only hear murmurs.

It was almost an hour before the talking stopped. It sounded like there was a brief argument, then he heard one or two women quietly sobbing, but that stopped too. Raymond could hear someone praying, then there was silence for at least ten minutes before Thompson opened the door and looked at Raymond. So did everyone else.

"Raymond." Thompson motioned for him to come into the room.

Raymond walked stiffly as he passed his relatives leaving the room. Cread patted him gently on the back, and his Aunt Esther whose eyes were still moist hugged him briefly. Deacon only nodded, then shook his head. His mother kissed him on the cheek with trembling lips, and hugged him tightly. Her eyes were moist, too. Thompson's house was like a funeral parlor. What happened, and why was he there?

Apprehensive, Raymond could only sit silently as his uncle gently closed the door.

"How are you doing, son?" Thompson asked softly.

"Fine, Sir. Thanks." Thompson was always serious, but

never as formal as he was that day. The last time he had called Raymond "son" was to tell him his father was in the hospital.

Thompson nodded. "You have any idea what we were discussing today?"

Raymond shook his head.

"It's about your friend Anthony, Raymond." Thompson took a few measured steps before looking at the floor. He paused for almost a minute before he continued. "He has become a threat to this family."

Raymond was confused. "Anthony? How, Uncle T?"

Thompson turned, leaned forward, and placed his hand on Raymond's shoulder. "Your friend Anthony has not been truthful. He was sent to investigate a family secret, something that has been kept quiet for more than ten years." Thompson shook his head only slightly, then continued. "If anyone ever finds out what happened back then, if anybody had a clue, the family would be destroyed. We can't let that happen."

Raymond was only vaguely aware the family had experienced something that was too awful to talk about, but he sensed that now was not the time to discuss it. "What do you want me to do, Uncle T? You want me to talk to him?"

Thompson lowered his head again before raising it to look at Raymond intently. "It's gone beyond talk, Raymond. He is too close." Thompson paused. "He has to be taken care of."

"Taken care of? How? Wh...?"

"You've been chosen, son. He's your friend; therefore, he's your responsibility. It's up to you to protect this family."

Raymond sat, waiting for Thompson to laugh or something.

Thompson turned to Raymond and placed both hands on his shoulder. "Remember Raymond, first and foremost, the family is everything."

"The family is everything," Raymond repeated softly. As often as he said those words at dinner, at meetings, and anywhere else the family gathered, it never seemed as significant as it did then.

Raymond was stunned. He sat in silence trying to understand. Thompson and the other elders had left some time ago. Thompson had told him about that night in 1948. There was no question in Raymond's mind that what happened then needed to remain a secret.

Raymond sat staring blankly at the wall, searching his mind for an answer, looking for an out, but knowing there was none. The once familiar house where the family sometimes gathered seemed different, strange, and even cold. Raymond experienced a storm of feelings. He was furious at Anthony for misleading him. He was confused as to why Anthony had to die. He was scared for Carla. He was mad at the crazy white people who got them into this mess in the first place. He was depressed thinking about the outcome, but most of all, he was fearful.

How had it come to this? Why was it so important for Anthony to expose his family? Why would he lie like that when all the family ever did was treat him like one of them? It was true, he saved Raymond's life, but now he was putting the lives of so many more in jeopardy, and for what, a story?

Cread volunteered to do what had to be done, but Thompson declined his offer. It was vital that Raymond understood the importance of protecting the family. When Raymond became the head, it was hoped that he would not be faced with similar decisions, but if problems arose, it was important that he take care of them. Cread understood.

Thompson instructed Raymond to meet with Cread, who would develop a plan for Raymond. When they met that afternoon, Cread took Raymond for a ride.

"How you feeling, nephew?"

"Confused. Scared."

"That's understandable. You need to understand though that this is not unlike the sacrifice we had to make back in 1948. In a perfect world, there would be none of this violence, but we're in a country that was built on violence, and we have to adapt. You understand?"

Raymond nodded.

"When I was in the war, I was so terrified it was painful. In our first battle, grown men were crying, shaking, and scared to death. Many of us died, but we carried out our mission. We knew it was imperative that we conquer the enemy, because they represented evil, and evil had to be defeated. Now, your friend Anthony is not evil, like many of those enemy soldiers weren't evil, but he represents evil when he tries to uncover a part of our past that we had no intention of creating. We were reacting to a wickedness that wanted to destroy our family.

"If Johnny had been hung back in 1948, it would signify that we had no control over our future. That anytime, anywhere, somebody else could dictate how we lived our lives, and we couldn't have that. That was not our history. This is the same type situation, Raymond. We have to be in control of our destiny. No one can hold dominion over us. We have to do what's best for our family. If we don't, then our ancestors' struggles were in vain."

"He's harmless, Cousin Cread. I bet Anthony has no idea what's really happening." Raymond hesitated, "If it's true that he's writing a story, why don't we go burn down the newspaper?"

"That's not practical son, and he would still know. What's

important now is that we get to him before he is able to present this information to his bosses."

"What about Carla?"

"She doesn't work for the paper. Anyway, I don't think she would take what she knows any farther. I have a good feeling about her." Cread pulled back onto Thompson's street, glancing at Raymond a few times. They entered the house, and Cread directed Raymond to the basement. Cread went to retrieve the liquid poison from Aunt Dahlia, a potion whose formula had been passed from generation to generation. Then they discussed the plan in detail.

## · XXXV ·

Anthony had received another letter. It was the same style as the last one with bold, underlined type.

TIME IS OF THE ESSENCE!!!!!
PROTECT YOUR LOVED ONES!!!!

He crumbled it and threw it in the wastebasket without thinking twice. Anthony hadn't slept at all the night before. He tossed and turned fitfully, finally arising at 3 A.M., tired and confused. With few exceptions, almost everything that he had ever planned in his life had come out right. But the biggest plans of all; making a major impression at the newspaper to establish his career, convincing his father that he could be successful on his own, winning Carla over, and fulfilling his promise for Emmanuel, were all in jeopardy.

Anthony tried to convince himself that what little Carla heard at the Williams reunion still didn't mean the family was involved. It was possible, but the men could have been talking about hunting.

He had learned something at the Williams's gathering the day before. Anthony finally found out what the word *family* meant. Before then, neither he nor probably any of his friends would have thought that colored farming families like the Williamses existed. No one he knew had a family like that. It just didn't add up that people as kind and gentle as they were would jeopardize their entire future by being involved in harming anyone.

Carla was right, of course. If he wrote anything about the family even remotely linking them to the missing men, it would destroy them. No one would allow whatever happened to go unpunished even though it may have been justifiable. Was the story worth it? The conflicting emotions made his stomach turn and his head hurt. He lay down one more time.

Four hours later, Anthony was still awake. He pulled out the envelope he was given by Whiting and pulled out the other reporter's notes again and began to read. So much violence he thought.

Why?

Another three hours passed before Anthony looked again at the note the reporter wrote to Mr. Whiting. What he needed most at the moment was guidance. Without any forethought Anthony dialed the operator for the number of the *Washington Post*. After going through two secretaries, he was connected.

"Jerry Forte speaking."

"Mr. Forte, this is Anthony Andrews from the *Arkansas Sun*."

There was a pause. "How can I help you?" The voice was cold and distant, but Anthony paid it little attention.

"I'm following up on an assignment you had when you were with the paper. Racial atrocities?"

There was another pause. "Yes?"

"I thought I would touch base with you and see if there was anything you wanted to share with me that wasn't in the folder you gave Mr. Whiting."

Forte snorted. "Whiting."

"Yes. Anything you want to share with me?"

"No."

Anthony was surprised at Forte's attitude, but pushed on. "Can I ask you something?"

"What's that?"

"Did you ever receive any threatening letters?"

"No. Probably wasn't there long enough."

It was slowly becoming evident that something was strange about the man, but Anthony continued. "I received a couple of letters that threatened me if I didn't find out information about what happened in Evesville."

"Evesville? What about Evesville?"

"It seems like some people in that town came up missing, and a black family might have been responsible. You aren't familiar with the place?"

"No. I'm afraid not."

"What about Dr. Edward Washington?"

"Look, Anthony, is it?"

"Yes."

"I was at that paper for two months. Didn't anybody tell you that?"

"No. I didn't know it was that short a time."

"I was at that paper long enough to find out that it was not the type environment I wanted to work in."

Anthony had been listening closely not so much at what he was saying, but how he was saying it. "Excuse me for asking," Anthony said, "but are you colored?"

There was a longer pause.

"How can you tell?" Forte asked.

"I don't know. I guess it's just something we know."

"Yes...yes, I am," Forte answered.

"So, you were the first black hired there?"

"They didn't know that."

"You mean you passed as white?" Anthony asked incredulously.

"Yes," Forte said softly.

"Why would you...?" Anthony's voice trailed off. "Why did you leave the paper?"

There was another pause. "I think you'll find quickly enough that everything is not as it seems. Because they thought I was white, they felt that they could speak freely about their colored folk. I've been in many circumstances where people took me for being white, but I have never heard the venom spewed that I heard at the paper."

Anthony was stunned. "Whiting too?"

"Especially Whiting."

It took a moment for it to sink in. Whiting a racist? How could that be? Whiting treated him with the utmost respect.

"I - I find that so hard to believe."

"How long have you been there?" Forte asked.

"More than seven months."

"That's interesting. No problems?"

"No. A little jealousy, but nothing overt."

"Then I suspect they have something they want you to do that can't be done by a white person."

"In other words, I'm being used?" Anthony asked skeptically.

"I'll tell you what. If you heard the way they talked about our race, there would be no question in your mind."

Anthony wondered if it was the racial atmosphere or Forte's inabilities as a journalist that resulted in his short stay. He was more curious though about his dishonesty. "Are you still passing?"

"No. I've learned my lesson."

## · XXXVI ·

The conversation with Jerry Forte confused Anthony even more. Why would the paper need him to find out anything? Was it Evesville? But then wasn't he the one who found the story, or was he sent there because they knew he would pursue the story? Whiting a racist?

It was early in the day, and the street was quiet. The owners of the house were still away, which was good, because he needed some sleep. Carla was at the library until late afternoon, so he would be able to get at least a few hours in before the evening.

Anthony slept restlessly for a few more hours before awaking at 3:30 P.M. If what Forte said was true, then he was being used. It could be that Forte was not a good reporter, regardless of how he represented himself, but what he said didn't appear to be a case of sour grapes. Anyway, he was at the *Washington Post*, and had been there for some time. That paper didn't keep incompetent reporters. Plus, he had had to go through two secretaries to talk to him.

Anthony ran over what transpired during the interview and during the subsequent months. Was there anything during those times that indicated he was being used? Nothing came to mind.

Anthony devised a simple plan. There was an obvious way of finding the truth.

Anthony retrieved the phone. "Hannah, this is Anthony. Is Mr. Whiting in?"

"Hi, Anthony. He's in a meeting, but I know he wants to talk to you. Just a minute."

"Anthony, how you doing there, son?"

Anthony took a deep breath. "Not so good, Mr. Whiting."

"What do you mean not so good?" Whiting asked as his voice bellowed through the phone line.

"I'm afraid I don't have enough to make a believable story."

"What!" Anthony could imagine being there and hearing Whiting's voice reverberating throughout that office. "What the hell are you saying, boy?"

He called me *boy*. That's a first, Anthony thought. "I've run into a dead end. None of my investigations are coming up with anything conclusive."

"What about the witnesses?"

"Unreliable. It seems that each one of them had a vendetta against the families."

Whiting started laughing. "Okay, Anthony, you had me there for a minute. So what's the real scoop?"

The word *boy* remained on his mind like a bad taste in his mouth. That one word alone carried so much weight that Whiting really didn't have to say anymore. Anthony had his answer. "That's it, Mr. Whiting. I'm not kidding."

"Well, damnit, you damn well better be!" Whiting's voice had lowered to a snarl. "You better have your ass back here with a story as fast as you can make it, or you're out of here. I'll make sure you never work for another newspaper in America. You hear me, boy?"

"I hear you, Mr. Whiting."

Whiting changed his tone again.

"Who got to you? Were you threatened? Are you still worried about the letters? We can take care of that."

Now how could he take care of it? "No sir, but I wouldn't want to print something that isn't true."

Whiting snarled, "You're fired, nigger. You understand? Come back here, clean out your desk, and get the hell out of our offices."

Anthony's face burned and his heart pounded. All that he had worked for was going up in smoke, but it was worth it. He was so stupid. Why hadn't he seen it coming? At the same time he was admonishing himself though, he felt a huge weight lift from his shoulders. There were no more conflicts, at least with this issue.

Whiting was still ranting. This was the first time Anthony was faced with this pure a hatred since he watched Emmanuel hung, but it had the opposite effect than either he or Whiting would have imagined. Anthony started laughing uncontrollably. The laughter started with a snicker then gathered momentum like someone falling down a flight of stairs with nothing to grab, until the rasping sounds, coming from somewhere deep inside him, began to hurt. Tears rolled from his eyes in torrents that he couldn't stop if his life depended on it.

All of the pent-up fear and frustration that had accumulated in the past years was rolled up and evicted by the pealing sounds of uncontainable mirth; but it wasn't really mirth.

Anthony knew exactly what it was because he had experienced it with Naomi. The demons were being released again, and he felt good about this one since he had a strong feeling they might not return any time soon. But, it was even more than that. It was the silliness of the man on the other end of the line thinking that he had any control over him; it was the audacity of people who felt they needed to live their life employing intimidation and manipulation; and, he laughed at his own stupidity, which blinded him because he was so trusting and so singularly focused on an objective without any consideration for its outcome.

For that brief moment, the laughter did more for Anthony than running ever did.

The other end of the line remained silent. Anthony took another deep breath, wiped his eyes, waited a few seconds for any response, then hung up the phone, thus closing the door on that phase of his life.

The sun was setting as Anthony sat in the dormer area of the house, still savoring a feeling of euphoria that came with his newfound freedom. His gaze drifted to the street outside. Drexel Avenue was quiet. A lone man walked slowly up the street as if he had no particular destination in mind. At first Anthony paid him little attention, but something made him look again. It was strange for a person walking this street to be loitering. The block was full of working people, most who walked with a purpose.

It took Anthony a while longer to recognize the lone figure. It was Raymond. Now Anthony was confused, because he had never seen Raymond walk like that with his shoulders slumped and his head down.

Directly after he saw Raymond, Anthony noticed a car turn onto Drexel from East 105<sup>th</sup>, driving at a normal speed, until the occupants also saw Raymond. Anthony could see one of the men pointing frantically at him as the car slowed to a crawl. It almost appeared as if the men in the car were stalking Raymond, who seemed to be engaged in deep thought. Anthony straightened up to get a better look, but couldn't identify any of the passengers through the car window. It didn't look good though.

Sensing danger, Anthony raced down the stairs. Once outside, he looked around before picking up a short, thick tree limb. He almost slipped as he turned the corner of the house running at full speed toward the men. The car had almost caught up with Raymond before Raymond finally noticed it. It pulled into a driveway in front of him and three men jumped out.

"Raymond!" Anthony was three houses away when he yelled at his friend. The three men turned for a second. Anthony recognized Trey and figured the muscular, bald-headed one was Roach. The other, a short stocky man wearing black jeans and a black sweatshirt, was a stranger.

Anthony rushed toward them with only one thing in mind. The driver stayed in the car. Three against two he thought as he hurtled toward the group.

With their attention directed toward Anthony, Raymond sucker-punched Roach, knocking him down. Trey leaped, but Raymond sidestepped him and kicked the fallen Roach to keep him down. The man in black reached in his pocket when Anthony hit him on the side of the head with the branch, then tackled him.

Trey recovered quickly and jumped Raymond from behind, holding his arms to his sides. Roach got up while Anthony and the groggy stranger wrestled on the ground. The man hit Anthony with his fist making Anthony temporarily lose his grip on the tree limb. Anthony was hit once more as he tried to stand. The blow buckled his knees and he staggered before he finally retrieved his weapon. Swinging with all his might, he knocked the man in black out cold, and broke the limb in half.

"Two for the price of one." Roach sneered as he reached into his pocket and produced a gun.

Anthony raised the broken tree limb, stepping toward Roach who laughed. "What are you going to do with that, punk?"

Anthony continued toward him. "Can't do that, man." Roach looked surprised, but not enough to lower the weapon, which was four inches from Anthony's chest.

Anthony could feel his heart banging. His breath came in gasps as he waited for the bullet.

Suddenly a calm came over him, and death became secondary. Emmanuel's body flashed through Anthony's mind, and he remembered how helpless he felt that he couldn't stop that boy from dying. This was a second chance. If he were shot, he would at least be shot trying to save someone's life.

Anthony dropped the tree limb and grabbed at the gun, bending it toward the ground. A surprised Roach tried to turn the gun toward Anthony, but Anthony had a death grip on his wrist. At the same time, Raymond swung his head back, bloodying Trey's nose and causing him to stumble. He then swung at Roach again, hitting him in the jaw. The gun fell to the ground. Raymond kicked the gun into the bushes, whirled a stumbling Trey around, and knocked him against a tree so hard that his head made a cracking sound on contact. Trey stayed down as Raymond then jumped at Roach.

Before Roach could throw a punch, Raymond kneed him in the groin. Roach went down to his knees and Raymond continued to kick him until he was almost unconscious. Anthony retrieved the gun and gave it to Raymond who held it toward a defeated Roach's head.

Air was coming in gasps as Raymond tried to catch his breath. Finally recovered, he knelt down and said evenly, "Either you let this go, or I or somebody in my family will kill you." Raymond pushed Roach over so he could look him in the eyes. "Is that what you want, man? You want to die? You can't kill all of us, but as God as my witness, if I die, you'll die, and your friends will die."

Anthony watched as Roach's eyes dimmed. Any fight he had in him was gone. He stayed down, not saying a word, but they all knew what his answer was.

Trey and the stranger were still on the ground. The stranger was slowly recovering. Everyone had forgotten about the driver. Anthony was surprised he hadn't jumped out, but after Raymond walked toward the car with the gun pointed at the driver, he knew why. Cread had quietly pulled up sometime during the fight and held a pistol to the man's head.

Cread walked around the car to the sidewalk. "My young cousin has never been wrong. You obviously didn't get the message the first time. I hope you don't have to die before it sinks in. You don't mess with this family, especially not this one." He motioned to Raymond and Anthony. "Get their wallets."

Anthony reached down to get Trey's and Roach's wallets. Raymond retrieved the other two. Cread emptied each until he found their driver's licenses. "Now, I know where to find each of you if I have to."

Raymond emptied the gun and threw it in the backseat of their car. He let Roach and the stranger pick up Trey then watched carefully as they piled into the car.

Residents of the street had gathered during the clash. All seven of the people were strangers to them, and the people were upset they were causing such a disturbance on their quiet street. The distant sound of sirens approached as Raymond and Anthony piled into Cread's car to leave.

"Raymond, you dropped this." Anthony handed Raymond a vial.

Raymond took it, fingering it briefly before throwing it into the sewer. "It wasn't anything," he mumbled.

***

Thompson looked up in shock as Cread parked the car in front of the house and Raymond, Cread, and Anthony piled out of the car. "What happened?"

"Roach tried to jump me again, Uncle T."

"Tonight? Right now?"

"Yep."

Thompson made a snorting noise. "I'll be damned. So what happened?"

"I was going over Anthony's house when this car pulls up in front of me. Anthony comes running toward me with this tree limb and steps in front of me to stop Roach from shooting me. It was Roach, Trey, and two other dudes. We fought. We won." Raymond looked at his uncle. "With the help of Cousin Cread."

Raymond turned to Anthony. "What were you thinking?" Then Raymond recoiled slightly. "You're bleeding."

Anthony looked down to see blood slowly seeping through his shirt. It surprised him too because there was no pain. The guy I was fighting must have had a knife," Anthony said as he rolled up his shirt. "I never even saw it."

Cread looked at the injury closely. "You were lucky. It's not too bad. Just a flesh wound."

Cread went into the house to retrieve bandages and an antiseptic.

Thompson was at a loss for words. He looked at Raymond, then at Anthony, then at Cread, who had returned with a clean shirt and was cleaning away the blood. It was probably the first time he was ever rendered speechless in his life. He finally gathered himself to ask, "What was going through your mind, young man, that you would sacrifice your life like that for someone else?"

Anthony winced at Cread's ministration, and then shook his head as if it was still a question in his mind, too. "I figured it was my fault that Roach and his guys were even on the street. I think they were coming for me and saw Raymond."

"Why?" Raymond asked.

"I saw Trey the other day, and I think he figured out that I was the one who warned you. I think it might have been a coincidence that Raymond happened to be on the street at the same time." Anthony turned to Raymond.

"What were you coming to see me about anyway, Raymond?"

Raymond, kneading his right hand, started to answer, but was interrupted by Thompson.

"What about Roach? How long is this going to go on?"

"It's going to be all right, Thompson," Cread said.

"And Trey," Thompson said, shaking his head. "I never did like that boy."

"I don't think we have to worry about Roach or Trey again," Cread said emphatically.

"You won't have to worry about me either," Anthony said. Everyone turned as he wearily sat on the steps, his head in his hands. Anthony was quiet for a minute, then he said quietly. "You know...I love you guys. I love this family. When I thought Raymond was going to be shot..." He shook his head slowly. "All I could think of was what a waste. Your family has shown me nothing but love even though I was...different. You accepted me, and all I could think of was writing a damn story."

Anthony shook his head a few more times before standing and walking toward the sidewalk. None of the men said a word. "I don't know if you or the Coulters were the reason those men are missing or not, and I don't care. I'm through," he said as he raised a hand.

"Where are you going, son?" Thompson called out.

"Home. Call Carla. Arrange to get back to Arkansas."

"You can call her from here," Aunt Dahlia said.

As usual, Aunt Dahlia was where nobody expected her to be. How much did she hear? Anthony wondered.

"You part of this family, boy. Family don't have to ask to use the phone. Just pick it up and dial."

Anthony stopped to look at Aunt Dahlia and the men. Everyone nodded. They never ceased to amaze him. Here he was hours from writing a story that could possibly implicate them and maybe even destroy them, yet they still accepted him.

Anthony smiled. "Thanks, ma'am. I guess I will." He bent down to hug Aunt Dahlia.

She patted him on his arm. "We love you too, son."

## · XXXVII ·

Cread drove Anthony over to Carla's where she met Anthony at the door.

"Hi, Cread." Carla waved as he began to back out the driveway.

Cread stopped the car. "You have a good man there," he said to Carla before pulling away.

Carla looked at Anthony. "You sounded different over the phone." She looked again. "And you look different. Did something happen?" Carla put her hands to her mouth as she looked closer at Anthony's face. "Who did this to you?"

Anthony shrugged. "I was in a fight, but I'm okay" Anthony hesitated. "I'm not investigating Evesville anymore."

Carla was clearly agitated, but waited for him to continue.

"They were using me, Carla. The paper only wanted a colored reporter so they could find out what happened to those missing men." Anthony paused. "There's so much to tell."

Carla took Anthony's hand and led him up the stairs. They sat on the sofa as Carla applied ice to his bruised face. Anthony told Carla very little about the fight. It was more important that she know about his childhood, witnessing the hanging, and the problems it sometimes caused as he became older.

"Oh my God, Anthony. How did you feel when you saw that?"

"I felt like...I was drowning, and there was nothing I could do about it. After that, I asked my parents every day if they saw anything in the paper about a boy who was killed. They never did, and I felt even worse then. There should at least have been a story. That's when I decided I would be a reporter. I pushed everything else aside to accomplish that goal, so if there were ever another incident like that, I would write about it. It became an obsession, driving me to be so focused that nothing else mattered."

Anthony then told her about everything that transpired. Carla held his hand the entire time, listening intently as Anthony told about his conversation with Jerry Forte, Whiting, the fight with Roach, and his pledge to the Williams family. She occasionally gasped or murmured sympathetically before hugging Anthony tightly. Anthony grimaced.

"What's wrong, Anthony."

"I got cut too."

Carla covered her mouth with her hand again, "Oh my God!!" she said as she pulled up the shirt Cread had given him. Tears formed in her eyes.

Anthony held her. "It's all right Carla. It's over now."

It took a while for Carla to calm down before he continued. "I was tricked, and I was stupid for thinking I was getting by because of my ability."

"It's okay, Anthony," she said soothingly after she had settled down. "That's what life is about, growing and learning. I always felt you were a good person."

They sat silently on the sofa for a while, then Carla sighed. "I have to tell you something. It hasn't been a smooth life for me either." She took a deep breath. "When my husband, Harold, died in a car crash, we were arguing. He was drinking. I felt his death was my fault. After that, I was like a zombie. I dated once." Carla stood and walked to the window. "I couldn't drive for a few years because every time I got in a car, I lost it.

"When I first met you, I felt something. I can't explain it, but something tugged at my heart for the first time since I met Harold." She looked at Anthony and smiled. "But when we began to talk, I was so disappointed, Anthony, knowing that our philosophies on life were so incompatible. You just don't know."

Anthony stood. "I felt the same way, Carla. I felt something too. You were different than any woman I ever met, and every day I was away from you, I thought about you. I thought about how it would be when we would see each other again. I even thought about how it would be coming home to you, waking up next to you, holding you..."

Anthony hesitated. "I guess I thought that if I didn't get involved, didn't deal with what was so obvious, I could get by without being affected." He looked into space for a moment. "But I know better now."

He took her hands, as they looked at each other, comfortable at last in each other's presence. She touched his cheek gently and looked down as he caressed her arms, her hands. He kissed her softly on the forehead, her cheek, then trembling, unsure, he kissed her lips. She wrapped her arms around his neck, and melted into the curve of his body.

PART III

## · XXXVIII ·

A nthony dreaded going to the paper. It was almost as if he was the loser, as if the reason he was leaving was because he couldn't cut it as a reporter. He was sure that would be the company's explanation. Another inept Negro reaches too far and falls on his face. He knew the truth, though, and the more he thought about it, it became increasingly clear to him that he was the only one who needed to know.

Thompson shared with him during one of their discussions that any time you seek approval from the same people who are trying to hold you back, you've already lost.

Hannah greeted him as if nothing happened. "Hi, Anthony. Let me know if you need anything." She touched his arm lightly.

"Thanks, Hannah. Probably a big box?"

"No problem."

There wasn't much to take. There were some family photos,

a marble paperweight his father had given him, some books on investigative reporting, notes and folders for random thoughts, and several pens he had collected over the years. He would leave the plant he bought. It would probably die anyway, he thought, with all the poison in the air.

It was business as usual at the paper. No one came to say good-bye. He could hear Whiting's voice coming from one of the offices, but he never appeared. Everyone's behavior was predictable. Leave the wounded to die, alone.

Hannah waved daintily as Anthony backed out the door. He had parked his car in the alley next to the building so he wouldn't have to walk so far. Anthony looked once more at the building that held all his dreams, his hopes, and his aspirations, then sighed. There was so much to learn about this world.

After putting the box in the car, Anthony backed out into something stabbing him.

"Wh...?"

"This is a gun you feelin', boy, and I'd love to use it. So would he," the man said of his partner who had moved to the other side of Anthony. "So walk over to this car behind you real careful like, and get into the back seat with my other friend there."

The two men walked on each side of Anthony as a third man in the back seat opened the door. All three had guns out but hidden under their coats. Anthony looked around for help, but there was no one in the alley except Anthony and the men. Hannah had gone back into the building. The quiet partner shoved Anthony roughly into the car.

Anthony's first thoughts were to fight, but all three had guns. Would they shoot him here if he tried to fight? Probably, he answered to himself, so he would wait. Maybe he would have a chance later on.

"We have some questions for you, boy, and you better have some answers," the man in the backseat said as he tied Anthony's arms with a rope cord.

The man who first confronted him turned in his seat to look at Anthony. "We're going to take you somewhere where you can answer some questions about those colored families. We know you know something. You were up North too long not to have found out something, and you're going to tell us everything you know."

Anthony felt almost detached. There was no fear, just wariness. Somewhere in Cleveland, he had lost his fear of violence. He looked at each of the men, trying to memorize their faces. Because they didn't hide them probably meant that they were either going to kill him or they didn't think that he would be taken seriously by the authorities if he reported the incident. Or worse, maybe they were the authority.

"Why is it you white trash always have to have the Negro do your work for you?" Anthony asked in an even tone. "Why don't you ask the families themselves, or are you too scared?"

The three men jerked around in unison to look at Anthony as if he was an alien from outer space. The blow to his jaw from the butt of the forty-five caliber Colt sent a searing pain racing down the right side of his body aggravating the bruise on his face and the knife wound in the process. Anthony winced, but didn't utter a sound. His eyes narrowed as he lunged against the man in the back. Another slap from the barrel of the gun knocked his head into the door, causing him to become dizzy and faint.

He lurched once more as the car started to back up and then suddenly stop. "Goddamnit, get that damn car out the way!" the driver yelled as he rolled down the window, waved his hand, and jammed the horn at the same time. Another car had pulled up behind it, blocking its access to the street.

Through glassy eyes Anthony watched as four men exited their car and slowly approached. "How y'all?" one of them said as he peered in the backseat.

The voice sounded familiar, but Anthony couldn't see very well. As soon as the man scratched his head with his left hand, he recognized him. It was Bobby Joe Byrd. He slumped back into the seat. All the fight in him was gone.

After turning around to look, the driver changed his attitude. "Bobby Joe! What you doin' here?"

"I'm about to ask you the same here, Milton. What y'all doin' here?"

"We on a mission. Got this coon back here. Going to get some information."

Byrd cocked his head as if he were talking to a kid. "Now, is that your job or ours, Milton?"

"Well."

"Well? Milton, I don't know how many times I have to tell y'all. We've been working on this boy, waiting and watching for almost three months now. Now suddenly you going to come in here and whisk him away? Is that fair, Milton?"

"Look, Bobby Joe. You know I ain't interested in messin' with your work. We got impatient. That's all. I figured we could find out everything we needed to know in a few hours," the driver said as he stepped out of the car. He motioned for the man in the backseat to unlock the door. The driver glared at the four men then opened the door and pulled Anthony out. "But he's all yours, Bobby Joe." The man sneered at Anthony. "You don't mind if we join you though, do you?"

Byrd's voice was angry. "Yes, I do mind, Milton. I haven't quite got over that you just about stole somethin' of mine."

Anthony raged inside. They were talking about him like he was livestock.

The driver raised his palms to Byrd and returned to his car. "Like I said, Bobby Joe, he's all yours. Didn't mean no harm." Milton's driver didn't seem as willing to give in to Byrd and kept his hand on his gun. Byrd's man saw this and stood between the driver and Byrd as one of the other men with Byrd walked Anthony to the other car.

"I'm sure you didn't, Milton, but understand, I'm disappointed in you. There's enough business out here to take care of without us steppin' on each other's toes." Byrd closed the door to his car. "You boys take care of yourself."

Once the car pulled away, one of the men in the car let out a low whistle. "Another minute, and we would have missed them."

"Yep. We were lucky today." Byrd turned to his new passenger. "How you feeling, Anthony?" Anthony didn't answer. "You're going to be fine now."

Fine? Anthony thought, but he still didn't say anything.

One of the men in the backseat looked closely at Anthony's bruises before he sat back seemingly satisfied with what he saw.

They drove without saying a word for at least a half an hour. The car eventually turned off the highway to a narrow dirt road that led into a wooded area. Anthony's heart began to beat faster as he pondered his situation. They drove for another five minutes before they reached a clearing. All Anthony could think of was his family, the Williamses and Carla, and all of the things he wanted to say to each of them before he left here. He thought of Emmanuel too, and his heart beat even faster. Is this how he felt just before he died?

There was a small white house with a pond in the front. A barn and a stable were farther back near the beginning of another wooded area. Anthony couldn't make out much more. His eyes were still blurry.

"Untie him."

"You sure?"

"Yes," Byrd said impatiently as he walked in front of them to the house. He held the door open as the four entered with an unsteady Anthony.

The house was a neat little cottage with bear rugs throughout. As his sight improved, Anthony was able to make out more detail. The walls were all painted off-white. The furniture was all rattan, but covered with different colored throws and knits. A strange thought crossed Anthony's mind as he looked around. If he were visiting, he would feel welcome—that is until he saw the gun rack on the far wall with a least ten rifles or shotguns.

Anthony was prepared to fight for his life. Whatever was going to happen was not going to be good, so he would have nothing to lose. He would rather die fighting than be killed like some docile lamb.

"Sit down, Anthony. You want a beer or something?"

Anthony sat warily. His body coiled. "No."

Byrd also looked at the scar on Anthony's head. "Not too bad," he said as he shook his head. Byrd walked to the kitchen. "Look, I apologize for causing you so much anxiety." Byrd's speech pattern had changed ever so slightly. "For you to understand what's going on, I need to explain something to you and to tell you some history. It may not have seemed like it, but I've always been on your side."

*FBI.* Anthony thought, slightly relieved, as he leaned back against the sofa.

"You sure you don't want that beer?" Byrd said as he popped the top on his own can.

"No," Anthony said, still cautious.

Byrd sat down in front of Anthony. "Let me tell you a story.

My granddaddy, William James Byrd, was in the Civil War. In 1863 he was fighting with Cabell's Brigade near Backbone Mountain. He and about one hundred fifty other confederates were holed up at the base of the mountain, but a barrage of Union artillery forced them to retreat into a shallow valley with almost no means of escape.

"My father was wounded. Most of the soldiers were either killed or wounded by all the firepower they had, but the Union soldiers didn't want to cross the open area, fearing the confederates weren't firing because they were trying to trick them like they did so many times before.

"Granddaddy was able to drag himself into the woods before the Union boys found out what the real situation was. After crawling a few miles, he came onto this farm near Waldron where the colored people were the only ones left. Two young colored boys picked him up and carried him to the barn. An old Negro woman came out and tended to his wounds. They took care of him for more than two weeks. That family even hid him from some Union soldiers who stopped along the way."

Anthony thought that was odd, but made no comment.

"My granddaddy probably would have died without their help. He was grateful but confused since they fought to maintain a way of life that would keep people like them enslaved, so he asked them why they helped him. The old woman looked at him and told him because it was right, and anyway, she said, 'I know you. You have a good heart.'

"That scared Granddaddy silly, because he had freed most of his slaves, since he and the other men on his plantation were going to war. She couldn't have known that since he didn't live in those parts. Nor could she have known that he always treated them like the human beings they were, and never once abused any of them.

"Anyway, he asked what he could do for them once every-thing was set back right. The old woman only asked only one favor: That he live his life in the best interest of her people. That was it. He promised that he would.

"After the war, the Klan formed these illegal governments and damn near ran everything in some of the towns while the men fighting in the army were still away. Former soldiers were forming militias to take some of these towns back from the Klan, and folks like them. When my granddaddy got back, he formed his own militia. Mind you, the other militias were not formed to help Negroes, but my granddaddy's was. He found men that felt like he did about the mistreatment of colored folk, so they fought the Klan for two reasons."

"I think I'll have that beer," Anthony said.

One of the men brought back a Budweiser. "Me and my brother Johnny heard all the stories about the Negroes they saved from hangings and beatings. What kept him and his men out of trouble with the folks who had no problem killing innocent people was that they were underground. They were more secre-tive than the Klan, and they only struck at night, intercepting some of them KKK boys before they could do their dirty deeds.

"We thought that was exciting, and right, so when we grew up, we decided to form a militia ourselves. We kept that same secrecy and were able to infiltrate the Klan and work from the inside."

"So you provided information to the FBI?"

Byrd grunted, and his partners laughed. "Sometimes they're more dangerous than the Klan, Anthony.

"What we did was stop hangings and beatings, even if it meant hurting or even killing some people. Anyway, one of the Klan members named Rafe Alan Tucker got in a fight with my brother Norman because he was trying to stop the men from raping a colored woman they caught outside town. Rafe Alan got so mad at my brother that he shot and killed him."

Bobby Joe Byrd took a deep, ragged breath as he continued. "When I found out, they say this man Rafe left town. Nobody would tell me where he was. I heard different stories, but nothing for sure until one day, I heard he might be in Evesville."

They killed those men, Anthony thought. He breathed a sigh of relief. It was Byrd and not the Williams or the Coulters.

Byrd motioned one of the men to get him another beer. "By the time I get there, he was missing again, and there was this rumor that all these Klansmen had come up missing."

Anthony slumped. It wasn't Byrd and his men.

"Everybody was scared to death." Byrd continued. "At first I thought there was another militia operating around there. I searched that town and asked questions, and finally decided the Coulters or the Williams family might have had something to do with it."

Anthony slumped even further, but also looked off, trying to appear as noncommittal as possible.

"It's okay, Anthony. I damn near know that one of them families did it now, but that's okay. I also know those missing men are dead. What I wanted to confirm was if the man who shot my brother was one of them who was killed, so I wouldn't have to keep looking for him."

Anthony shook his head in disbelief. "All this time. What about the shooting?"

"What shooting?"

"When I was visiting the Jacksons, somebody shot at me."

"That could have been anybody, Anthony, but I would bet money that it was a colored person."

"A colored person? Why?"

"Bad news, rumors, and folks minding other folks business travel fast down here in the South. Colored people look out after their own. If folks thought you were trying to find information that they didn't think you should have, those shots were a warning," Byrd responded.

One of Byrd's men added. "Once you started asking about Evesville when you were in Wynne, word was out. Some folks took exception to you digging up the past."

"What about the letters?"

"What letters?" Byrd asked.

"I received letters threatening me and my family."

"I'm not sure, but I have an idea," Byrd said.

"Who?" Anthony almost snarled the question.

"Could be Whiting." Byrd looked at one of his partners for confirmation.

His partner nodded. "Probably."

"Why?"

"He didn't want you to lose focus. Whiting is Klan, you know," Byrd said.

At this point, nothing surprised Anthony. "No. I didn't know."

"He's up there in the ranks. He just keeps it secret. I don't even know if his bosses know. He's also a member of the White Citizen's Council."

Anthony remembered that group. They were the ones who protested the integration of Central High the most vehemently.

"I still don't understand why I was hired though. Why did he want those families so bad?"

"You have to understand. All the good ol' boys in that area wanted to take both those families down a notch for different reasons. There was some...imbalance in that town. You know what I mean, Anthony?"

Anthony shook his head.

"Many in the town thought the Williamses were too proud and that the Coulters were too wild, and they were kind of afraid of both of them families. That's the last thing you want in a small southern town, is white people who are afraid of their Negroes. They were especially afraid of the Williams family. It was something about those people that you didn't mess with them for nothing. When that incident with the kids happened, a whole bunch of them got after the Coulter boy, but they were hesitant about taking on the Williamses, so they recruited some other folk from outside."

"Them boys were probably scared shitless," one of the other men said laughing.

"One of the new people who showed up was Whiting's nephew."

Anthony sat transfixed. He leaned forward as Byrd laid out the story.

"Whiting recruited Jebediah Ray Alford about four months before he turned up missing with that group, and he felt responsible to his family to find out what happened. If something bad happened to the boy, it was Whiting's duty to avenge it."

Anthony shook his head. "So, I was hired for the sole reason of getting some concrete proof that one of the families did it. Why didn't they go to law enforcement?"

"Without a sheriff—who by the way turned up missing, too—the boys from out of town didn't have much to go on. The Coulters appear to have left before the men ended up missing. It's possible they could have come back for revenge, but we doubt it."

"But what about the Williamses?"

"The Williams family, from what I hear, were the nicest people you could meet, but I think many of them knew that if you looked under the black skin of one of those upstanding colored citizens, you would find a fighter. I never met them, but some of the boys knew them, and you could tell by the way they talked about them that there was respect there."

"Or fear." One of Byrd's men chuckled.

Anthony shook his head. "So, I was hired to uncover the families and find out if they killed and whom they killed."

"That's about it, Anthony. You see, the Klan is losing membership. Even with the integration issues, an occasional visit by Dr. King, and a few other smaller incidents, folks don't seem to have the passion to join the Klan like they used to, but that incident in 1948 has stuck in the Klan's craw like a fifty-pound boulder. If they were able to find out who did it, it would serve as a recruiting tool and help them to rebuild."

The tallest of Byrd's men added, "That don't mean that coloreds aren't still being mistreated, hurt and sometimes killed, but it ain't always the Klan that's doing it."

Anthony nodded. "Now what?"

"If I could find out if the man who killed Norman was one of them boys that's missing, I would truly be indebted to you, and I could go back to taking care of business."

"I don't know, Mr. Byrd."

"Bobby Joe."

"I don't know, Bobby Joe. If I hear anything, I'll make sure you're the first to know though. What's his name again?"

"Rafe. Rafe Alan Tucker. He was a potbellied man, five-eight, probably weighed about 220 pounds with a scar going across his forehead. Ain't much to go on, but that's all I know."

"I'll try."

"That's all I can ask, Anthony. Thanks." Bobby Joe Byrd held out his hand. Anthony took it as they shook firmly. Byrd's partners extended their hands too. "Here's my number in case you need to reach me." Anthony tucked the paper carefully in his wallet. "Let's get you back to your car."

Anthony hesitated. "Do you know this Sheriff Cottingham?"

"Not well," Byrd responded, "but I know he's a good friend of Whiting's. Why?"

Anthony stood at the door. "It just seemed kind of strange that he would call me back from Cleveland just to ask me some questions."

"It was probably just to scare you," one of Byrd's men answered.

Anthony nodded. That made sense based on everything else that was going on. "What are you going to tell the other men who were after me?"

"Those were some of Whiting's boys. We're going to string them along awhile like we scared you to death, and tell them that you really didn't know. If that don't work..." Byrd shrugged and looked at his men. They shrugged in response. "We'll have to work out something else."

· XXXIX ·

*Is this how men scheduled for execution feel?* Anthony wondered. *Every day you're alive is a good day?* The apartment
door opened interrupting his thoughts. Carla looked radiant. It
was going to be a good day. She ran into Anthony's waiting arms
and he flinched as a sharp pain shot through his side. "Oh
Anthony. I'm sorry. I was just so happy to see you, I forgot."

"It's okay. It just hurts a little."

He held her tightly as they kissed for almost a minute. Carla
smiled as he moved inside the door, until she spotted the new
scar.

"What happened?" she asked, frowning.

"Ran into a doggone door."

Carla sighed. "You're going to kill yourself if you don't
watch where you're going."

A smile flickered briefly across Anthony's face.

279

"I missed you, Anthony." Carla sat next to him. "So what happened at the office? You didn't call me yesterday you know," she said in a playfully accusing tone.

"I'm sorry. It was late when I returned. The only person who talked to me was Hannah. Neither Whiting nor any of the others ever came by to see me. I wasn't even there as far as they were concerned."

"Just as well."

Anthony told her about Bobby Joe Byrd, but omitted the part about his would-be kidnappers.

"That's weird. I've heard of the militia, but I didn't know that any of them did that."

"And you're a history major," he chided. "I was as surprised as you, but what's most interesting is that they're still operating."

"That is interesting, but there have always been good people around," Carla said.

"I found out something else, too. Did you know Whiting was Klan?"

Carla frowned. "It wouldn't surprise me based on the how the *Sun* treats colored folk in their paper."

"Yeah. I guess I overlooked a lot of things."

"They're no worse than many other papers though. Maybe all of them are run by the Klan."

Anthony laughed. "No telling."

Carla placed one hand on her hip. "So, what are your plans?"

"My short term plan is revenge. I told you about Jerry who worked at the paper before me?"

"Yes."

"I think he would be willing to help me."

"With what?" she asked.

"Just wait, my dear. All will be revealed to you in time," Anthony said playfully as he ran his hand through her hair.

The *Washington Post* headline read, "ARKANSAS NEWS-PAPER EDITOR IS KLAN." The paper identified William Bradford Whiting as one of the members on a roster that was stolen from Klan headquarters. The forty men on the roster were all identified as well as any positions they held. Two were preachers. One was an alderman. Whiting had hired two members. Six were law enforcement officers, including a deputy sheriff, and two others held positions in city government.

The fallout was not as harsh as Anthony would have liked, but Whiting did lose his job. It seemed that the paper took his idea about using Anthony to increase colored readership seriously.

Editorials in the *Arkansas Republic* lambasted the *Sun* for not knowing of Whiting's Klan involvement. Of course no one from the *Sun* would talk to the *Republic's* reporters, but that didn't stop the *Republic* from covering every angle of the scandal.

Six separate articles were written over a three-week period about the newspaper. The most damaging editorial was the last, which posed the question of why any colored person would ever buy another *Arkansas Sun* knowing what they knew now. It further went on to observe that the only colored reporter the paper had was fired.

Of course there were some Arkansans who could care less and even cheered the newspaper for hiring Whiting in the first place, but there was also a large number of residents who were upset. The articles caused a chain of events that held the rapt attention of the state's residents for weeks.

The editor of the *Sun*, Charlie Hargrove became so upset

about the *Republic* articles, that he challenged the editor of the *Republic* to a duel. This led to another article in the *Republic* questioning Hargrove's sanity. Four cartoons resulted from the challenge. One had Hargrove with a pin-sized head on an over-sized body trying to stab the *Republic's* editor with a blunt pencil while being held back by a midget. To add insult to injury, the *Republic* hired its first black reporter. The paper trumpeted the employment with the headlines "THIS IS FOR REAL." The move endeared the paper to the colored community.

Distribution numbers at the *Sun* began to drop, causing expenses to exceed revenues for the first time since the paper started production. The paper let some staff go, and coverage became weaker, resulting in an even steeper decline in readership.

Anthony kept track of everything. He felt vindicated when one of the *Republic's* stories listed his credentials, then stated that he was more qualified than almost any other reporter that had ever worked for the *Sun.* If anyone should celebrate the demise of the paper, it should have been Anthony, but he actually felt sorry for those staff members who lost their jobs. He knew many of them. The ones he worked with were generally good people and dedicated workers.

The telephone rang, breaking his train of thought. "Well, that seemed to do the job," the voice on the other end of the line said.

"Yes it did, Bobby Joe, and I appreciate it. With your and Jerry's help, this turned out better than I could have ever imagined."

"Any word on the missing Klansmen?"

"I haven't had a chance to talk to the Williamses about it, but give me time."

"That's all I've got is time, Anthony. Keep me informed."

"You bet. Don't worry, I'll find out one way or the other." Anthony felt he owed Bobby Joe Byrd that.

## · XL ·

The apartment was quiet, which enabled Anthony some time for introspection. Mentally, he felt better than he ever had, but he still worried that the devil was lurking back there somewhere, its hand poised.

As if on cue, Carla came through the door. After one glance she asked, "What's the matter, honey?"

Anthony smiled. Besides being pretty and smart, she was intuitive. "I've been thinking," Anthony responded as he pulled the yellowed folded piece of paper from his pocket and laid it on the table next to him.

Carla glanced at the piece of paper. "About what?"

"If we're going to be together, you need to know everything about me."

"There's more?"

Anthony nodded and motioned for her to sit. "After I saw the hanging, I tried, but I was never able to control this fear of violence. The pain and dread I felt when I was around it would sometimes almost cripple me. It's probably still lurking back there, but it seems to have faded in Cleveland after our fight with Roach."

Carla listened as she gently caressed his hands. "You weren't afraid then?"

"It never crossed my mind. Before then, when I ran and exercised, it gave me some control and maybe a false sense of security, but it's all I knew how to do, except for this," Anthony pointed to the folded paper. "I felt if I read this often enough, I would eventually overcome."

"What's in it Anthony?"

Anthony took the aged piece of paper from the table and gave it to her. Carla carefully unfolded it and began to read the words written in a younger person's handwriting.

*August 15, 1948. I saw a boy hung yesterday. His name is Emmanuel. It could have been me but it wasn't. I saw a boy die because he was colored. I don't know what he did, but nobody should die like that. Emmanuel was probably a good boy who would have turned into a good man if they would have let him. I hope Emmanuel rests in peace.*

Then written at the bottom of the page almost as an afterthought was another sentence.

*I'll never die just because I am colored.*

Carla wept as she held the piece of paper.

"Ever since that happened, I've been searching for that quiet place inside me. You understand?"

Carla nodded.

"I - I feel closest to it when I'm with you."

Carla squeezed his hand with one of hers, and wiped the tears from her face with the other.

Two weeks passed with Anthony looking every day at classifieds for jobs in his field. As he expected, even with the color barrier being broken at the *Republic*, there was little or nothing in the state. It was becoming apparent that he would probably have to move if he wanted to pursue a career in journalism. This caused him some anxiety, since he had no idea what Carla's plans were.

One night while Anthony was cleaning, Carla gave him a folder with the Williams family name on it. "I've found some more interesting facts about this family."

"Like what, Carla?" Anthony asked as he went through the papers.

"Thanks to the Mormon archives, my students were able to trace the Williamses as far back as the late 1700s. It appears there were two brothers, Tchi and Douga, and a sister, Sitan, who were shipped together. They landed in New Orleans and were sold to a trader called Farro Munson. He didn't keep them that long, and subsequently sold them to the Caldwells from Mississippi. It also appears the Caldwells died without any heirs. The family was then sold to the Shaws and brought to Arkansas where they remained until after the Civil War.

"There are some things that are strange though."

A few months ago Anthony would have ho-hummed this information, but he was extremely curious about *his* family now. "What's that, Carla?"

"For one, it doesn't appear that the family took any of their master's names. Usually the slaves took the master's name after they were freed. It appears that at some point, they named themselves.

"Secondly, the family was never split. All three of the siblings married and had kids, but they all remained together, moving from one family to the other."

"I don't understand."

"More often than not, a plantation would sell off a kid or one of the adults for money or breeding. It's unusual that a family would stay together like that during their move from one plantation to another. There's almost always a split."

"It could be that they were lucky."

"It could be, but something else is strange. For instance, in looking at the death record of the Caldwells, it seems like the father, mother, and two sons all died at the same time. There wasn't much other information about them, but I would be curious to know what happened on that plantation."

"Maybe Aunt Dahlia or one of the other elders knows. You want to talk to them about it?"

"I did have some conversation with Aunt Dahlia. She has a wealth of knowledge about their history, but I don't know, Anthony. We've been prying into their affairs so often, they're probably tired of us by now."

Anthony laughed. "You're right." Then he shuddered.

"What's wrong, Anthony?"

"I just thought of something."

Carla waited.

"You know when Raymond and I had that fight with Roach and his boys?"

"Yes?" Carla answered.

"Raymond dropped a vial."

"So?"

"When I first saw Raymond walking down my street, he looked so downhearted." Carla sat next to Anthony as he continued. "He never came over to my place except the one time he walked me home, and even then, he didn't come in."

"What do you think he wanted, Anthony?"

Anthony lowered his head. "I may be paranoid, but I think Raymond was going to kill me. I think the Williams family found out why I was there."

Her eyes widened as she put her hand over her mouth to cover the quiet shriek. "No, Anthony! No!" she said emphatically.

"I gave him the vial back. He looked at it then threw it down the sewer. Now why would he do that with something that fell out of his pocket?" Anthony paused. "And how did Cread get there so fast, unless he was following Anthony to make sure the job was done?"

Carla sat looking stunned, constantly shaking her head.

"They needed to protect their secret, Carla. If they were involved, what would stop them from killing someone as insignificant as me?"

"And the reason they didn't was because you saved Raymond's life?"

"And because I promised not to write the story. I would bet money."

"So what are you going to do?"

Anthony paused, looking into space. "Nothing. What can I do?"

Carla shook her head again. She stood, walking to the window then turned abruptly. "You know, I would be afraid to be around them."

"We don't have anything to worry about, Carla. I saved Raymond's life twice now. Aunt Dahlia said I was family. I believe her."

"You saved Raymond's life the first time. That didn't stop them from trying to kill you!"

"Yes, but they know I'm not going to write the story."

"But you still *know* the story."

Anthony stood. "Not all of it. Anyway they said they forgive me. I believe them." He said the last words with such finality that Carla dropped the subject.

## · XLI ·

Someone shot Bobby Joe Byrd." Anthony gently placed the paper on the kitchen table. It was morning, and he was just reading the previous night's news. He felt guilty that he hadn't known sooner. "I have to go see him."

Violence seemed to lurk around every corner, Anthony thought. When would life be normal again? Why was all of this happening?

"I'll go with you," Carla said.

"No!" Anthony almost shouted before explaining in a calmer voice. "It might be dangerous."

"And it won't be for you?"

"I can't expose you to this stuff, Carla. The farther away from it you are, the better. I would kill myself if something happened to you."

"You're going to kill yourself anyway, jumping into these

situations. At least call some of your friends to go with you," Carla pleaded. "Don't go alone, Anthony. "

"Okay. I'll do that," Anthony answered, knowing that he wouldn't. None of his friends would understand, especially not Donald. He hadn't told them anything about Cleveland or the attempted kidnapping outside the paper because he knew they wouldn't understand. If he went to visit Byrd during the day, there should be no problems, and if there was, he could handle it.

"I'll wait until noon and go. That way Joe can make it during his lunch hour."

Carla nodded. She appeared satisfied with that.

At 11:30 A.M., Anthony drove over to the Veteran's Administration Hospital. It appeared a normal day. He stopped at the front desk, looking around, then in a lowered tone asked if Byrd could have visitors. The receptionist checked her files and said yes, but only for short periods since he was under strong medication.

Anthony looked around again before taking the elevator to the fourth floor. Room 421 was around the corner, according the floor nurse, so Anthony headed in that direction, still cautious as he approached the room. Four men were already there when Anthony entered. He recognized two of them from the house in the woods. The other two seemed to recognize him. They nodded as he entered.

"Anthony!"

Byrd was in good spirits, even though his voice was subdued and raspy. One of the men moved so Anthony could get closer.

"How you doing today, Bobby Joe?" Anthony asked as they shook hands.

"A lot better than yesterday, and even better tomorrow. Do you know everybody here?"

Whatever medication he was given, seemed to have no effect on Byrd at all. Anthony looked around, nodding at the two men he had met before. "No, not everybody."

"This here is Harley, and this is my cousin Otis."

The two stood to shake Anthony's hand. "Glad to meet you," they said in unison.

"Anthony here is...was a reporter. But then y'all know that." Byrd waved his hand, weakly.

"Who did this, Bobby Joe?"

"You know, they say if you're looking for something and can't find it, quit looking, and it will find you." Byrd's face twisted into a painful frown. "I'm sorry I wasn't paying enough attention."

Anthony looked up as one of the men started laughing softly.

"Damned if Rafe didn't pull his tail up from between his legs, come out from whatever hole he was hidin' in, and stick it to me."

"So he's alive?" Anthony asked, relieved that he wouldn't have to bother the family again about their past.

"Well..."

Out of the corner of his eye, Anthony noticed one of the men shifting from one foot to the other. Another had his head down. His question was answered.

"At least that's one problem you don't have to deal with," Anthony observed.

"True, but like that, a... Hydra? You know, the woman with the snakes in her head? You kill one and two more appear?"

Anthony nodded, surprised that Byrd knew any Greek mythology.

"Whiting and his boys sent him."

"How did you find that out?"

By only the slightest of movements, the same two men gave him the answer to that question too. They had their own means of finding out, evidently.

A thousand questions ran through Anthony's mind. "What happens now, Bobby Joe? Where does it end?"

"I don't know, Anthony, but one damn thing for sure, it ain't over."

"It sure as hell ain't over," one of Byrd's men said.

A nurse came into the room. "What are all you gentlemen doing in this room at one time?"

The two men who were sitting stood as she entered.

"There can be only two of you in here at one time. You all know that."

"Sorry, ma'am," two of the men said as they looked at Byrd for direction.

"Why don't all you all go outside for a minute? I want to talk to Anthony a while."

After the men and the nurse left, Byrd became more serious. "You know Whiting is upset with us that we pulled the cover off him and he was fired from the newspaper. Somehow Whiting and his boys found that I might have been the one who got that list, but he blames you as much as he blames me, so you need to be careful, Anthony; we're outgunned here in the city, and my cover is gone."

Anthony shifted in his seat. "I can take care of myself."

"It's not just you that you have to take care of."

The statement hit Anthony like a sledgehammer. Carla, his mother, his father!

"What do you think I should do?"

"I'm going to have to think about this one man. This is a heavy one. I wouldn't be so concerned, but I know Whiting, and he's a vindictive man. I believe he called Rafe out so he could kill me like he killed my brother. He's the worse kind of snake."

A series of jumbled thoughts raced across Anthony's mind. He could call the police, but for what? Nobody had done anything yet. He could move, but his family would still be in Arkansas. He could do nothing and hope the situation would blow over, but the likelihood of that happening was slim to none, according to Byrd. He could get the *Republic* to write another story, but he didn't have enough evidence, and if what he suspected were true, the perpetrators would probably be long gone. He could kill Whiting, but how? He had never killed anyone in his life.

Byrd interrupted his thoughts. "One of my boys is going to give you something." Byrd's head rose as far as it could from the bed as he looked at Anthony sternly. "Take it, practice with it, and get it into your head that if necessary, you'll use it."

"Otis!"

The tallest of the men eased back into the room. Byrd nodded, and as smooth as a magician, the hard, cold steel of a revolver pressed against Anthony's hand.

Byrd looked at Anthony with his penetrating stare. "No matter how right you are, sometimes it comes down to this."

"How was he?" Carla asked.

"He'll survive. The wounds weren't critical," Anthony responded.

"Did he say what happened?"

"Only that he was at the wrong place at the wrong time," Anthony said evasively.

"Who went with you, Anthony?"

Anthony turned to see Carla's arms folded and her mouth turned down in a frown.

He figured he had better be especially straight with her on this one. Anthony found it hard to even tell Carla a small lie. There was a bond growing between them that made him want to tell her everything. "No one. I couldn't get anybody on such short notice."

"You sure didn't call Joe, because he called while you were gone." Carla pouted. She always looked the most beautiful when she became upset.

Anthony approached her from behind as she turned away, wrapping his arms around her waist. "Look, Carla. They wouldn't understand. These guys are so removed from this stuff that it would take a century to explain. I don't have the time."

Surprisingly, Carla smiled. "My, have we changed."

"I guess we have," Anthony said as he hugged her tightly, nuzzling her ear. *Maybe that's what staring death in the face does to you,* he thought.

## · XLII ·

Carla agreed to move north with Anthony, who worried most about his parents. Moving them, even if they were willing, would be a monumental task. It was really out of the question, though. His father would never leave a profitable business like the funeral home, especially since it had been in the family for so long.

Nobody appeared to be looking for him, though, so if he moved, hopefully it would be over. In two days he was going to leave to interview with the *Call and Post* in Cleveland. It was a small, colored newspaper, but Anthony didn't care anymore. It was more important that he feel comfortable.

Carla had talked to people at Baldwin-Wallace College and Western Reserve University. They would travel to Cleveland together. Anthony looked forward to talking to the Williamses again. Carla didn't. She still wasn't over the fact that they might have tried to kill him.

Two days went by fast. Carla finally met Anthony's family. Their reaction was predictable.

His mother took Carla's hand and wouldn't let go as she alternately hugged and beamed at her. "It's so nice to meet you, Carla. Anthony's told me so much about you."

Anthony smiled as he watched Carla, nervous at first, warm up to his mother in a matter of seconds.

"So you're a professor? Are you tenured?" His father was all business, but it didn't take long before even he was beaming as Carla modestly deflected most of his questions.

"I've heard a lot about you, Mr. Andrews. It must be a wonderful feeling becoming so successful at such an early age."

Anthony swore he saw a hint of blush on his father's face.

Anthony and Carla almost missed their plane saying goodbye. His parents acted as if they were going to Russia. His father hugged him for the first time since he was a small kid. His mother hugged him even longer, but he could still feel the tension between the two.

"I found this motel on Euclid Avenue. It's the closest place I could find. You think that would be all right?" Anthony asked Carla over the drone of the plane.

"I'm sure it will be, Anthony." Carla held his hand. "I understand why you're so drawn to the Williams family, and even though I'm still a bit leery about them, I won't question you about them again."

Anthony smiled and squeezed her hand.

Anthony called the Williamses as soon as they checked in.

Thompson Williams answered the phone. "When are you coming over, Anthony? Everybody is waiting to see you."

It felt good to hear those words from someone he admired so much. "Carla has an appointment tomorrow morning, and I have one tomorrow afternoon, so how about tomorrow evening?"

"That's fine, son. About seven o'clock?"

Anthony checked with Carla and confirmed. "We're looking forward to it."

Carla gave him the funny look she usually reserved for their arguments. Anthony understood. Even though she wasn't going to express her concerns, she still had them.

"It's going to be all right, baby, I promise you." Anthony was delighted. Thompson had called him son.

The closeness of the Williams family still amazed Anthony. They all gathered in Thompson's house to eat. It was evident Carla was still apprehensive, but she eventually gave in to their charm. Raymond and Myra were there looking like two newly-weds, even though nothing was decided. Even Cread was gracious. It was the first time Cread had ever offered his hand to Anthony in a greeting. That gesture meant everything to Anthony. Hopefully, it would help in alleviating Carla's concerns.

Carla eventually sat down with Aunt Dahlia. They talked like old friends. "We have a rich history, dear. Someday when you settle down and have some time, we'll talk about it," Aunt Dahlia said, patting Carla's knee.

"I look forward to it, Aunt Dahlia. As a matter of fact, I would be honored if you shared it with me."

Aunt Dahlia smiled at Carla, holding her hand. "You're such a blessing."

Eventually, Thompson, Raymond, and the other men gathered on the front porch.

"How did the interviews go?" Thompson asked Anthony.

"Very well. The owner of the *Call and Post*, Mr. Walker, is a very knowledgeable man. I like his style."

"When are you going to know?" Raymond asked.

"He said I was hired. We have to work out some other matters, like pay and starting date."

The men nodded.

"You didn't tell us much about what happened after you quit the paper, Anthony," Hilton asked.

"I didn't quit, I was fired." Anthony told them everything, including the attempted kidnapping, and Bobby Joe Byrd.

Cread was quiet up to that point, but shifted in his chair and grunted. "Seems to me like you might need some help down there, son."

All of the men agreed except Deacon. "We live up here now, Cread, not down there. We've had enough violence in our lives."

"Anthony is one of us now, Deacon, and the family is everything. If he needs our help, we're obligated to give it to him," Cread said.

Anthony glowed as he listened to the two men, but felt compelled to interrupt. "Man, you guys have done enough for me already. Once I move up here, everything should be fine."

"Well, it's evident that some folks still don't get the message," Cread said gruffly.

"What's that, Cread?" Thompson asked.

"That we aren't going anywhere, and there's nothing they can do to make it any different."

"Amen," the men chorused.

"Yeah, that's the sad part about this great country. If all the energy that some used to keep us down was used to build this nation up, we could be even greater." Hilton leaned back in his chair as everyone listened. He shook his head. "That night in the woods never should have happened. Why anyone would want to hang two young men like that is still a mystery to me."

Cread grunted. "Control, Uncle Hilton. It's always been about control."

"They beat that young Coulter boy with bats after they hung him," Hilton said in disbelief.

Thompson gently put his hand on the old man's shoulder.

Anthony felt like he was standing in front of a blast furnace. The rush of heat hit him with the force of a speeding truck. "I was there," he said in a hushed voice.

"How could that be?" Thompson asked. "You lived in the city, and you couldn't have been more than a teenager yourself."

"We were visiting cousin Mathis."

"Junior Mathis?" Hilton asked.

Anthony's shoulders slumped. "Yes. Joe's father. When you said bats, it all came together. I was in the woods when I heard noises. I saw them hang the Coulter boy. I saw them beat him."

Cread nodded knowingly. "I knew there was something about you. I could tell it in your eyes. Tell us your story."

When Anthony finished, Deacon put his arm around Anthony.

Hilton looked at Anthony and patted him on his back. "You know our family never talked about what happened after our incident in the woods. Nobody among us said a word about it, but we need to talk. Maybe if we had talked about it back then and got it off our chest, Hopson might still be here today. It isn't right that a man keep that much turmoil boxed up inside."

Thompson glanced at Raymond who had turned away when they mentioned his father's name. In all their discussions, he hadn't talked to Raymond much about his father because like everyone else, he hadn't really understood what happened the day he took his life. Thompson did notice that Hopson drank a little more, talked a lot more, and didn't always make sense, but he never imagined that those were warning signs from a man that was going to commit suicide.

Thompson's shoulders drooped briefly as he thought about it. Thompson should have understood the signs, but he didn't.

Nobody did. The "woods" had gotten to Hopson. It had gotten to all of them in one way or another. Thompson glanced at Cread who nodded. Thompson took his hand off Hilton as if to give him approval to proceed.

"We all family here now. Anthony, you've been through some rough times like us. Although you haven't killed anybody, Raymond tells me you were willing," Hilton continued.

Anthony hung his head.

Deacon went to shut the front door so no one else could hear the conversation.

"I know I pray every night for forgiveness for what I had to do. It isn't right to have to take a man's life," Deacon said.

Cread spoke quietly and respectfully. "You're right, Deacon. It isn't right, but sometimes it's necessary."

Ransom spoke in his high, lilting voice, sounding like he was on the verge of crying. "That night affected everybody. It changed us. We saw a side to us that I hope the kids will never have to see."

"I look at those kids, though, and it makes everything we did worthwhile. They were worth the sacrifice we made. They were worth losing a part of our soul," Hilton said. He looked at Anthony again and then at Raymond. "Raymond, I guess your uncle Thompson told you what happened back then, and Anthony, I know you did some investigating, but I want you two to know the whole story. We need to tell it for our own sake."

Thompson sat quietly as he thought back to that night.

*The night air was damp and still as he and the others gathered in the woods to wait. There were no sounds except for the occasional shuffle of feet as everyone tried to get as comfortable as they could. Thompson tried to make out the others, but it was so dark he could see no more than a few feet. How would they be able to see them if and when they came?*

*The Coulter boy had been hung, so they had moved Johnny in with other relatives, just in case. Sometimes, the Klan came straight to the house, shooting, burning, and looting before carrying their victim off—if the person was still alive. That wasn't where the family wanted to fight. The invaders were big on surprises, so they planned to surprise them first.*

*It was Saturday and some of the Klan talked about a "picnic." Usually, some white person would come to warn them. Tell them not to go to town or not to go past somebody's farm, but nobody warned them this time. Nobody.*

*Word got back to the family, confirming their worst fears, and after a lengthy debate, it was determined that the family had no choice but to fight. Running was out of the question. The family would run from no one.*

*Thompson sat with the others that morning as they developed their plan. It was a simple one based on their knowledge of hangings in their area. If the Klan did what they did in the past, a group of them would probably come to the clearing in the northern woods. They would shoot off their guns to celebrate and go through their ceremony.*

*They would then proceed to grab whoever they were after, torture them until the next day, then hang him or her. Sometimes it occurred after church in front of town folk with packed lunches, but because the Klan feared retaliation from the family, they would more than likely kill their captive in private like they did the little Coulter boy.*

*Two of the family had scouted the area earlier in the day. You could drive down Heck's Road ten times and not see the entrance. There was only one narrow path into the clearing. It was wide enough to accommodate one car at a time. Cread had picked a spot to hide near the edge of the clearing. He figured this was where they would come—if they came at all.*

*It was where they had come when they got Mr. Crenshaw, the cook at Barley's; Joe Elders, a quiet farmer who bothered no one; Mrs. Morgan a housekeeper; and old John Berry. They knew this because Farley Johnson's farm was a mile away, and he had heard the faint sounds of the guns before they hung Joe Elders, riddled him with bullets, and then burned him. No one ever found out why. Mr. Johnson had heard the guns again before they dragged Mrs. Morgan from her house and eventually decapitated her for supposedly mouthing off at a white woman.*

"Nobody knew what we were going to do. Neither Johnny nor any of the rest of the family knew a thing. We had to keep it a secret from everybody," Hilton said.

Deacon spoke, "I tried to talk everybody out of it. There should have been a way to come to a peaceful resolution. Martin Luther King, Jr., would have found another way."

Nobody responded for a minute.

Hilton finally spoke up. "If there was another way, Deacon, we would gladly have done it. But lives were at risk, and not just Johnny's. We had no choice."

"If Johnny was killed, not only would it have devastated us, but most of us would be dead or in jail right now. You know we couldn't have let that stand, Deacon." Cread added. "This way was the best way."

Thompson remembered vividly what happened next.

*Less than an hour had passed, but it seemed like an eternity. Saturday was usually a day for him, and the rest of the family, to get together to rest and play. Depending on the season, they would be running, throwing a ball, laughing, or sitting around talking and eating. He wondered what his sister and his younger cousins were doing about now.*

*The noise from a faint clap of thunder penetrated his thoughts at that moment. Somewhere far away it was raining. He wished he were there instead of in the woods. He wished he were anywhere but in the woods.*

*A shiver ran through him as he thought about what he and the others were about to do. There were eight of them waiting in ambush, ready to take the lives of other men because of their deep and abiding ignorance. Thompson hoped they wouldn't show, hoped they would forget the whole matter and stay the hell wherever they were.*

*Whatever lingering thoughts or hopes he had were interrupted by the droning noise of approaching cars. It was another minute or so before he saw the wavering lights penetrating the darkness. His stomach lurched. He felt as if he were the victim. The fear he felt rushed through every part of his body, almost freezing him from moving.*

Shoot low, *he told himself.* Shoot low. *His cousin Cread had told the men gathered there that people had a tendency to shoot high in the dark. He rubbed his hands against his thighs, trying to stop the shaking. There was a faint flurry of movement around him as everyone prepared. The growing sound of the cars was as ominous as an army of tanks advancing on an enemy. He was sweating profusely, furiously hoping that his clammy, shaking hands would be able to perform.*

*The cars entered the clearing one at a time and formed a circle before the occupants exited with their guns. There were four cars carrying fourteen of them. They were dressed in white gowns without the masks. When they met in the middle of the circle, the light from the beams made them look almost ghostly. He could see them clearly through the bushes. Some were laughing; some were serious. He looked around for the signal. There was none. What was Cread waiting for?*

*Seconds after he asked, he saw the match. His pulse quickened, knowing that this was the time. Tonight he would take a human life. He shuddered violently at the thought as he slowly raised his rifle.*

"We had to kill all of them," Hilton continued. "If even one were to get away, it would have meant death to us, and death to a lot of other colored people in town."

In awe, Raymond asked, "What did you do with the bodies?"

"We took them to the deepest part of the woods to a small clearing and buried them side by side in a three-foot grave that we dug the day before."

"Then we prayed over them," Deacon added. "We prayed over each one individually."

*We prayed before and after we killed them knowing full well that God would want no part of people like the Klan or people like the Williams men had become,* Thompson thought to himself.

"We sprinkled cayenne pepper around the area, so animals wouldn't disturb the place," Cread continued.

The men sat quietly for a while.

"Do you think they would have published this story if you had written it, Anthony?" Deacon asked.

Anthony was still reeling from the realization of what the men had done. They did do it, but it was clear now. They had to. It was the type of family they were. He couldn't picture them doing anything but that, protecting their family. In reality, in the back of his mind, he thought they might have. Crawford Reardon had given him his first clue when he said he heard gunshots. Having learned so much about them, plus what Carla told him at the family gathering... Anthony sighed. Deep down, he knew back then, but he had suppressed it.

It was out now though.

Then it dawned on him. Emmanuel, the boy he had named in his mind, was Hosiah Coulter. He finally knew the little boy's real name. Hosiah Coulter. Anthony repeated his name again and again.

Anthony felt a mixture of pride and awe mixed with relief. The men had shared their deepest secret with him. He belonged to the family, and the family belonged to him.

Anthony looked around, lost in thought. The men waited. Deacon repeated the question. "Do you think the paper would have published this story?"

Anthony came around, deliberated for a while, then answered, "Probably not, at least not the ambush part. I'm not sure that any white paper in the North or South would write about white men on the way to killing a colored kid being killed themselves. Those aren't the type of stories they would want anybody to know about."

Thompson nodded. "Aunt Dahlia would say, 'Until the hunted have their own historians, tales of the hunt will always glorify the hunter.' "

Hilton continued, "There were eight of us. Three of our cousins were from out of town, so they and Ransom drove the cars back to Mississippi and dumped them in a lake."

"Did the Coulters have anything to do with all this?" Anthony asked.

Cread grunted. "Naw. When the boy was hung, they acted like chickens with their heads cut off. They didn't know what to do. We tried to get them to go in with us, but they were already packing. As far as I know, they ran out of town and didn't look back."

Anthony looked at Cread. "What about the missing sheriff? Do you think the Coulters had anything to do with that?"

"I doubt it seriously." Cread answered.

Hilton shifted in his chair. "There was a rumor that the sheriff heard about the hanging and was going to try to stop those boys from coming to get little Johnny."

All the men turned to Hilton.

"It's just a rumor, but a couple of the farmers did hear some white men arguing with Sheriff Jefferson the day before those boys came out to the woods. I'm getting this third hand, so you can't put much weight on it, but from their account, there was some shouting and loud noises coming from the sheriff's office early that evening. Somebody shouted "nigger lover", there was a shot, and then everything got quiet. Old Mr. Fambrough and his cousin heard the argument and hid behind a shed when the sheriff's door opened so they wouldn't be noticed, then they left the back way. Left their groceries and everything."

Thompson slid his hand across his chin. "So you think that the same folks that came to the woods were responsible for the sheriff missing?"

"It's hard to say," Hilton answered. "But it makes sense. If he was going to try to stop them, they very well could have killed him too. The sheriff was a fair man. He might have tried to stop them."

"When I went to Evesville, the sheriff's office was torn up, and there was blood on the wall," Anthony offered.

"That makes sense from what I heard." Hilton said. "The sheriff could have been killed. I never said anything, because we never talked about the woods again."

Hilton hung his head. "Once we completed our business, we had to leave. We hoped the other families would follow. It was the only way to insure that there would be no retribution against innocent folks." Hilton said. "When we split up, it was more heartbreaking than anything else that happened to us. Not being able to see all the family together was worse than death."

"The family is everything," Thompson said quietly.

"The family is everything," the men repeated.

"The family is everything," Anthony said as they followed Hilton's lead and stood in a circle holding hands. As soon as he joined hands, a surge of energy rushed through him. The feeling was like nothing he had ever experienced before. It was as if they had transferred part of their strength to him.

It scared him.

Afterward the men sat long into the night saying little, each in their own world. Hilton was the first to rise. "I'm going to turn it in. An old man needs his sleep."

Anthony's eyes narrowed, then widened as Hilton stood. "Have you always used that cane, Uncle Hilton?" he asked cautiously. "I've never seen anything like it."

"It's a walking stick, Anthony. And no, it's not the first time. I pull it out now and then when I need strength."

Anthony took a deep breath; his voice was almost a whisper. "Is there any significance to the snake that's carved into it?"

Hilton eyebrows raised, then he smiled briefly as he looked back at Anthony. "They say there is..." he responded as he slowly descended the steps.

## · XLIII ·

Anthony called his family every day. He had a strong need to be with them. After arriving back in Little Rock that evening, he ate a light supper with Carla, then headed to Pine Bluff. His mind kept going back to that day when his parents had their argument. Thinking about it still pained him. He wished there was something he could do to make things right between them.

It was ten o'clock when Anthony crossed Highway 104. He was getting drowsy, so he was happy to know it wouldn't be much longer before he got to his destination. It was then that he noticed the old grayish-looking Buick behind him. It was the same Buick he had seen ten minutes earlier. He remembered it because there were so many men in the car. In the South, a car full of white men was a source of apprehension for any black person, but especially when driving alone. That same rush of anxiety he felt in Evesville slowly twisted its way through his stomach. Whatever drowsiness he had was gone.

Anthony continued to glance at the car through his rearview mirror as he continued down Route 65. It remained behind him. Anxiety had turned to dread, causing Anthony to grip the steering wheel so tight that his hands hurt. Anthony slowed his Chrysler to let the other one pass, but it slowed down with him. It was then that he noticed the headlights of a second vehicle behind the Buick. It had slowed too.

There was no other traffic on the highway, so Anthony figured that the cars must have been following him. Anthony couldn't see the driver or passengers in the Buick, but he guessed they were either the men who tried to abduct him outside of the *Sun's* offices or some of their associates.

He tried to collect his thoughts. Going to his parents' house was out of the question. The gun Byrd had given him flashed through his mind, but it was in the trunk. There was only one other option. He would have to outrun them.

From the looks of the Buick, it had to be at least ten years old, if not more. Judging from what little he could see of the exterior, it didn't seem to be in that good a shape. His Chrysler on the other hand was six years old and in very good shape.

Anthony gunned the motor as he approached Pine Bluff. Traffic was still sparse. Being a week night, the town had pretty much shut down. Hopefully, a police car would see him speeding and stop him.

His car shot past eighty miles per hour as he continued along Route 65. When he looked in the rearview mirror, Anthony was surprised to see that the two cars remained right behind him. He revved up to ninety miles per hour, but still could not shake them.

A sign indicated that Route 79 was a mile away. Anthony decided to take it. The cars seemed content to stay behind him. His Chrysler swerved, almost losing its grip on the road as Anthony negotiated the turn. On Route 79, they continued to drive up to speeds of ninety miles per hour, for what seemed to Anthony like forever, before the gray Buick pulled alongside. A window rolled down and the barrel of a gun appeared. Anthony gunned the motor again and ducked at the same time. The car stayed abreast of his.

"Pull over," the man with the gun commanded. Anthony slowed the Chrysler as the two cars slowed with him. He glanced at the men, but still couldn't make them out. When he had slowed to about thirty miles per hour, Anthony sped up again. It only worked for a few minutes before both cars pulled up behind him.

This time when the Buick pulled alongside Anthony, the man shot. Anthony ducked again before he realized that the man was not shooting at him. A loud sound was followed by the slap of loose rubber. He panicked as the Chrysler swerved on a lacerated front tire. Braking only made it worse as the car, now speeding out of control, skidded toward the woods on the right side of the road. It slid sideways before ramming a tree on the passenger side. Shaken, but not hurt, Anthony pushed open his car door and ran blindly between the trees into the woods.

A dirt path wound between the trees. Anthony wasn't sure if he should follow it, but the alternative of running off the trail would mean he would make more noise, and it would slow his progress. He could hear car doors slam as he raced cautiously down the trail, avoiding the hanging limbs and tree roots. He worried least about being caught from behind. Taking the path, he eventually reached the edge of a clearing.

He paused to decide his next move as voices, speaking in urgent whispers, pierced the otherwise quiet forest. Anthony chanced running across the clearing, but three of the men spotted him. They took off toward Anthony with rifles and shotguns raised. Anthony sprinted to a small cluster of trees before dashing to another dense area of the woods just as a shot rang out.

As the echoes from the sound of the shot faded, he could hear the heavy pounding of feet coming toward him, then the sound of the men chasing him stopped. He stopped too. There was no noise except Anthony's breathing. Thoughts began to flow. What would Raymond do? What would Thompson do? What would Cread do? But those were interrupted by the sound of someone approaching again, but at a slower pace.

Anthony hid behind one of the larger trees and waited. He needed a plan to get out of there alive. There were probably six to eight men. It would be no problem to outrun them, but he couldn't outrun the bullets. The clearing was probably his best bet still, but how could he get there with no cover and so many people after him?

The crackling sound of dead tree limbs and dead leaves as the men neared snapped Anthony back to the present. It sounded like three to four men, and they were approximately fifty yards away. The swish of tree limbs and bushes against clothes indicated they were closer still. If he moved from his spot, he would make the same sounds they were making and give his position away. If he stayed there, they would eventually find him.

Perspiration ran into Anthony's eyes as he contemplated his fate. The snapping tree limbs gave Anthony an idea. A dead branch lay against the tree. Anthony picked it up and waited. At least he would have a weapon.

From the noise they made and the tops of the swaying foliage, Anthony could tell the men were within ten yards. In desperation he changed plans and picked up two more dead branches. He threw them, one after another to the far side of where he thought the man farthest from his tree would be, hoping they would think he was running in that direction. It was a trick he played with his cousin Joe in the cornfields on Cousin Mathis's farm.

Seconds later, Anthony heard a quick movement then a shot. A man screamed in pain. Another howled, "Damn, damn, damn. Somebody help me! I shot Leroy."

As the shooter's cry echoed through the woods, Anthony ran in the opposite direction.

## · XLIV ·

nthony could hear men running toward the wailing shooter as he circled the path he thought they would travel to get back to what he hoped was the clearing. The trees and brushes only allowed him to move at a snail's pace, but at least he had a destination. Hopefully, crossing the clearing would put distance between him and the men, and with any luck, save his life.

It took a while, but he finally reached it. As he entered the clearing, Anthony heard the footsteps of what sounded like one man coming out of the woods. He looked around, desperately seeking shelter. The pear trees were too far apart to provide a cover. There was a small hill to his left. The larger oak trees were...then it hit him like a thunderbolt: the pear trees, the hill, the towering oaks, and this clearing with flowers. He had been here before. This was where the agony began. This was where he had witnessed the hanging. The pain that seared his brain and raced through his body, immobilized him for a moment.

His stalker broke into the clearing and stopped. Anthony glanced back to determine the distance between them. It was lucky he did, because the man had raised his weapon. Anthony ducked and leaped sideways as a shot rang out. It was a rifle shot. That was good. It meant that the man had to have a good aim, and in this darkening place, the chances of him hitting anything were slim. The man started to run toward him. Anthony reached the other side of the clearing and waited a second behind a tree before taking off, making sure to keep trees between them, but also making sure he could be heard.

Painful memories resurfaced as he leaped over the same hidden ditch he had fallen into thirteen years earlier. It was like yesterday that he ran in fear for his life, and now here he was again, running, but with a plan this time. Anthony picked up another branch and hid behind another clump of trees, stomping both feet in rhythm, making the sounds of a man still running. The noise of broken brush and limbs let Anthony know the man was closing in. Seconds later he heard what he had hoped for, an "hmmmph" followed by a large crash, then a howl.

Anthony held the branch high and peeked around the trees to see the man rolling in pain on the ground. With the man's features now visible, Anthony almost reeled, dizzy from the realization. It was the squat one, the one he remembered so well. It was the one who carried the rope that hung Hosiah. His rifle had fallen and his leg, obviously broken, was twisted at an odd angle under him. Terror filled the man's eyes as he grabbed the rifle. Anthony jumped into the ditch to wrestle it away from him. The same fear that he saw in this man was the same fear he probably created when he appeared before colored people with his white sheet. What was going through this man's mind now? Was he ready to die, or was he thinking, hoping his life would be spared?

When Anthony raised the gun to his shoulders, the man cringed, raising his hands in front of him pleading, "Don't." A stain spread slowly across the front of his pants.

Anthony's hands trembled as he pictured this man putting a noose around Hosiah. He tightened his finger on the trigger, then released it without firing a shot. He wasn't a killer, not yet, but he was two seconds from being one.

Anthony turned to move back through the trees, but a rage enveloped him that was so strong, he had to turn back. Tearing tree branches away as he approached, he leaped out of the thick group of trees and raised the rifle again. Anthony's temples throbbed. The man made a mewling sound when he saw Anthony reappear. He lurched with his one good leg, trying to escape before letting out a short cry, grabbing his chest and collapsing.

Anthony lowered his rifle for the second time. Cread would have shot him without any hesitation, but he wasn't Cread. Anthony climbed out of the ditch and ran with the rifle toward the distant farm, barely visible in the waning light. He paused briefly among the corn stalks, but there was no noise to indicate that anyone was following.

Anthony moved closer to the farmhouse, but not too close. He had no idea who was living there since Cousin Mathis moved. Instead he walked cautiously until he was at the far end of the cornfield near the road before lying down, exhausted, to wait for the light of dawn.


Anthony hitched a ride back to Pine Bluff in an old colored farmer's truck. The farmer's face was filled with a million wrinkles, but there was an odd mixture of dignity and youthfulness in his voice.

"What are you going to do with that rifle, son?" the farmer

asked, looking at the weapon.

Anthony looked at the old man and shook his head. "It's a long story, sir. A very long story."

The farmer nodded and said nothing else during the ride. He was kind enough to let Anthony off at his parent's house. Anthony rewarded him with ten dollars; thankful he didn't have to walk very far with a rifle wrapped in a potato sack.

Neither of his parents was at home. Anthony took a shower, changed clothes and called his father to ask permission to borrow a car after explaining that his had failed him. The stress-filled drive back to Little Rock seemed like days instead of hours. It wasn't until he reached the outskirts of Little Rock that he began to calm.

As soon as he entered the apartment, the phone rang. It was either Carla or his parents wondering what happened. He was wrong on both counts.

"Are you okay, Anthony?"

It was Byrd. "Now I am," Anthony responded.

"I heard what happened last night," Byrd offered.

The man never ceased to amaze Anthony. "How could you know what happened last night?"

"One of my men was there," Byrd responded.

Anthony sat down, still weary from his ordeal. "Why? How?"

"My man was with the group that was chasing you. He was at his wit's end trying to determine how to save you, but, as it ended up, you didn't even need him."

Anthony waited for Byrd to continue.

"When the guys found that you tricked them into shooting each other, they became a little nervous. Then when they found Tatum laid out in the ditch dead and saw that his rifle was missing, they came to the conclusion that chasing you wasn't in their best interest." Byrd laughed, "Ain't no fun when the rabbit got the gun."

Tatum. Anthony mouthed his name. It would be etched into his brain forever.

"They carried the two dead men out of there and didn't look back," Byrd grunted.

Anthony shook his head. "The fat guy, Tatum, must have died of a heart attack."

"Well you can tell me about it later. Right now, I think you need to move out of the apartment and lay low for a little while."

"Actually I was getting ready to move up North anyway. I'll just have to do it sooner," Anthony pondered out loud.

"Probably a good idea," Byrd responded.

"What about you. What are you going to do, Bobby Joe?"

Byrd sighed. "I don't know Anthony. I can't stop what I'm doing now. I'll just have to find a different way of doing it."

## · XLV ·

Matters had quieted down a bit although Anthony's cautiousness might have had something to do with it. He stayed at Carla's place and hardly ever went out at night. Although he took the gun that day at the hospital, it lay where he first put it, in the trunk of his damaged car under the spare tire. The rifle was still wrapped in the potato sack hidden under some old papers in the same trunk.

Sitting next to Carla one night after everything was arranged for their move, Anthony realized that through all the chaos in the past few days, not once did he have a panic attack. It was the second time he was confronted with a violent situation and the devil had slept through it.

There was hope.

"I felt something in those woods, Carla."

"What is that, Anthony?"

"When it struck me that those were the woods where the little boy was hung, I started to panic, and all of the pain I carried all those years surfaced, but then I got this rush, and I experienced the same feeling that I got when I was in the circle with the Williams men. When I was behind that tree, and then when I held the rifle pointing toward the man in the ditch, I finally felt that I was in control. Anthony looked at Carla to see if she understood anything he was trying to say. "It's hard to explain, Carla, but I left something in those woods when I was a kid. I left part of me there. Last week I feel like I retrieved some of it back. I'm beginning to feel whole again. Do you understand?"

Carla looked at Anthony with tear-filled eyes. "I can't even begin to understand, Anthony. I don't want to tell you I do when I don't, but I'm so happy that you feel the way you do. What you've shared helps me to understand you better and love you more. That's all I can do."

Anthony knew it was hard to understand. What he loved most about Carla though was that whatever the situation, he knew deep in his heart that he could depend on her to be there for him.

His thoughts shifted as he looked at her sitting there, more beautiful than ever. The Williamses came to mind. He owed that family—his family, everything. They showed him strength, and that love triumphed. Through all that they had overcome, there was no bravado, no boasting. And although he was sure they knew fear and apprehension, it wasn't a permanent part of their lives. They seemed to accept things as they were, then quietly do whatever was necessary to rise above it, maintaining control of their lives in the process.

He could see why no one would suspect they could kill. Nobody would ever see it coming.

Carla looked at Anthony, lips pursed, hands clasped. At that moment a feeling coursed through him that he had never felt before. Anthony knew he loved her, but what he felt for her at that moment was so deep, that there was no question about their future. He returned her gaze and held her closely.

The radio began to play a Ben E. King song in the background. It caught both their attention. It was *Stand By Me.*

Anthony and Carla's eyes locked.

"I want to have kids as soon as possible," Anthony whispered.

Carla raised her eyebrows as she smiled and placed her hand on her chest. "What brought this on?"

"There is so much we can teach them, so much all of us can share. I want them to learn how to move through this world quietly, at peace, yet understand all that can harm them and how to prepare to confront it. I want a family like the Williams family.

"I want them to know the power of a strong family. I want them to know so many things. I want you to be their mother, and I want to have you in my life forever."

"...so that means?"

It was hard for Anthony to say it even then, but he knew in his heart what he wanted. "You're going to have to be little patient with me."

"Is that a proposal?"

"Yes," he said softly.

"Are you sure you're ready?"

Anthony lowered his head in thought, then raised it, looking into her eyes. "I'm more sure about this than anything in my life." Anthony took her hand. "And whatever it takes to make it happen, I'll do it."

Carla slid into his arms as if she had been there all their lives. They held each other for a long time before she responded. "Okay, Anthony. If you're sure, I'm sure," she whispered.

# EPILOGUE

*Fall 1962*
*The Woods*

A nthony sat on the L-shaped hill and reflected upon all that had taken place since his first visit to the woods that summer in 1948. It had taken him almost a year from the second time he had entered here before he could return to the scene of the dreadful events that had altered his life forever. He had to, because it was important to him that, at least once, he leave the woods on his own terms, not running, not scared, not even mad.

He moved from the hill to walk the path he used as a kid when he first entered the woods. Little had changed in fourteen years. The meadow, the flowers, the trees were all as he remembered. Anthony leaned against a tall oak tree. As he looked closer at what would have been his secret place, he realized that there in fact had been a change. Some of the trees were taller and the beautiful array of flowers that had provided so much serenity at the beginning of his first visit had spread even farther throughout the calm, quiet meadow.

Eventually he approached the path he had used to escape. Anthony walked it in silent contemplation. The path was smooth, except for the footprints of a small animal. Anthony smiled. His gaze followed the impressions on the ground until they faded into the distance among the shrub and the trees.

He had left footprints there too. Twice—one at thirteen years of age and the second at age twenty-six. Both times he had been running in fear. The first in horror at a scene he hoped he would never see again in his life; the second, from men who were intent on doing him severe harm. Only the second time, Anthony had more familiarity and, consequently, more control. Not much, but certainly more than he did the first time, because he had learned.

And he had grown. Grown like the trees that surrounded him. When he first left the forest, he was a scared, confused young man. When he graduated from college, he was less scared, but just as confused about his direction and his purpose. When he was confronted with circumstances that threatened his life, he learned that confusion was not an option. He would have to make choices—and quickly. During each stage of his life, he had been presented with both challenges and opportunities.

Anthony smiled again. There was a reason people had come into his life because each in their own way had contributed to his growth: his wife Carla; his mother and father; Whiting; the Klan; Byrd; the Williams family. Some had presented him with questions. Some had presented him with answers, and in the end, he was satisfied with the choices he had made.

He and Carla, who had returned with him and was waiting in the car, had been married close to six months. It was hard to explain to anyone what their union had done for him. Just her presence had changed him. It had made him stronger, but most of all, it had made him more peaceful.

Anthony's father appeared to have heeded his advice. His mother was happier than he had seen her in a long while. Byrd moved to Mississippi because, as he related to Anthony, "there was so much more work to be done there." Whiting had dropped out of sight, but Byrd's last words dampened any joy he might have gotten from that news. "Be careful, Anthony. You never know what hole he might slither out of next."

Anthony's ex-girlfriend, Naomi ended up marrying Victor Carson, Anthony's next-door neighbor. Anthony was surprised, but happy for her. He even sent a gift.

And the Williamses—they hadn't changed at all. They couldn't change. Their life was steeped in tradition that succeeding patriarchs would keep alive. That's how they survived. It was how they achieved. Why change things that had worked for centuries? Raymond, who was in his first year of college, would ably follow in his Uncle Thompson's footsteps to lead the family, and they would continue, hopefully without any more conflict, to live and better their lives through one another.

Anthony looked at the largest of the towering oaks. The Williams family was like that great tree with its roots planted firmly in the ground by love, by respect, by ritual and by history. If there was such a tribe as the Snake Walkers, every Williams would be a member. Anthony had become knowledgeable about many things, but it had taken some time before he found an answer to his own question: What would a child need to know to be able to walk through a nest of poisonous snakes without being bitten? And who better than Cread to explain to Anthony that nothing on this Earth should be feared, just understood. That would be the premise.

It had been slow coming, but Anthony had finally begun to comprehend. He also realized that as much as he had learned in the past few years, there was so much more to know about himself and about life. He turned to walk away, picking a few flowers for Carla, then looking once more before leaving the woods. Echoing in his mind was a quote he had heard from a professor at college, "Every door represents an exit and entrance." Anthony smiled. If there were going to be more stages in his life, then there would certainly be more exits.

Anthony let out a sigh of relief as he walked toward the car. He felt cleansed as the sun's rays washed his face. Carla looked more beautiful than ever as she stood by the Chrysler, waiting. Anthony turned to look at the woods for the last time. He had left a lot of bad memories there. Although he hoped that he had left the devil there too, he knew he hadn't completely. According to the men in the Williams family, you never do. But armed with the knowledge he had gained over the last few years, and coupled with the friends and alliances he had made, Anthony felt a cautious optimism about his future, his entrance to the next stage of his life, and the challenges it would surely bring.